MY MOTHER WAS SCREAMING. . . .

The walls of the tunnel were soft, and purchase was easy to find. I was, in fact, changing the form of the solid rock and hollowed space through which I was making my way, digging, scratching a trail. The tunnel buzzed like the aura of an earthquake. I was all but deaf, and there was no heat to detect. There was cold. Behind me, my mother, and ahead of me, a solid, porous and dense.

The cold was more solid than anything else, and I fell into it. I heard a prolonged, desperate and oddly musical sound, like plainsong pleading, and the echoes of it everywhere, through the segmented tunnels like finger bones through the mountain and through the bones of my own phalanges clawing now at cold turgid air. My mother was screaming. . . .

HIGH PRAISE FOR
MELANIE TEM
acclaimed author of *Revenant, Prodigal,*
and *Wilding,*
winner of the Bram Stoker Award
for Superior Achievement in a First Novel
from the Horror Writers of America

"Spectacular." —Stephen King

"Melanie Tem makes a very able guide through these deepest regions of fear. . . . She may well be the literary successor to Shirley Jackson and be destined to become the new queen of high-quality, psychologically disturbing horror fiction. . . . MELANIE TEM'S WRITING IS A CRY FROM THE VERY HEART OF DARKNESS."
—Dan Simmons, author of *Summer of Night*

"Outstanding . . . Not since Faulkner have I read a writer's work which could set me thinking so many ways."
—*The Post Journal* (Jamestown, N.Y.)

"Tem has a knack for getting beneath the skin to the ambiguities of fear and desire and she never flinches from depicting emotions in all their disturbing complexity."
—Lisa Tuttle, author of *Gabriel*

"Melanie Tem doesn't tug at the heartstrings; she twists them until you scream."
—*From the Time Tunnel* newsletter

"Melanie Tem writes excellent horror with deep understanding of real families and their conflicts."
—*The Denver Post*

"STUNNING. . . . Anyone interested in domestic, personal or childhood horrors, anyone who doubts that this genre . . . is still capable of raw human truths could learn a thing or two from Ms. Tem."
—*Fangoria*

"Most of the best-known authors in the field of dark fantasy are men. It has not always been this way. In the nineteenth century such novelists as Mary Shelley, Jane Austen, Ann Radcliffe, and the Brontë sisters chilled many a spine. And today, a number of talented women are taking their places beside Stephen King and Dean Koontz in this male-dominated field. At the forefront of this group is Denver's Melanie Tem."
—*Rocky Mountain News*

"Some of the most emotionally acute prose to appear in horror since Shirley Jackson's *The Haunting of Hill House.*"
—*Necrofile*

"Melanie Tem knows intimately the terrors that haunt families. Put aside V. C. Andrews and John Saul. The Shirley Jackson of *We Have Always Lived in the Castle* now has company."
—Edward Bryant, *Locus*

Also by Melanie Tem

MAKING LOVE *with Nancy Holder*

PRODIGAL

REVENANT

WILDING

DESMODUS

MELANIE TEM

A DELL BOOK

Published by
Dell Publishing
a division of
Bantam Doubleday Dell Publishing Group, Inc.
1540 Broadway
New York, New York 10036

ISBN: 0-440-21504-8

Printed in the United States of America

Published simultaneously in Canada

December 1995

10 9 8 7 6 5 4 3 2 1

RAD

For my daughters,
and for my sons,

because, male or female,
it's not easy to be strong and honorable
in this world.

And for their father,
who shows us all how.

ACKNOWLEDGMENTS

I can't give thanks and acknowledgment enough to Trey Barker and Karn Koske, my able assistants, who were pressed into emergency service and who managed to save both my sanity and this book. They are both writers themselves; watch for their work.

Thanks, too, to Julie Deden and Bill Estrada of the Colorado Division of Rehabilitation, for speedily providing me with nifty adaptive software and patiently training me in its use.

CHAPTER 1

The alarm had sounded. The message had gone out, buzzing and clicking through the Tallus compound on a higher, more urgent frequency than ordinary communication. Reported by sentries who were seldom pressed into duty and who did not always get details right, the message was sketchy; all we knew at first—all we needed to know—was: DANGER.

Rapidly, details emerged, passed from one to another like partially digested food. Rory was causing trouble in town—typical male foolishness without even the usual level of male self-restraint. Some kind of fight. Some kind of disturbance. Some kind of drawing attention to himself and, by extension, to us.

Avoidance of—aversion to; terror of—this sort of trouble was a constant and formative of our individual and communal lives because it could so easily jeopardize the entire community. Rory, obviously, had not thought about that, or he had not cared, or he had intended to jeopardize the community. In every generation were one or two or a few boys whose recklessness reached such depths; almost never did they live to adulthood.

My sister and our mother went in after him. He was, after all, their son and grandson, and it was still, barely, summer so he was still, barely, their responsibility. I shuddered to think what would happen if he pulled something like this two months hence, down in Ambergen, when the women were asleep and we men, stewards then, had to take care of things. I was, in fact, wryly surprised that he had not already done so, last winter or the year before, for his delinquency had by no means appeared suddenly or out of whole cloth. I did not let myself think about that.

"Come on, Joel."

I looked at Ma askance. "Why do I have to go?" To my own ears I sounded like a truculent adolescent, not much unlike Rory. Indeed, I generally felt less than adult when I talked to my mother, or to any woman for that matter. Such diminution had its advantages, chief among them the dearth of female expectations, so I was nonplussed by being ordered along, even mildly indignant.

"You and Pete. This could get physical. Come on."

Pete and I did not even exchange glances.

There was no point. We just trudged to the garages, waited for an indication of which vehicle we were taking, hunkered down in the bed of the old Chevy pickup, and waited more or less stolidly while Alexis and Ma got in, Alexis driving.

We had backed out of the garage and turned onto the driveway, which curved and dipped for more than a mile from the compound out to the dirt road, when the truck stopped, roughly enough to throw Pete into me and me against the wheel well. Pete rolled his eyes and I heaved a sigh, exaggeratedly heavy but foreshortened so Ma would not catch it.

Among the men, there was a whole secret language like that, sighs and eye-rollings and exchanged looks and particular postures and gestures that the women, if they noticed at all, did not try to intercept or interpret. If they had, they would have found them laughable. "If men ran things," this code pretended to assert, "things would go better. Vehicles would be braked smoothly. Teenage boys would be kept in line." But even in the winter, when there were no women around to hear us, we never said such things aloud, and most men probably never gave them coherent thought—not for fear of female retribution or mockery, really, but because responsibility even just for words or thoughts like that would have been too much for us, let alone any such actions.

Through the back window of the cab, we heard raised voices and saw Alexis gesturing angrily. Then Ma got out and, leaving the door ajar as if to show her intent to make this quick, came around to us. "Let me see you."

Neither of us knew what she meant at first. Then Pete said, "Oh, right," laughed a little, and hauled himself up onto all fours. When Ma circled her fingers around each other in long concentric circles, he grinned sheepishly and pirouetted on elbows and knees, awkwardly, of course. Noting that his long and bulky flannel shirt obscured the avial humps on his shoulder blades and made his arms look shorter than they were by creating the optical illusion of a lower-slung waist, and that his straight red-brown mustache all but hid the tips of his teeth where they protruded between his lips, I realized what Ma was inspecting for: that in town we could pass, long enough to get Rory without causing a greater stir.

Ma was wearing a voluminous slicker with a hood, which caused me to reflect that it was a good thing this was a rainy late-autumn midnight and not a morning in, say, June; her appearance might still be a bit odd by town standards, but it probably would not give rise to downright astonishment. From an inside pocket she took a roll of double-sided adhesive tape and handed it up to Pete. "For your ears."

He grimaced but did not really object. He made a tube out of a small piece of tape and carefully stuck it behind his left ear, then made a fold in the ear and pressed it back onto the sticky surface of the tube. He waited a minute, shook his head, leaned sideways. The tape held. He repeated the process with the right ear, then faced Ma with his eyebrows raised. Narrow-eared like that, he looked ridiculous, and even Ma laughed, but she nodded approval. "You'll do."

She looked me over as though she had never seen me before, trying, I knew, to assume a townsperson's perspective. She had me loosen my belt so my pants would sag, and I thought that, while this would disguise my scoop, I would look like a middle-aged gang-banger wannabe, but I did not bother to tell her so. She insisted I trim my nails. This was no easy thing, since naturally they were long, thick, and curved, and Alexis had twice lain on the horn before I was done. If Ma noticed her daughter's impatience, she gave no sign; certainly it did not agitate her in the least, while it made me so nervous I nicked myself.

Finally she was satisfied, and we got on our way; Alexis floored the accelerator so that Pete and I slid toward the back of the truck bed, but Ma must have said something to her—or her own common sense rose to moderate her maternal instincts, brash now as they so often were—because the truck settled into a steady if too-rapid pace.

Leaving Tallus like this, such a rare occurrence, made the season seem farther along than I had realized, the year farther gone. I well knew the date, but the women's sleep and our trip south were triggered by weather conditions more than by the calendar, and I had thought we had more time than this. The passing landscape had a decided autumnal aspect, almost wintry. The deciduous trees overhanging our long private driveway and then the gravel county road had already begun to lose their leaves, and those that remained were colorless and soggy. The sky was a thick, wet gray. There was no breeze, but the air was chill.

I reminded myself, with both relief and resentment, that it was not up to me to decide when we would leave. I would be told when to take up my assignments. Until then, there was no point in worrying about it. There were plenty of things to worry about—most immediately, my nephew Rory.

I pulled my pea coat under and up around me, wishing that I had worn more layers of clothing and that my hair were longer and thicker to cover more of me, though enough hirsuteness to keep me warm would surely have drawn unwelcome attention in town. That was probably one of Ma's reasons for insisting that I be part of this rescue mission—I would not stand out as much as, say, Miles or Stockard, with their more admirable pelts.

Apparently I had been harboring the hope, secret even from myself, that my mother had chosen me for my competence or some other positive attribute, because the realization that it had probably been for my looks offended me, hurt my feelings. Sullenly I settled into a corner for the long ride.

"What do you suppose he's gotten himself into this time?" Pete mused.

"Who knows? Who cares? We'll find out when we get there."

"Do you think he has a self-destructive streak? Or is it just the process of individuation?" Pete had been studying psychology. His persistence, the very fact that he was *interested* in all this, annoyed me and struck me as borrowing trouble. I wanted only to make myself as comfortable as possible in this extremely uncomfortable situation and, literally and figuratively, ride it out. Nevertheless, and even more annoyingly, I found myself responding in a way that would give him more to speculate about—and, therefore, more to talk about. "I think he's more homicidal than suicidal."

The instant I said it I wished I had not, because Pete, predictably, bared his teeth and sank them into it, treating this observation far more seriously than I had. "Do you really? Homicidal? Do you think he's that dangerous?"

Now I had to defend what had been essentially a throwaway comment. There was no reason to think I could successfully do that. This, I thought morosely, was why men habitually did not offer —did not *have*—opinions about much of anything. "I think he's more of a danger to the rest of us than he is to himself," I said reluctantly.

Pete made thoughtful noises, which was not a good sign. I did not want to engage in further frustrating conversation about a subject utterly outside our purview. I suspected that the women could do something about Rory, if they chose to; there were not many things that, individually or collectively, the women could not affect. It was, in fact, quite possible that they were taking action and Pete and I simply were not privy to their strategy. But Rory's misbehavior, its wider meanings and deeper implications, were pointless for us to consider.

I did consider them, though, if only superficially, my unwillingness to think deeply about troublesome matters serving not to quiet my ruminations but only to keep them specious and therefore more nerve-wracking. I thought about Rory as a child. He had not been an especially appealing child—always obstreperous, often defiant, and sometimes mean. But the spring he was six, we had spent a fair amount of time in each other's displeased company while his mother gave birth to his brother Sebastian, then discovered Sebastian's multiple handicaps and enlisted veritable hordes of females, including our mother and Rory's then-four-year-old sister Meredith, to support her in her grief, tend the infant whose needs were apparently not like those of other infants, and decide what to do with him. Regarding this last, I did not know and did not want to know what the options had been.

It had not been a good summer. I knew not a thing about child care and had no interest; this was not a job for men. And we had not much liked each other, Rory and I. We still did not much like each other. But for some reason, memory had limned those months with pleasantness, which carried over when I thought about him now. To my displeasure, I retained a certain affection and sense of responsibility for the boy.

I was spared further risky musings and more conversation or avoidance of conversation with Pete when Alexis threw open the driver's door and flung herself out. Still speeding, the truck careened, and Ma reached across to grab the wheel, barely keeping us on the road. Alexis, as was her wont, was screeching. "This is stupid! I can get there faster on my own!"

She took off through the woods toward town. Already she was clicking and squeaking, as if she could locate her son from here. Perhaps she could; it was a given that women had higher-developed echolocation skills than men. Pete and I listened to her until the trees and the divergence of her route from the truck's obscured her.

Ma had slid over behind the wheel. Just the top of her shiny-hooded head showed above the seat, and I wondered if her feet even touched the pedals. But it never would have crossed my mind to doubt that, one way or another, she would handle the truck. Women always handled things. In particular, my mother always did.

The truck fishtailed a few times, but she got it under control before any damage was done to either the vehicle or its trajectory, and we continued on our way. Pete cocked his head in the direction Alexis had taken, and the tape behind one ear popped loose as the muscles strained to fan. Myself, I heard nothing but engine and tire noise, drizzle on cold metal and glass, leaves damply falling, the skittering and flittering of small warm-blooded creatures we passed too quickly for me to identify. I thought Ma and Alexis probably cataloged, so readily as to be almost subliminal, every living thing that ever crossed their paths, but I was just as glad to allow some of them to escape my notice.

After a few minutes Pete gave up trying to follow Alexis's flight. He folded up and secured his ear again, half turned toward me as though to say something, thought better of it. We rode the rest of the way in a silence that he might have called companionable but was, to me, merely the welcome absence of chatter. The older I got, the more I valued peace and quiet, and the less of either I seemed to get.

We were well into the outskirts of town before I realized it. Instinctively, feeling ambushed or—worse—on the verge of being ambushed, I gathered myself, wrapped myself smaller and tenser. In my nearly fifty years, I had been to town perhaps twice, and the place did not sound at all familiar. The heat of it was dense and animated, confusing.

When I was a child, Ma and a few other adult women had had to go into town once every month for supplies. There had routinely been extensive preparation: careful scheduling to minimize the number of stops, rehearsal of speech and bearing, disguise that seemed playful to me when I was very young but that I soon recognized—was forced to recognize—as deadly serious. If we ran out of something before the month was over, it was understood that we would do without until the next appointed shopping time. While the shoppers were gone the community buzzed with an undercurrent of anxiety, though we all went about our daily business as we always must; when they returned, there was no celebration, but there was widespread communal relief.

The relationship of Tallus to the town had varied throughout the history of both, and I never knew much about it. Women were the keepers of the past—historians, storytellers, mythmakers, genealogists—and bearers of the future because they knew how to plan and prepare and were constitutionally able to imagine beyond the next night or the next season. I, being male, had enough trouble navigating the immediate present, the immediate past, the very near future.

I did, though, have a vague impression that there had been times when Tallus was almost entirely self-sufficient. Ma had alluded to elaborate farming and livestock operations where now there were only gardens, orchards, and a few animals more pet than prey—enough work in themselves. When I thought about it at all, I supposed that back then the community had boasted more and better tailors, toolmakers, carpenters, entertainers than when I was growing up, and/or that those recent ancestors had been less restless, less greedy than we were.

Even more dimly, I was aware that once we had had far more contact with our neighbors, and that this had been an ugly and hazardous period all around. This had to have been a very long time ago, when the Old Women were young or even before they were born—a perspective almost impossible to maintain; considering the Old Women at all was like leaning out over a seething pit, and considering them when they had been something other than Old Women induced profound disorientation and dread. It had been before there were any investments and then, while the investments were proving themselves, before we had had agents in distant cities and foreign lands.

Now, lately, we were mutating into another sort of self-sufficiency that I scarcely comprehended. Tallus had been wired. We had stepped into cyberspace. I was not even sure I had the jargon right, but the results were legion: Financial matters could be handled with nary a personal meeting, phone call, postal delivery, or stroke of the pen. Orders for groceries and other supplies could be placed via modem, and the only interpersonal interaction required was the dispatch of a single representative to meet the delivery truck at the end of the driveway. The children's home-schooling, for generations hotly debated among educationally minded women, now had access to vast data banks and infinite permutations of source materials, not to mention all the tools for teaching and self-instruction I kept hearing about. Youthful enthusiasts—and my mother, too, which galled me—claimed that before long we would not have to deal directly with anyone outside the community. I did not argue, naturally, but I was skeptical, more in a futile attempt at self-protection than out of any knowledge or intuition.

Alexis had indeed located her son well before we got there, causing me to wonder why we had taken the truck. Maybe Ma and Alexis had anticipated that Rory would give them trouble and refuse to come home under his own power. In any case, I never would have questioned the decision, and I did not even think about it for long, because my attention was claimed by a commotion in a little half-block park and by Pete's hissed "Shit."

Before I had managed to scramble out of the truck—before I had even resigned myself to the patent necessity of doing so—I picked up heat and motion and incipient motion from perhaps a dozen warm-blooded bodies in the park. One of them, closest to us and separated from the others, was my sister. The others were particles circling around each other, drawn to and repelled by each other, all these forces combining to create a seething whole. I had not expected to be able to isolate Rory among them. I was sure Alexis had done so from some distance away; I was sure Ma was doing so now, as she flew out of the truck and across the sidewalk to Alexis's side and past, black raincoat billowing.

Sensory perceptions began to sort themselves out as Pete and I approached the crowd. I could hear individual voices, discrete breathing patterns, footsteps and the sliding of hands on weapons. Young men, all of them, townspeople, with Rory surrounded.

Alexis was squeaking madly, summoning her son, but nobody in the park was paying her the slightest heed; Rory was simply ignoring her, and the others would not have heard. I noticed now, through the painful haze of the bright gray glow from the security lights, that all the boys were wearing a uniform—baseball caps with the bills turned sideways, khaki pants sagging below their knees. I had read about gang costumes but had never seen them before, and, once I recognized what the outfits signified, my first reaction was amusement, for they really did look ridiculous, like pompous children, playing and posturing, out of their league. And they were so *young;* it was hard for me to tell their ages in comparison to Rory's, but I guessed none of them to be older than he was, and he was only seventeen, I thought, eighteen at most. Although I knew they were dangerous, could be lethal—especially to us—it was hard to take them seriously.

It was also hard to determine precisely in what way they were threatening Rory, although the sense of threat was palpable. In the approximate middle of their rough circle, he stood half bent, shoulders arched in fighting stance. He was shorter and slimmer than most of them, although among us he was on the stocky side. I was struck simultaneously by how much he resembled them

—the same fearful bilateral symmetry, the same imploded and furious energy, the same hot blood —and by the differences in physical configuration and internal structure that set him so apart.

Alexis shouted, "Rory, get your ass over here!"

Rory, of course, immediately set his stance and growled, "Go fuck yourself." The others, of course, hooted with derision. The sheer dumbness of my sister's move amazed me, put me on some sort of unaccustomed alert.

Alexis was fairly atwitter with frustration, both because Rory was not minding her and, worse, I knew, because she did not dare be as forceful as it was possible for her to be. "Joel, Pete, what the hell are you guys doing? Don't just stand there! Go get him!"

Pete cocked his head at me as though listening for a reaction but did not wait for it even if I had had one. He plunged into the melee. I remember hesitating, but I followed, it being unimaginable to me what I would do if I did not do that. "Be careful!" my mother commanded, and I knew she was not urging caution for our safety so much as reminding us to fight circumspectly, not to use everything we had, not to betray any skill we did not absolutely have to use.

As it turned out, we served primarily as decoys. The gang turned on us, away from Rory, and I heard his yelp of indignation; whatever was going on here, he was by no means entirely an innocent victim.

One big kid swung his stick at my knees and I leaped easily over it, restraining myself from going too high in the air. Pete dived up and sideways into another one's neck; I heard the rubbery rustling under his shirt but I doubted any of them would hear it or would have any suspicion about what it was.

Pete was dancing. When I realized what he was doing, I was impressed by his creativity and quick thinking. Several of the punks were guffawing. Pete pirouetted on tiptoe and executed several minor flying leaps, then took off across the park, diagonally away from my mother and sister, who had taken hold of Rory's arms. Hooting and brandishing their clumsy clubs, all the attackers but one chased Pete.

I was so sure that the herd instinct of these boys would be as strong as ours that I did not at first realize this one had stayed behind his fellows, his sights on me. Instead of taking him on directly, as I should have done, I moved toward Alexis, who was handling Rory alone and having trouble with him. I was not sure what she would want me to do, but I knew I was expected to be available to her.

This drew my unwelcome escort toward them, too, just as Ma came at Rory from above. I heard her tiny body slash through the air like the flattened head of a spear, followed by Rory's startled outrush of breath as she tackled him. Then she had hold of the back of his collar and the back of his belt. He was bigger than she was by quite a bit, but, with strength that thrilled me even though I had always known it was in her, she lifted him off his feet and started to carry him off. Although it was a risky, brazen thing for her to do and was sure to complicate things, I very nearly applauded.

"Rat face!" The kid's taunt was a bit breathless, I thought. "Shit, it's the fucking Flying Mouse!" as if that were an insult or a joke. I all but chuckled at his puny meanness, but Ma's hissing, suddenly vicious, made it clear to me—and to the hoodlum himself, apparently, for he grew quiet and started to retreat—that this was no laughing matter.

Screeching and swearing mightily, Rory had twisted himself upside down and wrapped arms and legs around his grandmother's torso. With the right torque, his bite would be fearsome, and I thought I should go to my mother's aid, but my impulse was too scattered to act on. I hovered helplessly.

Ma easily tossed Rory to Alexis, who easily caught him. As she carried him off, in scoop and claws, in the direction of the truck and Tallus, I heard her whispering to him in a decidedly nasty way, "You little son of a bitch, who do you think you are?" and, despite my own anger at him, I wished she would not call him names and would not ask him a question that pierced so surely to the heart of the matter.

Ma went after the kid who had so injudiciously followed me. He ran, but pointlessly. She swooped around in front of him and came up from underneath to sink her teeth into his throat. He gave a gurgling sound, surprisingly brief and muffled.

I had never known my mother to kill before. I had, in fact, never known anyone to kill before; there had never been any need. The eruptive smell of the boy's blood nauseated me, excited me, made me salivate. I understood why she had to dispose of this foolhardy witness, but I could not myself have done it, and my mother's ability to take such decisive, violent action was appalling.

She carried the limp body off to the far side of the park, where there were trees and a little band shell. I heard her teeth slash his throat, which was strange, and then tear at other parts of his flesh, and I realized, with grudging admiration because I never would have thought of it, that she was disguising the kill.

A cacophony like rising wind, interspersed with footsteps and shouts, approached from behind, and Pete shouted for my help in fending off his attackers. As if to some signal inaudible or incomprehensible to me, the entire mass of them stepped back, reassembled, and attacked. Pete was buried; I could not see him, and, much more alarmingly, I could neither hear him nor detect his body heat.

My mind went utterly blank. I had no clue what I should do. I was not used to making decisions on my own, and certainly not decisions whose consequences were this enormous.

It could not have taken long, in real time, for me to do what I did, and I was never aware of making a conscious decision; indeed, if I had been I might well have been paralyzed. Before I knew it, I had sprung into the mob—which, for all the metaphorical appeal of regarding it as an undifferentiated mass, a single and single-minded creature, was, in fact, comprised of a finite number of separate organisms, each in some or many ways vulnerable.

My teeth punctured the first flesh they encountered and drew blood. Invigorated, I flung the kid aside and went for the next one. I met with very little resistance, perhaps because I could move faster than they could, perhaps because my method of attack was a surprise to them. It was fortunate that their only weapons turned out to be makeshift clubs, which they found difficult to manipulate at such close range; had they been seriously armed, of course, the rules and stakes of combat would have been considerably different. But, whatever the reason, the bottom line was that they were no match for me, assisted belatedly but significantly by Pete as he worked himself free, and cutting through them to Ma and Rory was really rather easy.

The two of us shot upward, enough to escape but still well under control, and then out of the park. I was sorely tempted simply to take flight. Had it not been two o'clock in the morning, had our opponents and observers been other than drunk, stoned, and otherwise unreliable, even the minimal amount of airborne locomotion we indulged in would have attracted troublesome attention, and there would have had to be more casualties; as it was, we were taking a risk less calculated than, later, in the retelling, Ma and Alexis would make it out to have been.

Alexis, now with Rory rather meekly at her side, caught up and took over. By the time we got back to the pickup, she was well into a hissing, spitting torrent of vituperation that took in all males, past, present, and future, with her son as the perfect exemplar of every enumerated character flaw. By the time we were on the road—Rory in the cab between his mother and grandmother without so much as an objection on his part; Pete and I relegated to the open bed again—it was hard to think of the rescue, which actually had been rather daring, as having had much to do with me, except for my uncomfortable sensation of having committed an act out of character for myself and my entire gender. I was hungry, and by the time we got back to Tallus I had managed to make pervasive in my mind the worry that the sun would come up before I had had a chance to eat.

CHAPTER 2

I had a strong, if delayed, reaction to the incident in town, intensified by the fact that I was obviously not supposed to be having any reaction at all. We were not exactly forbidden to talk about it—a direct ban would have accorded the thing too much importance—but formidable distraction was created, chiefly the announcement that we would leave for Ambergen at the end of the month.

This was not nearly enough time for proper preparation. The hurry panicked me nearly to the point of paralysis, although I surmised its purposes and even, somewhat dully, concurred with them. Having to get ready so hastily would keep the gossip about what had happened in town to a minimum, and, on a more practical level, what had happened in town made it seem wise—not imperative, but certainly advisable—that we get out of there as soon as possible. Anyway, the weather was changing; a solid argument could be made that the season had already changed.

I was badly shaken. No one else seemed to be, and so I rapidly began to doubt the authenticity of my distress. Obsessively, I made mental lists of the things I was upset about, as though that would anchor them.

I had dreams about the kid who had died. When I woke—sometimes a dozen times a day—into broad, painful daylight, I could not remember any distinctive feature, but in the dreams the multiple sounds of him were finely detailed and terrible. "He was a punk," Pete said dismissively the one time I brought it up to him; I never mentioned it to Rory for fear that I would be telling him something he did not know, or that he did know and would say something crass, and I never would have said anything to Alexis or Ma out of some deeper and less definable fear.

Then there was the persistent vertigo, that peculiar mix of terror and a nearly sexual excitement that burbles up sometimes when you make a precipitous drop or climb, or when suddenly a void opens below you. Although we had not been followed back to Tallus and night after night there were no repercussions, I knew we had come very close to both disaster and adventure, though I would have been hard-pressed to describe the precise nature of either.

Even more unsettling, I had been forced to perceive myself in a way so uncharacteristic as to border on the unnatural, and I did not know what to make of it. I had made decisions, taken action, and undeniably influenced subsequent events. I was finding it very difficult to integrate any of that with what I had always known about myself, and the resulting incongruity was, I knew, part of what was making me physically unwell.

I awoke hard, although I had not been soundly asleep. It was almost dusk. I had to get up. I would much rather have slept through the night, but I had things to do. Even if my overdeveloped superego had allowed me to go back to sleep, my sister or my mother or some other woman would have come pounding at my door any minute, and the nervous anticipation of being rousted—gently by Ma; indifferently by any other woman, brooking no nonsense; as unpleasantly as possible by my sister, who delighted in startling me so that I shook and was queasy for hours—made it impossible for me to catch another few minutes' sleep.

I eased myself down from the loft. My head ached. My shoulders and ankles were stiff after immobile hours in the sleeping position, as they often were these early evenings of my middle age. Moaning and groaning, cracking my joints, I made more noise than was necessary as I made my way through the dimming house, but none of the other men showed any signs of agitation; most of them did not even stir.

I scowled. They would have to get up soon, too. I was not the only one who had things to do, even though it often seemed that way to me.

Getting up in the evening was almost always an unpleasant experience. Seldom did I feel rested. Seldom did I happily anticipate the night ahead. Even through the drawn shades, the house was uncomfortably bright. It was also crowded, and dank from communal sleep. It smelled faintly sour, faintly coppery.

Despite the early hour, more than a few of the women were up, getting ready to go out for breakfast. Hunger would wake them successively earlier in the evenings now as winter approached, and they would eat more and more every night until just before they settled down for their winter sleep they would be doing little else but eating. I did not know how they did it. I did not know how most women did most of the things they were expected to do. Poorly socialized though I might be, and chronically dissatisfied with my lot in life, being male had always seemed less trouble than being female.

Alexis and our mother were up, of course—my sister because she was as poorly adapted to the female role as I was to the male and she always had trouble sleeping, even in the middle of winter, Ma because her advanced age both allowed and required her to prepare extensively for hibernation. Sebastian was crouching on the kitchen floor, all at odd angles, as far away from his mother and grandmother as he could get and still be in the same room. He was sipping bright red blood through a bent straw out of a plastic Vikings cup that he held in both hands. Despite his general obliviousness to the world around him and inability to perform basic functions for himself, he obviously knew enough to release the anticoagulant in his saliva, for the blood flowed freely. Wanting some turned my stomach, and I closed my ears.

"Joel," my mother exclaimed in some alarm, squinting up at me. "You're up early. The sun's not even down."

I made the mistake of saying, "I'm hungry."

Predictably, Alexis advanced on me and shook her long loose finger in my face. "Get yourself under control, big brother. It's still summer."

"Technically," I muttered, and she cocked her ears sharply, ready to take me on, but Ma said her name and she subsided. To escape her superciliousness and Ma's chronic worry, I went on through the kitchen and out the back door into the courtyard.

The air was alarmingly crisp. The twilight seemed deeper than it was because of the enclosing buildings and the trees even in partial leaf. In summer, sounds and smells of the outside world scarcely penetrated into this inner sanctum, which was where most of the real life of the colony took place. Any echoes of sound or heat from inside out were likely to be our own. From here, it was quite possible to be persuaded that we were a world unto ourselves. In autumn, though, as the deciduous trees bared and the dominant color of the surrounding landscape changed from green toward olive drab and the time for migration drew near, we all began to feel more and more exposed.

I could pick up no scent or body heat in here from any mammals other than family, and I was too famished to wait for something to wander in with nightfall. I would have to go out. Sighing, I checked that I had the key ring in my pocket, which I always did, and strode along the walled path to the small-vehicle garage. Not for the first time, I wished I did not have to eat. I backed the quarter-ton Ford pickup out of the garage and up the driveway.

Starting just a few feet from the compound, hardwood north-temperate forest came right up to both shoulders of the driveway, a mass of flora whose individuals were no more discrete than I was, say, from my cousins or nephews. In the truck's headlights, things were flying, but they would have been of no interest to me even if I had sensed them by some mechanism, other than vision, which could afford me more detail. Foreshortened perspective caused the parallel lines that formed the driveway to converge behind me almost immediately, obscuring the compound I had just left. I tried to reassure myself that, within the memory of even the eldest matriarch—about whom I did not like to think in even this glancing way—no one had stumbled onto Tallus or come hunting. But I could not imagine why.

The long driveway ended at the long narrow dirt road, and I took the turn away from town. I had traveled this road in one way or another hundreds, perhaps thousands of times in my life. I knew where I was going. A certain foolish nostalgia came over me, a familiar if silly feeling this time of year as we prepared to leave Tallus and go south to Ambergen for the winter. I did not like to move. If we ever tried to stay up here year-round, there would, of course, be hell to pay, but I loathed change, even predictable, cyclical change. The fog that gauzed the woods and the countryside only intensified my melancholy.

I followed the road where it curved to the left and stopped the truck in unbroken woods. Though I did not want to be out in the chill, I dared not drive any closer to the neighbors' pasture than this.

Airborne, it was easy enough for me to leave no visible marks of my passage on the ground, but I had to make a conscious effort not to make any noise that my prey or their owners would hear.

The little herd of handsome buckskin and sorrel horses crowded nickering up to their side of the fence when I offered apples from my stash in the bed of the truck. I observed them, one after another, considering the velvet noses, the soft underlips, deciding on the tender spot behind the ear where the skin was thin and the pulse close to the surface raised the temperature discernibly. They mildly stomped their feet and shuddered their hides, as though I were a pesky horsefly, when I leaned from the top rail and nuzzled their fragrant necks.

I did not take more from them than I needed; the temptation to do so was loathsome. Their loose lips and big square teeth closed over each apple in my palm, savored, played, took their time, while my thin lips and blade-teeth worked quickly and efficiently, without much pleasure for me or harm to any of them.

Depressed and still sleepy, hunger slaked but far from satiated, I drove home. The fog had thickened. The woods and the lowering sky wrapped themselves around me, chill and damp, swarming. Again and again, for cold fleeting instants, I would think I was lost, though that was not possible as long as I stayed on the road; then spatial and temporal orientation would swim clear again. Eventually, though it should have been a short ride, I came upon Tallus, and had the sense that I must have driven past it and circled back more than once without being aware of it.

Though I had lived there all my life and never considered living anywhere else—except Ambergen, of course, which was part of the same cycle yet as different from Tallus as it was possible to be and still sustain our collective life—I had to admit that the place was quite impressive for its subtlety, its intricacy, and its ancient functionality. From the county road, the driveway turned off like any other driveway, through trees and clearings, down a hill too small to give a pretense of hiding anything. At the bottom of the slope, before it started upward again toward the lake, lay the buildings of Tallus, a good-sized ranch, perhaps, with numerous outbuildings and a large but not otherwise notable main house. Or perhaps a passerby would think it one of those tiny towns with no visible means of support and, in fact, few visible inhabitants. Happily, no curious student of indigenous lifestyles or local history had ever been moved to stop and investigate.

In all parts of the world except Antarctica and some few Pacific islands, branches of our extended family had established communities with widely diverse physical and social structures; although it was hard to believe, I had been told that some even lived in towns, among townspeople, in a kind of symbiosis that horrified me. Our branch had lived at Tallus, unmolested and apparently not much noticed, for many generations—since, I thought, we had come out of the ancestral caves, although I was more than a little vague about anthropology.

I parked in the garage, checked the gas gauge, got out stiffly, and locked the pickup. As usual, especially at the end of summer when my controls were slipping, I had to try the locks several times before I could remember for certain that I had pressed them down, and then I did not know whether I had turned off the lights.

Finally I let myself in through the big front door, which was as public an entrance as we had, and went through milling women to the other side of the house, facing the hidden courtyard, where our communal private life took place. This aspect of Tallus, the real thing behind the facade, was nothing like any of our neighbors' places, and I shuddered to think of the interest it would engender among them. No matter what the official female position, I found it implausible that someone at some time had not wondered or would not wonder about us, and all the various interiors of Tallus were what they would speculate about.

Here were wide, deep overhangs constructed to accommodate those of us who roosted in large groups, and cozy nooks for those of us who roosted alone. Doors large and small pocked the face of the house along the ground and at midlevel and up in the high peaks. Windows all had tight shutters. There were balconies big enough for an individual, stairways leading nowhere at either end, railings guarding no edge, because these architectural forms followed functions rather different from those our neighbors would have expected.

The interior courtyard itself was as big as many a meadow, and had been designed by our forebears to give the impression both of open space, when we hankered for freedom, and of home. Soon it would be too cold to be outside except at the earliest and latest hours of the night, which always made me sad. Not being able to sit on the porch or hang in the hammocks around the courtyard was a sure sign that it was time to go south.

That evening like most, the porches were teeming with men. Some lounged on the steps. Some tipped precariously backward on kitchen chairs to prop their feet on the railing. Some lay supine or prostrate on the narrow shellacked floorboards. Two or three had fallen asleep again, their bodies swaying gently like fruit, round as apples, elongated as ripe bananas.

My cousin Ted stumbled out of the house, holding his belly and groaning in anguish that was not entirely mock. Ted and I, along with dozens of others, had been born the same summer and had grown up more or less together under virtually identical conditions and with virtually the same upbringing. But he'd always looked considerably older, which had made me envious when we were teenagers and came to cause me both relief and consternation as we entered middle age. Ted gave the entirely deceptive impression of having lived a hard life.

My uncles Perry and Sydney were carrying on a desultory argument about the pennant race. They had no good reasons for their opinions, though, and neither of them could follow a coherent thought from beginning to end. Myself, I took the Twins, but I did not find it interesting enough to talk about.

I could hear and smell my cousin Miles, passing gas from both ends in belches and farts, long before I saw him in the doorway, backlit by the dining room chandelier and frontlit by the gibbous moon. The kids were teasing him, and he was reacting ponderously. They poked at him. He whined and complained and tried to slap them away, but they were too fast for him. He could never anticipate what they were going to do next. They had him listening all over for things that were not there; they'd make rapid flipping motions just close enough to his nose to get his heat detectors going, then retreat out of range and sit perfectly still when he tried to find them. They made raucous jokes at his expense and nagged him till he laughed, even though he could not possibly get the punch line and would have been insulted or hurt if he had.

It was mean, but not extreme enough to force me to intervene. Maybe one of the women would come out and stop it.

Our labored breathing filled the partly enclosed space. Our body odors mingled and accumulated. Footsteps crunched over the layers of discarded carapaces, fruit rinds and seeds, birds' feet that littered the porch like peanut shells on a barroom floor, then subsided as each man found a place to settle.

I remember musing groggily that before long we'd all have to rouse ourselves for the autumn trek south. I remember vaguely dreading the effort that would take and vaguely looking forward to it. That was a typical conflict for a man at this time of year, and a mild one at that, as much a part of the seasonal routine as the weather change and the preparations for the trip themselves. I had no reason to anticipate that anything out of the ordinary would happen this year. But then, I would have been unlikely to take note of any clues or portents if they had presented themselves, so habituated had I become to noticing no more than was necessary in order for me to perform my limited assignments. It was not up to me or any other male to see the big picture.

From overhead and in front of me, my mother

said my name. Heavy-lidded and -limbed, I struggled to turn toward her, against the erratic motion of the glider and my own torpor. "Hello, Ma," I managed, as though I had not talked to her mere minutes ago and did not talk to her countless times every night three out of the four seasons of the year.

The moment she sat down next to me, a comforting rhythmic swing was established. It was annoying that I had not mastered a glider, of all things, and further proof, as if any were needed, of my general clumsiness in the physical world.

She was a small woman. All of us in the Desmodus branch of the family were rather small. Many cousins towered over us, legs twice as long as ours, shoulder span twice as wide. We were not the smallest; my cousins Barbara, Mitchell, and Stockard, and their myriad children and grandchildren, were positively tiny, and with that brilliant red-orange hair they looked like little jewels, a comparison that seriously irked them. But we were small, and my mother was small among us.

She patted my knee, then flexed her fingers so that her curved nails dug in only slightly, a signal she had employed since my childhood that she wanted my attention. The truth was, she always had my attention.

My mother touched me a lot as I was growing up. She would smooth my hair or tousle it. She would grab me and kiss me through my half-hearted preadolescent protests. She was quick to swat and quick to soothe with a stroke of her hand. One of my earliest memories, from when I was an only child and life surely was better, was of snuggling with her in bed on Sunday evenings while my father got us breakfast. We had a game, the particulars of which I did not remember, which involved nipping and licking, her teeth and tongue gentle on my flesh. The game had stopped with my weaning. It embarrassed me that I sometimes wished we could play it again.

"You don't seem very interested in Theresa," she said, as usual wasting no energy on obliqueness or diplomacy. "What's wrong with you, Joel?"

It was a question, a complaint, that I had been literally or by inference hearing from her all my life, and it was unanswerable. I attempted a general disclaimer, which actually had some truth in it: "Give me a break. I'm almost fifty years old. I can't be expected to be all that interested in sex anymore." The whole truth—or, more of it—was that I had never had a particularly well-developed libido.

With some effort, I visualized Theresa. She was a very distant cousin whom I hadn't seen since she was a kid and I was maybe twenty-one. By that time, I had already been alternately fighting and succumbing to chronic depression, though I did not yet know it was something definitive enough to have a name. I did not remember Theresa from those days, only a few seasons when her parents had brought their enormous brood along and so she must have been with them.

Now she was—undeniably, but almost entirely in the abstract as far as I was concerned—quite an attractive woman: long limbs, small triangular face, short black velvety hair with a striking white streak through it. Despite her skilled flirtation that seemed to include me, however offhandedly, and a reputation for considerable expertise in the erotic use of fangs and claws, I had been able—or willing—to muster no more interest in Theresa than in anything else.

"Baloney," pronounced my mother, giving my knee a scolding shake. "I'm seventy-six years old, and I'm still interested in sex. Quite interested, as a matter of fact." I did not look away fast enough to avoid seeing her wink.

I could feel myself blush. Not for the first time in my life, I wished that my mother would not say such things to me. "Yeah, but you're a woman" was my weak rejoinder, and I laughed without humor.

"I won't be around much longer," she said. "Before I die, I want to see my grandchildren."

The first of these declarations was more than I could handle, although I obsessed about her death, had had waking and sleeping nightmares about it for most of my life. We were a very long-lived family; at least two of the Old Ones were rumored to be several hundred years old, and, though that sort of longevity was rare—and purchased at a high price—any woman could expect to live a good long time, thanks partly to hibernation and partly to female manipulation of the conditions of their lives. Still, seventy-six was getting up there, and I did not know how to think about or how to avoid thinking about my mother dying. So I said, "You have grandchildren. Three of them."

"If Alexis didn't have children, I'd be having this conversation with her, too."

"So she's a better child to you than I am. What else is new?" I was not sufficiently ashamed of my petulance to control it.

Characteristically, she did not attempt to pretend that what I had said was untrue. "So what's wrong with you?" she demanded again.

My mother did not like men. Most women I knew didn't; some of them were vocal and virulent man-haters. She wasn't like that. Her attitude toward us was more contempt than hatred, more disappointment and disgust than dislike.

She never tried to hide it. She would say, "I wish I didn't feel this way," which is more than I had heard any other woman concede. "But every experience I have with a male supports it. Show me I'm wrong, Joel. Give me reason to like and respect a man. You're my only son. Make me proud."

It was clear I had not. My mother loved me because I was her son, but I was no stronger, smarter, more reliable, or more moral than any other male.

My father, for instance. For a long time, hearing the story and parts of the story like a fairy tale, I could not imagine why she had married him, and the sheer waste of it infuriated me.

Pretty, cultured Grace, who'd had "all sorts of young men vying for my hand." Vivacious, ambitious, intelligent Grace, who "could have had any husband I set my sights on."

And Charles, well established as the local ne'er-do-well, a boor and a fool even then, already a drunkard, already a spendthrift, whose apparent sole distinction was that he could recite the works of the Romantic poets from memory.

Sometimes the thought of their absurdly doomed match made me laugh at both of them. Sometimes it made me sad. At heart, it shamed me, for the union that had produced me was at best tacky and at worst symptomatic of much that was wrong with our society. And it filled me with dread and determination never to perpetuate it, never to enter into any relationship that would test my essential masculine character. Cupid foiled by cupidity. Romance undone by congenital moral rot.

I remembered my father almost not at all. I was six when he left, and my sister Alexis was not quite two. Secretly I suspected that six was old enough to have retained more memories than I had, especially since Alexis claimed to remember things like the smell of his pipe, the red feather in his hatband, the time he either dropped or threw her and dislocated her shoulder. My memories were far less specific: I remembered being afraid of him. I remembered missing him. I remembered wondering where he had gone, and whether when I grew up I would go there, too; sometimes I imagined a place without women, but that was too fanciful and frightening and so I imagined another place much like this one, another wife much like my mother, another son much like me—a whole nested community of doppelgangers.

My mother had told me more than I wished she had. His mistresses used to call her to weep about his unfaithfulness to them. She used to pour his whiskey down the sink and hide the checkbook and the car keys. One spring he just wasn't around when the family started back north from Ambergen. In some versions, she searched everywhere for him even though she hadn't had enough rest and so was sick from it the entire year; in other versions her father and brothers went looking for him in the men's favorite hangouts but couldn't find a trace, and she knew nothing about it until she awoke back in Tallus in the spring, and she was just as glad.

When I was about six months old, he came into the nursery one night and, with paternal instinct as unerring as a feeding mother's, singled me out and spanked me for crying. I did not think I consciously remembered that, but Ma had related the incident so many times to me and to others in my hearing that I could no longer tell whether it was her memory or mine. She said she tried to stop him. She said she did stop him, but he had already hit me, I was already traumatized. Once I said, "No wonder I'm so afraid of everything," and my mother looked so aghast that I knew both that I was right and that I would never dare say such a thing to her again.

"I'm tired," I told her now. It was as good an answer as any to the query about what was wrong with me—not untrue, but fundamentally nonresponsive.

"You're depressed," she accused.

I shrugged.

"Before I die," she said firmly, "I want to see you in love and happily married. You hear me?" As usual, her concern for me served only to make me feel guilty. "Or," she conceded, to my considerable surprise, "happy at something. What would make you happy, Joel? What do you want out of life?"

I had no idea. I resented her asking; it even

seemed a little cruel, since I did not perceive that I had many options, but I dared not think of my mother as cruel. I said nothing, and she sighed but did not press.

Rory slammed out of the house and at the edge of the porch struck a pose like the one he had attempted in the park—feet in a fighting stance, one hand on a low-slung hip, jaw and chest jutting. Periodically, I concluded the kid was all attitude, no substance, no heart. This summation, like all others about Rory, did not hold, but while it was in place it afforded me some relief from puzzling over him.

Ma and I watched him, she with wary affection and concern, I just warily. Rory glowered around at all of us, his malevolent gaze lingering on poor Miles for a beat or two. Apparently he saw nobody worth causing trouble for. He stalked off into the gloaming. I marveled smugly at the wasted energy of youth, an evolutionary anomaly if there ever was one.

Ma sighed again. She sighed often and heavily in my company. She leaned over to kiss me. I was embarrassed by the intimate tickle of the soft whiskers that ringed her wrinkled old-woman's mouth and the coolness of the bare skin around her nose. She stood up, setting the glider in motion, and held out her hands. "Come on, son. Let's go look at the babies."

This was far too much activity for me in my

malaise. I protested. "Ma, I just ate. I want to rest. Anyway, it won't work. I've seen babies." On the steps, Ted and Stockard were having a rambling conversation about the weather and, although I found the weather utterly uninteresting as a topic of discussion, I flailed for something to say that would ally me with them and disengage me from my mother.

I was neither quick nor forceful enough. She tugged at my sleeve in such a way that I would have fallen off the glider if I had not hastily lowered my foot to the porch floor and then heaved myself up. We made our way among Perry and Ted and the others and out along the short walk to the nursery.

I was not nearly so blasé about the nursery as I wanted both my mother and myself to believe. There was something about those large snug rooms, fur-lined with the writhing little bodies of all those eternally ravenous babies, that never failed to stir me. It was not some clandestine yearning for children of my own; at that time, I was aware of not a shred of paternal instinct. But the smell and sound and feel of the mass of infancy—squirming, dribbling urine and thin feces like so many tiny squirtguns, reeking with that milky, shitty, furry odor peculiar to infants that women found so endearing and that made my already queasy stomach lurch, mottling the walls and ceiling with infinite variations on the colors brown and gray shot through here and there with an orange or silver highlight, and the constant cacophony, the constantly undulating body heat—my senses were seriously threatened with overload if I did not pull them back even farther than they habitually were.

Entering the room only as far as necessary for my mother to shut the door and seal in the incubatory warmth, I asked somewhat archly, "Anybody we know in here?"

Of course there was. Our colony was a large one, and even the matriarchs did not know everybody. But within this teeming plush would be dozens, scores of children whose lineage my mother—and, doubtless, I—had known for generations. I did not really care who they were. One baby was essentially interchangeable with any other baby, if you asked me. But if I could get Ma started on identification and genealogy, it would distract her, briefly, from my own filial shortcomings, procreational and otherwise.

Briefly, it did. Her face, beautiful in a way quite different from how it must have been when she was a belle, lit up. Clasping her long thin hands, she stepped lightly across the sticky floor to the nearest corner. When she stood on tiptoe to touch her fingertip to one or more of the plump little bodies, I unwillingly noticed how the unfolding of her arms and legs was a bit creaky now, a trifle inefficient. "This is Becky's little girl," she murmured, as if not wanting to wake the child although there was such a din of small squeaks and clicks and chitters already that surely no other sound would disturb. "And over there"—she pointed with fingers like the tines of a long-handled rake—"is Maryanne's son. This is the first night she's left him."

I did know Maryanne. A true scatterbrain, she was always taking a turn too fast and grazing a wall, or traveling great distances at breakneck speed when what she was hunting had all the time been under her feet. Her son was stout. He snarled unpleasantly. His nails curved like miniature scythes, and his belly made him resemble a glossy brown bowling pin. Carrying him with her would have made Maryanne very nearly immobile. The sacrifices of motherhood touched and appalled me, in an obscure sort of way.

Someone flung open the door behind me and darted past. I flinched at the influx of cool air and barely got out of the way. I did not hear who it was. A mother, though. She flew straight into the churning far wall, which to me was nearly featureless, and without hesitation found what was obviously her own baby among the masses. Its squealing grew frantic, much higher-pitched and louder until I thought I could not bear it a second longer, and then stopped when she pressed her mouth over its mouth and fed it.

My mother cooed. "Don't you just love babies?"

"Not especially," I said.

She sighed. Instead of asking again what was wrong with me, as she might well have done, she answered her own question. "Typical male."

Women said that a lot. It was such a commonplace observation as to be beneath notice, a throwaway line. Women would have said they meant nothing by it, it was only a manner of speaking. It neither required nor permitted a reply, although over the years I had considered and rejected many.

The thing was, everything stated and implied by that remark was correct. Men were, in fact, weak, childlike, unreliable. Men did require protection, caretaking, and structure. Men were incapable of functioning in their daily lives without women. It was women upon whom the community depended for the expertise, common sense, and fortitude to get us all through the days and nights.

A girl paused in the opening between this room and the one just like it that adjoined. It was my niece Meredith, taller and shapelier, it seemed, just since last night, when surely I must have seen her although I doubtless had not taken much notice. She was still gangly but—I saw before I could stop myself—had both hips and breasts. In body type and deportment she was like Alexis—compact, stocky, fiercely graceful—

but facially she was a healthier copy of her father David.

Meredith did not hear us. We observed her go back and forth, ministering to her charges. Ma said, with grandmotherly pride, "She's so good at this. I feel safe leaving the little ones with her all winter."

"She doesn't like it," I said a little smugly.

"How would you know that?"

I would have liked, at least for that moment, to claim that I was Meredith's confidant. But that was not true, nor was it very likely. I had to settle for having some domestic information that my mother lacked. "She and Alexis have been arguing about it."

"Well, she's of an age," she declaimed, employing one of those code phrases women used with each other, or with men to underscore our status as perpetual outsiders in our own culture.

I, however, understood what she meant. Perversely, not because Meredith's role in society much mattered to me but to score a point with my mother, who wouldn't tally it, I observed, "It won't be much longer before she'll have to sleep the winter like the rest of you. What do you think, next year?"

"Alexis hasn't said whether she's started her period or not. I do know she's worried about her."

People talked about how vulnerable men were, how fraught with danger the world was for us, and parents fretted openly about raising boys. My mother never did stop bemoaning the tribulations of being a good mother to a son—the *impossibility* of being a good mother to a son, she would go so far as to say, presumably commenting on how I had turned out. But I thought it must be equally difficult to raise a daughter with integrity, or to be a decent woman in that culture that accorded women such advantage.

Meredith, or one of the other young adolescents charged with baby-sitting, closed the connecting door. Ma took a last sweep around the nursery, both wistful and watchful. She could not resist adjusting a blanket, stroking a fuzzy head, murmuring an endearment. Hands in my pockets and eyes downcast, I stifled my boredom and waited. At last, we left.

On the way back to the main house, Ma said, "You know I worry about you." I took it as an accusation.

All I could manage was, "I know."

"You seem so unhappy."

"I'm not unhappy."

"Well, you're certainly not happy."

"No."

"You don't seem to have any purpose or meaning or—I don't know—*spirit* in your life."

"I get by."

"That's not good enough."

"It's good enough for me. You expect too much, Ma."

"You're my son."

I kept quiet, concentrating on forcing my body to move. I was really extremely tired, and my mother was quite capable of carrying on any conversation, especially this one, entirely on her own.

But she stayed quiet, too, and emotional discomfort quickly worked its way through my exhaustion. I had lost her interest. She was thinking about something else. Out of breath from exertion and sudden acute dismay, I gasped, "I had The Dream again last night."

Instantly her attention snapped back to me. She stopped on the path. I stopped, too. "You did?"

I nodded. "Not much this time. Nothing new." I was too weary and unfocused to come up with something new. The price of my mother's attention was effort, and I was willing and able to put forth only the most minimal.

She put her hands on my shoulders. The webbing that fell from her arms enveloped me. "Tell me about it." It was far more command than invitation.

Recounting The Dream to my mother was much like navigating at top speed through total darkness in a place only marginally known. I would speak a word or two, a rapid phrase, and then my ears would involuntarily close themselves off from my own words for a split second so that I could pick up their echoes from her. Orienting and reorienting myself in this way, I could make great imaginative loops, dizzying dives, complicated sheer climbs in my storytelling, minutely adjusting to whatever I sensed she wanted to hear.

At that point in my life, The Dream was entirely a fictional construct—which is to say, a lie. I seldom recalled any of my actual dreams, beyond the most rudimentary of sensations and images, the crudest of messages (hunger, for instance; blood), and certainly I'd never dreamed anything like the elaborate recurring Dream I'd taken to telling her. The Dream was the only lie I ever told my mother once I became an adult, but it went on and elaborated for years.

"Well," I began, as always not knowing what I would say until it came out of my mouth, "I was flying again. This time in broad daylight."

She moved her hands up to my cheeks. Her slender thumbs curled around my ears but carefully did not probe inside. I felt her nod. Anticipation trembled through her wrists and clawed fingers into the flesh and bone of my face, making my jaw tingle and my headache exponentially worse.

"I was caught up in one of those wind currents," I went on, making it up as I went along, hunting for the simplest images and most succinct descriptions possible so I could get this over with. "I was soaring up along the face of a cliff. A red cliff. Sandstone. Pocked." Ma liked details. Her hands tightened around my cheekbones, slid down to the sides of my neck. For her sake, I pushed my floundering imagination. "Oh, and I saw an inscription on the cliff wall. My name, and my birth and death dates, and a couple of lines I couldn't make out. Then the wind dropped me. Then I woke up."

She shook me a little. "You couldn't read it?"

In the grip of her fingers, I managed to shake my head. "Just my name and the dates. But the date of death was my fiftieth birthday."

Even I, having been present in my own imagination when this conceit was created out of whole cloth, was impressed. My mother was positively thrilled. She caught her breath, then hugged me fiercely. "I do love you, Joel," she declared out loud, and then we went on to the house.

Ma and almost all the other women were out hunting, and I had digested enough of my meal that I was not quite so bleary and logey and had started packing, when Meredith appeared in the doorway to the loft. I tried to ignore her, hoping she would get bored and go away, but she wouldn't be ignored. "Uncle Joel?" I thought she sounded embarrassed.

"What can I do for you?" I asked irritably.

"I, um, there's something you have to see."

"Meredith, I'm busy."

"It's, um, it's Uncle Miles. I think he's dead."

"Dead?" I echoed, stupidly.

"I didn't want to tell Mom. You tell Mom. She'll get mad."

I followed my niece, who was flying across the dark courtyard. My mind was racing. The syndrome that had affected Miles's mind carried with it all sorts of physical problems, most of which I had heard about only vaguely. I did remember knowing that he had not had a normal life expectancy.

He was lying, in unnatural angles and folds, under overhanging bushes at the edge of the courtyard. Gingerly I squatted beside him. There were odd indentations at the base of his throat and, I saw when I surprised myself by taking his hand and turning it over, at his wrists. His skin, usually smooth as a child's, was now furrowed with deep, dry, irregular wrinkles. He was very pale. When I lifted his head, I felt notches along the juncture of his skull and spine, but I did not know whether they had always been there or whether, new, they had something to do with his death.

His characteristically dull face had been altogether emptied of animation and expression. In death he looked not peaceful but erased. He had been attacked. Fangs had left tracks at half a dozen places up and down his neck; the tip of his nose had been completely bitten off; pulse points all over his body—under both ears, inside elbows and knees, at wrists and thumbs and ankles—had been bored. This must have taken some time. Something had gorged, feasted on Miles, while the rest of us had been going about our daily business.

"Something ate him," Meredith observed.

"Cool," said Rory, who had slunk up behind us.

CHAPTER 3

"We do have natural predators," Ma had pointed out sadly. "As a species, we do have enemies. And part of the price we pay for living off by ourselves is increased exposure to them."

"Hey, yeah, well, maybe old Miles had enemies of his own," Rory had suggested with relish. "You know, like, *personal* enemies."

"No need to borrow trouble," Ma had rebuked him. "We've got plenty of trouble of our own."

Now she stood beside me at Miles's funeral, intent and composed, apparently at peace. None of that peacefulness was accessible to me. We were strangers, although she was the person in the world to whom I was closest—in truth, the only person to whom I had ever considered myself close. The minister, somebody's cousin from another colony, said Miles's name, and it sounded like another cliché, like nothing personal at all.

Sebastian sat cross-legged on the floor, his

back to the subdued hubbub of the funeral. I kept thinking we did not have time for this; we had to get ready to migrate. Leave it to Miles, even in death, to get in the way.

Sebastian was making one of his odd, intensely irritating, repetitive noises, this one a chittering like an angry squirrel. Nobody bothered to tell him to stop, though from some parts of the crowded room it was hard to hear what anybody was saying about the deceased. There was not much to say, anyway; people were shamelessly making things up.

From behind, Sebastian looked almost like an ordinary child, perhaps younger than his ten years. I felt an unexpected tenderness toward him that I immediately put aside. His knobby knees made a W with the stem of his frail body. His blond hair was shaggy because it was rare that he would allow scissors anywhere near him. His hands gyrated as though he were fingering some convoluted stringed instrument or making unrecognizable shadow animals on an imaginary wall.

Seeing him head-on was always something of a shock, even though I had known him his whole life. It was not that his face looked old; it looked ageless, eerily unmarked by the passage of life and time, as though Sebastian had ways of keeping himself well out of both.

It would be inaccurate to claim that I knew

what he was thinking and feeling, that I could tell whether distorted and disjointed images and ideas were scattershot through his mind or whether his thought processes were abnormally focused. It would be fallacious to suggest that, then, I even felt any real connection with him. But I also held myself out of the melee of life, as much as I could, and in a perverse sort of way it seemed I might have something to learn from him. So I watched him, rather than think too much about what had happened to Miles. Sebastian was avidly self-stimulating. The process had always interested me, the way he refused virtually all external stimulation in favor of that which he himself could generate and, presumably, control. He'd been doing it ever since birth. With an unbecoming gleefulness, I wondered what he had done during his months of gestation, and whether my sister had known something odd was developing in her womb, and whether her attitude toward him of contempt and frantic pity and guilt and impatience and fierce overprotectiveness—only a distillation, really, of the attitude Alexis and most women held toward men in general—had taken root before he was born.

Sebastian had been about three months old when his father David, who even then hadn't been noticing much of anything outside his own immediate sensorium, had noticed him rubbing the back of his head with his fist. At first David had been mildly impressed that his infant son already possessed enough fine-motor control to execute such a precise, directed, repetitive motion. The obsessive quality of it had quickly become apparent, though, as the baby rubbed and rubbed, wearing a substantial bald spot on his scalp.

He had also taken to emitting a peculiar, sustained, flat noise, quite unbabylike in that it wasn't directed at anybody else. It was something other than babbling, the raw material of language to be shaped by adult reinforcement into intelligible speech. It was not an expression of any need that Sebastian wanted somebody to do something about; the noise had not changed in frequency, volume, or tone when he was hungry or soiled or when those conditions were remedied. Obviously he was producing the sound for his own private—not to say secret—purposes.

Or maybe, I had thought unwillingly, he really was trying his best, which was far from good enough, to communicate. Like a baby who would be lost forever if its mother didn't single it out, who could do nothing but call for her again and again and hope she was listening, maybe Sebastian was doing his best to be found.

Even if that were the case, he would not be calling for me. It was not my responsibility. He had a mother, a grandmother, and a sister.

While the generic eulogies for Miles went on,

Sebastian was emitting an extremely high-pitched and low-volume repetitive tone, out of the auditory range of those who saw better than they heard but well within mine. I heard it in the spaces between the bones of my skull. Both Alexis and our mother glanced at him repeatedly, wondering, I knew, if they should try to get him to stop or take him out of the room, thus risking an even greater disturbance, or hope he would wind down of his own accord before he completely disrupted the service.

Ted and David were crying. I suspected that David was more upset by the reminder of his own mortality than Miles's, but Ted seemed genuinely sorrowful. This took me somewhat aback. I would not have thought Miles had any real friends to speak of, and his only close relatives had been his mother, who, years ago, had been one of those—a few every season—who just did not return one morning from a feeding foray. As I recalled, Miles had been the only one of us to truly mourn her; she seemed to have been as marginal a member of the community as he was. The rest of us were his "family" only in the technical sense of bloodline, which, because it applied in one way or another to everybody in the colony, meant nothing personal.

The harsh reality was that Miles had been both personally unremarkable and of no practical use. In sum, he had drained considerably more resources from the community than he'd contributed. Only with much concerted compensation by the rest of us, and then only barely, had he been able to function.

We'd had to search for or outright fabricate ways to keep him occupied; there had been few things he could actually do. Assignments requiring intellect, common sense, concentration, or self-motivation had been quite beyond him. He could not be counted on to follow simple instructions, let alone to solve a problem, formulate a plan, or make a decision on his own.

Physically, he had had below-average strength and ambiguous health. Occasionally we had used him for manual tasks, but for the most part he was more trouble than he was worth. He had tired easily, or he wouldn't show up for work if he had a headache or a cold. If he was left unsupervised for even a few minutes, he would wander off, or he would just sit down where he was, the job undone all around him, and eat his beloved trail mix and wait for somebody to come back to tell him what to do. Unkind as it was, the truth was it would be a relief not to have to babysit Miles anymore.

Sebastian was fairly hooting now; people were turning their heads in his direction. Alexis started toward him, but Ma stopped her.

Alexis had been forced to leave him in the nursery much younger than she should have, because he could not be trusted to hang onto her. The last time she had taken him with her, they had come home early, Sebastian obliviously tugging at clumps of his hair and my sister trembling, furious and terrified. She told my mother, and I eavesdropped, that she had been speeding along with the others, just at the fall of dusk when conditions were optimum, and right in the middle of an especially precipitous dive Sebastian had let go; she'd barely been able to scoop him up.

But when she left him behind, she often had trouble locating him in the crowded nursery, because he would not answer her call. On more than a few mornings she'd just given up, and had either eaten the extra food herself, thus throwing off her own metabolism, or passed it along to some other mother who had a normal child, which Sebastian decidedly was not.

Despite this early abandonment, Sebastian had not been a failure-to-thrive infant. He had flourished, in his own peculiar way. He'd grown bigger, stronger, and stranger. He still could not reliably feed himself, would often not accept the food from his mother's mouth, or he'd take it and hold it as if he didn't know or care how to swallow. Alexis worried constantly and vociferously about malnutrtition and, indeed, he was stick-thin and ghost-pale. But he survived.

He never seemed to care whether he'd eaten or

not, just as he seemed unaware of being cold or tired. He could have a wound for days without calling attention to it until someone else noticed, as if he did not feel pain or was not distressed by it.

Which actually seemed to me a potentially useful approach to the world. To regard pain as simply beneath notice. Not to expect anyone to tend to you. Sebastian, of course, took it to the extreme, increasing rather than diminishing his physical dependence on others, but emotionally he was, to all outward appearances, quite literally self-contained. There was something to be said for that.

Sebastian had managed to foil, rather dramatically, my sister's formidable maternal instincts, and she was often distraught over him. The other women would commiserate, and our mother would point out that, although certainly Sebastian was harder than most, raising sons was always a trial. Alexis appeared to derive some comfort from this dubious sisterhood.

Miles could not have been easy, either. The minister, who had barely known Miles except as a kind of cartoon character, was saying something about childlike simplicity. I fidgeted.

Every once in a while, more often when he was younger, one or another of the more nurturing or civic-minded women would take Miles on as a project. She'd spend a lot of concentrated time with this man she had known all her life, getting to know the "real Miles"; I agreed that there probably was a part of the personality concealed under layers of conditioning and social expectation, in Miles as in everyone, but I did not agree that it should be considered any more "real" than the rest.

Miles's advocate would wax indignant that we didn't sufficiently respect him, which was, of course, accurate. Then she would begin experimenting with all sorts of approaches, behavior mod and "normalization" being the most popular, which seemed to me no less disrespectful than the mostly benign neglect with which the rest of us treated him.

She would turn vociferously accusatory or affect a quiet smugness as she pinpointed various supposed keys to unlocking Miles's core self and helping him reach his true potential. She might even take notes.

But Miles—implacable, impervious, impassive—had bested them all. This *was* his true self; he *was* living up to his potential. Sooner or later, all his self-styled advocates and his friends who used the word "friend" both too lightly and too purposefully got bored and gave up trying to change Miles into a contributing member of society.

That was the closest I could come to thinking about Miles himself. The lifelong impression he'd left was so flat and featureless that I couldn't catch hold of it. But he served as a way for me to think about men in general, my family in general, society as a whole, which was slightly less agitating than obsessing about getting on the road, although probably less useful.

Everywhere—horizontally across this community and others I knew anything about, vertically down through the generations—were men and boys who could barely make their own way in the world, or who could not, who had to be propped up by women. Sebastian, Rory, David, Miles, my father and grandfather, even and perhaps especially myself—all of us were damaged some way. Physically frail, mentally weak, morally bankrupt—none of us could be considered whole. I could not, in fact, come up with a single man, current or ancestral or incipient, who possessed a fraction of the positive qualities of the average, ordinary woman.

I was getting restless, and I was by no means the only one; Stockard was openly fidgeting, Pete had backed away from the crowd to eye something that skittered along the baseboard, and Rory and Meredith were bickering in loud, vicious whispers. The minister finished talking. Miles was laid to rest. We paid the minister and dispersed, and my greatest sense of emptiness came from the acknowledgment that we hadn't lost much.

Preparations for the trip had reached their

usual late-autumn fever pitch. I had my own list of tasks to attend to. But I squandered another few minutes watching Sebastian. He had found a cranny to squat in and turned his back to everybody else. I could not bring myself just to leave him alone. By pressing myself against one of the walls that formed his corner and then positioning myself slightly above him, I could listen directly downward and clearly hear what he was doing now. He was, apparently, bent on ravaging his own face.

The lips of all my sister's kids are, like their father's, loose, thick, wrinkled, and slightly protruding. Sebastian's lower lip hung in tatters now, like a serrated leaf.

Meredith's nose had the high bridge that made some visages on her father's side of the family look positively aristocratic, but that had been exaggerated in the boys so that, together with the lips and the undershot jaw, their profiles could be said to suggest dull savagery. The bridge of Sebastian's nose was scored now, two deep bloody grooves across it where he had raked it with his nails.

His cheeks were gouged, obviously both inside and out. The fold of skin around his neck, as if he had stuck his head through an old-fashioned ruffled collar, was drizzled with his blood. I must admit I kept watching him for a beat or two before it occurred to me to break the grisly spell.

Then, "Sebastian!" I exclaimed, and lost my grip and slid noisily down the wall.

Alexis came flying across the room, shrieking her son's name. She grabbed his shoulder. He was no more or less stiff than usual; his mother might as well not have been there. She managed to jerk his torso and then his head around so that he was de facto facing her. When she caught sight of his face she cried out, swore, and slapped him hard.

Everyone in the room stopped doing everything else and paid attention to the small domestic crisis in our corner, except the star of the show, Sebastian. Even as his mother raised her hand to hit him again, he stuck out his long tongue and bit down on it.

My hand shot out, virtually of its own accord, as though protecting Sebastian were an instinct not long dormant although quite unsuspected until that moment. I caught my sister's arm in midair and spat, "No, Alexis, stop it," shocking us both.

For such an extroverted person in such a communal society, Alexis often behaved as if she were accountable to no one. That came of being a favored member of a favored class. Like many mildly abusive parents, determined to keep their children from "turning out" badly and disgracing them, Alexis never would have thought to alter for the public her private behavior toward them.

To her—and most women would have agreed, most men would have had no opinion—her parenting of her children, especially of her sons, was at the same time supported by community mores and nobody else's business.

There I stood, grasping my sister's arm and not meeting her eyes. I had no concept of what to do next, either to proceed with my intervention or to abort it. More than anything else, I was excruciatingly self-conscious.

In the space of a split second, Alexis went from astounded to livid. A lesser woman would simply have jerked away from me or told me to get my hands off her, which I would gladly have done. Alexis curled her thumb and fingers back around my wrist and dug the nails in, with this one practiced and efficient movement causing me to long to break my grip and rendering me incapable of doing so. Nearly the same height, she brought her face close to mine. Her tiny black eyes glittered. Her breath was hot and sharp. "How *dare* you?"

I forced myself neither to stammer nor to apologize. Since we had been small children, essentially since her birth, my sister had dominated me and been roundly encouraged to do so; doubtless we were destined to live out the rest of our socially and genetically constrained lives without much alteration in the power dynamics between us. But groveling was not required. I declared, rather self-righteously, "Physical violence doesn't teach him anything. It just drives him further inside himself."

"Oh, Joel, you're such an *expert*!" Alexis was a champion sneerer. She retracted her upper lip from her top teeth, exposing not only their glistening points but also the pink scalloped bases where they rooted in her gums. She narrowed her narrow eyes until they all but disappeared. "Who do you think you are?"

There it was again, the fundamental and nonanswerable question. I made no attempt at a reply. I did, however, try to face her down, with equal lack of success. We stood there nose-to-nose, and I would not have been able to end the standoff.

Ma stepped in. "Joel." She never would have spoken my sister's name in that stern, morally indignant manner. "Don't you have anything better to do than get in other people's way? Or are you all ready to go?"

I was nowhere near ready, which she knew. I said to her, not to my sister, "Sorry."

"And Alexis, stop bullying your brother." To my ears, this maternal admonition sounded decidedly halfhearted.

With a final gratuitous stab of her claws and a venomous glance at Ma, Alexis let me go. As I turned to walk away, I realized that, sometime during our little imbroglio, Sebastian, the subject of it, had left his corner.

I scanned the room and found him on the far wall, arms and legs rotated in their sockets, causing him to look like a lizard climbing. His head was twisted oddly, too, so that he gave the impression of staring at me over his shoulder. I suspected that in truth he was staring at nothing at all, or at something the rest of us had no hope of seeing, and I just happened to be in his skewed field of vision. Nothing personal. Story of my life.

Meredith knelt beside him. Through the commotion between us, I could clearly hear her yelling at him. Sourly I reflected on the frustrations of the sibling relationship, which seemed to me to arise out of the dissonance between stubborn, baseless expectation and persistent reality. I could think of only a very few situations in which siblings would have chosen to relate if they had not been related. In the vast majority of cases, brother and brother, brother and sister, even sister and sister could tolerate each other only for brief periods of time or were active antagonists. This was true as children growing up; Ma had despaired over Alexis and me, but we had been no worse than almost anybody else we knew. Conventional, hopeful wisdom promised that siblings were, despite every appearance to the contrary, really quite close; that they would defend each other against an enemy from outside the family; that when they were adults they would be friends. I had almost never seen that happen. Unless they were engaged in intrafamilial warfare, siblings generally had as little to do with each other as possible.

Out of a peculiar and, I could only hope, fleeting illusion of comradeship with Sebastian, of all people, I surreptitiously waved and smiled at him. "Hey, kid," I said, meaning to acknowledge him in case he really had been making contact, to reinforce this rare socially appropriate behavior, and to defy my mother and sister. This last was pointless, too late and therefore essentially risk-free, since they both had left the room to attend to other things.

I had too much to do. I never saw any other man with a list, and by that measure alone my assignments seemed to me disproportionate, never mind that I had compiled the list myself.

One particularly odious task was to gather apples—ripe, overripe, and windfall, to suit the range of tastes—and sack them for the journey. Carrying our own food was critical because it allowed us to travel straight through the nights without having to stop to eat, which would have called unwelcome attention to ourselves and increased the odds of problems with insomniac locals, speeding long-distance truckers, and other nocturnal travelers.

But fruit was repugnant to me, and the

orchards were especially redolent this time of year. Just the thought of the sickly sweet odor turned my stomach. And the orchards were too close to the dens of the Old Women for me to feel anything but uneasy in their malevolent if hidden presence.

I had never been in the wakeful presence of an Old Woman. I had never heard one speak. I knew no one who had; I suspected Ma of having had some sort of personal experiences with them, but I had never queried and she would not have admitted it to me. They were said to awake only a few nights in a season, and there had been nights all my life when I had felt evil abroad; as a kid I had called it monsters, but now I had no name for it but Old Women, and that was enough.

Dragging burlap sacks for the whole fruit and lidded five-gallon containers for that which had decayed into pulp, I trudged on foot through the house, across the courtyard, through the buildings on the other side of the compound, past the dens, and into the orchards. Ordinarily, this would have been Miles's job. He had missed a lot of usable fruit, and he had always gobbled more of the very ripe than his stomach could handle, with the result that intestinal difficulties made him and everybody else miserable the first night or two on the road. But at least I had not had to do anything regarding apple collection except supervise.

The others were already there; I heard them as I approached, and thought for a moment, sheepishly, that they had started the gathering without being told. But they were feeding, indulging themselves and wasting time when there was so much to be done.

I just stood there among the trees for a while, indulging myself in outrage and disgust, thereby wasting time, too. A pattering, dripping, sheeting sound surrounded me, like rain except that it was confined to the area of the orchard; where there were no trees, nothing was falling from the sky. The viscous precipitation was composed of organic discard no one considered edible, partly digested fruit, and the nonstop excrement of those who perched above and around me and gorged themselves. I was drenched in it.

Unhappily, it had been a good year for apples, and there was still plenty of fruit on the trees and on the ground. Not one of the other men offered to help, and I preferred resenting their laziness to asking. It took me the rest of the night to collect all the fruit, store it in its appropriate vessels, pack it in the trucks for transport, and recuperate.

Early the next evening, Mitchell and I were in the process of closing up the attic for the season —nailing shut and shuttering windows, setting out traps, treating floors—when from the courtyard below we heard the first bellows from the lek. I groaned aloud, and Mitchell grunted. "Shit," he said. "Hard to believe we'll think fucking is fun after a few days in the tropical sun, isn't it?"

"I won't."

"Oh, sure you will. You're a creature of destiny just like the rest of us."

Mitchell was given to specious and florid figures of speech like that. He tended to get especially carried away around women, thinking to impress them with his erudition and wit, when in fact he was the subject of considerable female derision behind his back. With men, he was only mildly a buffoon, assuming just one of the numerous degrading roles with which men reduced themselves.

The shutter on the east window was stuck. I forced it and it snapped. I swore. The sudden bright sunshine sent needles of pain through my eyes and made everything look gauzy. When we came back in the spring, I wouldn't even have time to relax before I'd have to be back up here, making the windows accessible again for that first night. Seemed like a double waste of time and effort to me. But I didn't make the rules.

The commotion was loud and getting louder, even though the semicircular area used once a year as the lek was on the opposite side of the courtyard from our house. Irritably I wondered who was down there already. Rory, no doubt; my nephew's obsession with fornication, his enthusiasm for the female-prescribed male sex roles, was one of the numerous things he and I did not have in common. I heard, with familiar aversion, his mating call, an explosive cry like a guttural foghorn. He'd been practicing, probably in front of a mirror, to use his big lips to their full advantage, a fleshy megaphone. The suggestive, even obscene, call was a promise on which I had no doubt he could deliver.

Mitchell rose to it. He laid down his tools, straightened, scratched his groin. "Duty calls," he said to me, and left.

Duty did, indeed, call, but I delayed going down to the lek as long as I decently could, which was only until I'd pried the pieces of the broken shutter off the wall. All that remained then of the attic chore was to repair the shutter, and for that I had to go downstairs and out to the workshop, which meant crossing the courtyard and being visible from the lek. I might as well get this over with.

The lek was already crowded, which was not surprising considering that it was a small area expected to contain the expansive movements of mass copulation. Every time we went through this I was grateful, for this among a host of other reasons, that it happened only once a year.

Middleaged and out of shape though I was, and not much given to vocalizing the mating call, I was immediately set upon by two females, one of whom was the intrepid Theresa. I did my duty with both of them, although I doubted it would do much good. I was able to produce only a minimal amount of semen and, though of course I had no way of measuring the sperm count, I couldn't imagine that anything I contributed would actually produce offspring. It never had, as far as I'd been informed—the eternal male caveat—and at this point in my reproductive life it seemed even less likely. These two women would store my semen in their bodies until they decided they were ready to send ova into it, and then nothing would happen as a result.

If they knew that, it didn't deter them. "Thanks, babe," Theresa said happily. She kissed me on the cheek and walked away across the courtyard, her dressing gown flapping open from her shoulders like extra wings.

The other woman seemed older than I was, so maybe there would not have been much real chance of her getting pregnant anyway, or maybe she didn't want to and was, like me, just going through the motions. She tousled my thinning hair as she left and pronounced, "You're sweet, Joe." It wasn't unusual for women to get male names slightly wrong; men were far more likely to pay attention to details like that, because we'd had to, for social survival. Her name was Louise.

I sat for a short while at the periphery of the

lek, surreptitiously relaxing. Any woman monitoring my industriousness might think I was recovering from the exertion of sex, except my mother, who would cut me some slack anyway. Drearily considering how best to fix the shutter, even more drearily anticipating the long trip ahead of us, I thought about the haphazard nature of paternity. All a man had to go on was what women told him. I could mount a dreary argument that this fact of life was the single most important source of female power, but argument over a fact of life was patently not worth the effort.

Few men and fewer women were left in the mating arena. Mitchell was done; he would be glad to tell me later who had fucked him this year. Foremost among the younger males still going at it was, predictably, Rory, and I observed his copulatory action with a sort of weary amazement. I didn't think I'd ever been that young. I wondered what he thought of himself before, during, and after.

At the moment, Rory and a blandly pretty young woman were joined in a sexual ballet that took them across the ground and up into the air in truly breathtaking gyrations. Various appendages beat and swayed and crisscrossed, moving together in lockstep. I could see where they were joined, the pivot point of their dance, but both their organs were concealed in the tangle of her long golden hair and his shorter russet fur. Their cries, grunts, squeals, growls were loud in the lek and in the surrounding courtyard.

When they were finished, the girl glided off and Rory collapsed laughing in the dust. Laughing! Alexis went to him and hovered, to make sure he was all right—which he was, but no thanks to her. Deciding I'd had enough and, in any case, would be pushing my luck if I stayed here any longer, I proceeded to the workshop.

Once I set my mind to it, it didn't take long to repair the shutter. I was fairly competent at domestic tasks, though I detested most of them. I was hurrying back across the courtyard, which was crowded now with people getting ready for an extended vacation and showed no signs of the seasonal orgy, when I saw my sister again.

She was in the shadowy L of the big house, behind the kitchen addition, not really well hidden but not exactly out in the open, either. Meredith was with her. They were squatting on the ground, and someone was stretched across all their knees. Sebastian, I saw. He was characteristically stiff, but he did not seem to be struggling. I slowed but didn't stop, watched against my will and better judgment.

Alexis said something, and Meredith bent over her brother. Then Alexis looked up and saw me.

Abruptly she stood up, rolling Sebastian to the ground and sending Meredith back onto her hands. "Joel!" my sister yelled. "You have work to do! Get out of here!" So I did.

CHAPTER 4

The ripe, red, juicy watermelon, cut lengthwise to reveal its bloodless flesh that was so tantalizing to some branches of the family, went flying off the porch. It neither burst nor tipped upside down in the dust, which surely disappointed Rory, who had tossed it. "Fucking fruithead crap," he snarled, then struck a belligerent pose and waited for somebody to protest. When nobody did so soon enough to suit him, he added for good measure, "Fucking nigger shit," and waited again to hear what effect he had had.

Though I knew better, I fell for it. "You're kidding," I said, and stared at Rory and laughed. I could not help myself. He had said such things before, and I knew he was not making some kind of sick racist joke. But openly taking him seriously would have necessitated admitting how disturbed and dangerous he was, which would at least have implied an obligation to do something.

As so often happens, the threat I knew to be worried about turned out to be the wrong one.

"Fuck, no, I'm serious," he insisted, unnecessarily. "I ain't eating none of that shit."

Stockard, who was a fruit eater to his very bones, had clambered down and rescued the melon before any damage was done. Now he had his face buried in it so that it ringed his head like an extra collar of scarlet moist flesh. "Watermelon's great stuff. You don't know what you're missing, boy."

"What's the matter, Rory?" I demanded, challenging him as if we were already safely at Ambergen. "Afraid you'll be contaminated?"

Stockard was still talking with his mouth full. "I mean, there's nothing up here to compare with Ambergen melons and mangos and bananas, but this'll do for now." He raised his head and belched, and watermelon seeds flew.

I do not know what possessed me. "What have you got against fruiteaters, anyway? What difference does it make what somebody's food preferences are?" I would like to be able to say that I was trying to take his measure, to ascertain just how deep and virulent his racism was. But really it was just a way of egging him on without having to expend very much energy. Rory was an easy mark.

"It ain't natural," he declared, as if that were the end of that.

"And black people?"

"They ain't human. They ain't animal, either. They're some other thing, I mean, look at how their heads are made. And they get this disease. What is it, this anemia, no other human beings get." He pulled a face. "And you guys take their blood. Makes me puke."

"Their blood?" I said encouragingly.

"Tastes different. Tastes like poison."

A ripple of incredulous laughter spread through the men on the porch. Rory glowered and puffed out his chest.

He had little use for anybody who wasn't "like me," which meant he had little use for practically anybody, depending on how narrowly he was defining "like me" at any given time. I had heard him express extravagant contempt for our distant cousins who had noses like hammerheads, for those who did not migrate, for those—admittedly very few and more than a little strange—who slept at night and were awake and abroad in the day. Any species, gender, ethnic group, family, hair color, head shape, feeding habit, metabolic cycle, ear size not his own had at one time or another been defined as "other," with the result that Rory regarded himself—sometimes with pride, sometimes with fury—as a lonely righteous being in a corrupt and alien world.

He was just getting started. "We have to protect the purity of the species," he declaimed.

Unwisely I remarked, "The 'purity of the species' is already substantially watered down, if you ask me, and getting more so by the season."

He hissed in moral outrage. "No shit. And it's up to people like me to stop it."

If a woman had been there, she would have told him to stop talking like that; depending on her own sense of morality, she might have lectured him or expressed moral disapproval. My mother occasionally had gone so far as to talk about evil. To Rory and to his mother she would go on about how evil was hardy as a weed and needed no nurturing, only opportunity. Rory scoffed. Alexis defended her son and, infrequently, asked for advice, of which my mother had a store.

To me, in private, she had once or twice confessed that she thought Rory might be evil. I had heard her make this startling statement to Rory's father, as well, and wondered what her intent could be. Perhaps she had hoped to jolt David out of his solipsism. Most likely she had had no particular intent, had not given a thought to how such a conjecture might affect Rory's father. She would never have said it to Alexis.

Both David and I remained studiously silent when she said extravagant things like that. David waited the minimum acceptable period of time before he started talking about his own maladies.

I just tried to think about Rory as little as possible, even when he was the center of attention.

This time, the women were all, to one degree or another, disengaging from everyday life in preparation for their sleep. Only men were within earshot of Rory's ravings, and the most assertive response any of us could muster was Pete's bored "Oh, for God's sake, Rory, lighten up."

Rory swaggered across the porch, a caricature of the blustery young gladiator. Had it been a few weeks later, he'd have had a fight for the asking; many men, especially young ones, were wildly combative in the south. We were, in fact, getting close enough to migration that tension was palpable, and Pete's sons Josh and Ramsey stood up beside their father, springy on the balls of their feet and shoulders high, while Rory approached.

Then Sebastian came in a whirlwind out of the house, screaming "No! No! No!" stumbling and careening, catching himself somehow in midair enough to maintain his forward progress. Meredith was in pursuit.

Momentarily distracted from his pugnaciousness, Rory stared after his brother and sister, pronounced, "Fucking freak," and stormed away.

David gave a little groan. Gingerly he spread his fingers against his upper chest. "I've been having pain, Joel. Somewhere in here—" He frowned and moved his fingers slightly to the left. "—or here, maybe. What do you think it could be?" I rubbed my head, roused myself, and all but tumbled off the porch in my haste to get away. Rory had stopped toward the other side of the courtyard, but I could not bear the thought of trying to converse with him, and I found it hard to believe he had anything to say to me, either. He did turn off the path that I was following, and for the moment I was spared having to think about him anymore.

I made my way to the garage for the last inspection of the hibernacula before we hit the road. My mother was there, conducting her own inspection; once I had resented her poking and prodding in what was supposed to be my area of responsibility, but I had come to realize that she was checking details that were nowhere on my list and that I would never think to look for.

We worked more or less together for a while, and then she said, as far as I could tell apropos of nothing other than the shared activity itself, "This may well be my last trip south. I know you don't want to hear that, but I think we ought to talk about it."

Had I thought my mother was immortal? My resistance to the conversation she was trying to have with me was surprisingly intransigent.

"This year, I just might not wake up."

"Are you sick?"

"Not that I know of."

"Then why are you talking like this?"

"I have a feeling." She hesitated. "I've been warned."

"By whom?" I demanded sharply, wondering if Rory or Alexis had said something thoughtless or deliberately unkind. Though Ma was not thin-skinned and certainly had no need of a defender, I was ready to make a fuss on her behalf—which was, in truth, on my own. "Did somebody say something to you—"

"Joel," she said, and patted my hand. "It was an Old Woman."

My indignation instantly gave way to such instinctive aversion that it was all I could do to ask "What—what did she say?"

"She didn't exactly 'say' anything. But I've been warned. Or invited. I don't have another full year to live." Though I had known her bluntness all my life, it had lost none of its power to jar me. I'd come to see how this was one of our complex little games: The more forthright she was about issues I found distasteful, the more withdrawn and passive I became, which in turn elicited from her directness sometimes to the point of brutality in an attempt, I supposed, to force me to engage. The similarity between this interplay and the mother-son dynamic between Alexis and Sebastian was not, even then, lost on me.

"Joel, do you hear me? Do you understand what I'm trying to tell you?"

There was a spot in the corner of the roof of this first truck, not the oldest by some years, which would have to be reweatherized before next season, but I judged it—with some anxiety—to be sound enough for this year. I extracted my bulging notebook from my pouch and scribbled a reminder. The temptation not to bother writing it down, to rely on only a mental note, was strong because it was superficially easier, but from woeful personal experience I knew the validity of the stereotype that men would forget everything about matters of northern responsibility during the southern sojourn.

"There's something to be said for being done with all this," my mother persisted. "These last few years it's been harder and harder to come back." I felt a spurt of anger that I hastily tamped down, a buzz of fear that I sublimated into renewed manual labor.

Women often talked reverently about their annual near-death. They would describe it as life-changing or -centering, hallucinogenic or directly connected to the divine, depending on the woman and on the circumstances and obsessions of her waking life at the time. I had little doubt that most of these testimonials were in some way sincere. I had equally little doubt that they were intended to underscore the fundamental banality of masculine existence, of which no man needed to be reminded.

It was not precisely sleep, they told us, but a profound alternative consciousness that those who had not experienced it—preadolescent females, who would, and males of any age, who would never—could not possibly appreciate. I had never asked any of them, most particularly my mother, for details, but I'd not been able to induce enough self-protective skepticism to counteract the message that my life, and that of every other male, was congenitally incomplete, into which we were, by nature, unable to introduce either meaning or substance, because we slept only in segments of every twenty-four-hour period and not for months at a time.

I had a dim perception that some of the old women had similar feelings about their own lives in relation to those of the Old Women. Those creatures, though, were utterly beyond my comprehension—or, more precisely, beyond my willingness to comprehend. The thought of my mother communicating with one of them, in some pre- or post- or extraverbal way, made my skin crawl.

I hoisted myself down from the top tier of sleeping compartments, grimly noting once again that my joints were stiffer and my lung capacity less every time I did something like that. Panting, I stood in the chilly garage, pretending to be more preoccupied with my to-do list than I was.

Ma came to me. She did not touch me, but she positioned herself directly in front of me and so close that it was impossible to resist for long the impulse to focus on her. To my horror, she was crying, which, of course, was in some way my fault. "Joel," she said, the instant she had my attention. "I'm telling you that I will die soon. Don't you have anything to say to that?"

I shrugged. "What's to say?"

"Don't you *care*? Won't you miss me?"

"Sure."

She waited for more. I waited for cues, or for her to give up. Peering at my notebook, I did my best to concentrate instead on all the tasks—too many, but manageable—that I had to do before we left.

Finally, Ma sighed, a sound familiar from my earliest childhood, and shook her head. I understood that I had let her down again, and that it was not really my fault since it was in my nature to do so. "I worry about you, son," she declared, as though it were the first time she had ever said that.

"Don't worry about me, Ma," I recited.

"I did the best I could with what I knew at the time, but now that I see the kind of man you've become, I think I've made serious mistakes raising you. I'm sorry."

"It's okay. I forgive you for making me the kind of man I am." If she caught my sarcasm, she gave no sign. She patted my arm, commiserating, as if to say we both just had to make the best of a bad deal.

"You and Alexis both," she said mournfully.

Now here was something new. A distant adrenaline alarm informed me that it was also threatening. I had absorbed with my mother's milk her dissatisfaction with me, but I had never guessed she harbored toward my sister any feelings other than adoration and pride.

Ma was not finished. She sighed, heavily this time, and sounded far more distressed now that she was contemplating my sister's alleged ruination. "Alexis is so angry so much of the time. Hateful. I don't like having to say that about my own daughter, but it's the truth. Don't you think so?"

Of course I thought so. I always had. The startling fact that our mother thought so, too, had the potential of forcing me to reevaluate my entire family history if I allowed myself to take it too seriously. So I limited my response to "Oh, I don't know."

"I know you two are close," our mother said, and I did not snort or guffaw. "But she's always been hateful to you. I've spoken to her about it, but it makes no difference. Do you think somehow *I've* made her that way?"

Whenever a woman accosted me with intimate feelings, hers or my own, I was made uneasy. Especially I did not want to know the workings of my mother's heart. Still, it was an improvement over the earlier discussion of her imminent death, and therefore probably merited encouragement. I came up with a substantially noncommittal "In what way?"

"I know the way your father treated her has turned her against all men," she mused sadly. "And I know she's probably picked up some of my attitudes. But I've always tried to *say* all the right things to her about men. I can't be held responsible for what I think and feel. Can I?"

Lately I had become curious, in a mildly resentful sort of way, about the internal dialogue of my mother and other mothers of sons. Ma, for example, was a highly moral woman. In theory and in practice, she valued both honesty and kindness, and for the most part managed to deliver both. She would go out of her way to help someone in need, sometimes at considerable personal sacrifice, and she was the consummate community volunteer. She spoke up against all sorts of injustice, took up all manner of causes, personally and in skillful concert with others righted any number of wrongs.

So how was it that she could say to me: "People accuse me of being anti-male. I don't mean to be anti-anybody. But listen. How many times have I had the truck in the shop this year, and I still can't be sure it'll last the trip; he's supposed to be a good mechanic, but he either can't or doesn't care to do it right."

I did not bother to point out that a female mechanic might well have had the same problems; the truck had over 100,000 migratory miles on it. In reality, it wasn't a female mechanic. And she was right; this guy was doing slipshod work. Maybe she was right, too, that it was the best you could expect from a man.

"Show me I'm wrong, I tell them. Show me a man who can be counted on. Show me a man with common sense and common decency. Show me a man who could get along for ten minutes without women to keep this world going. I'd love to be proved wrong, but I don't even hope for it anymore." I could not, of course, show her anything of the kind.

Ma stayed there for a while, giving the impression of being even smaller and older than she was, of having collapsed in on herself. This was a habit that had become more pronounced with age; it seemed to be a sort of meditative state, a reflection and result of hibernation, perhaps even a rehearsal for death.

She used to do that every once in a while when I was a boy, more often during my teenage years. The older I got, the more I grew to expect such absences and even to find them relieving, but when I was little they had enraged me. I could remember climbing up on her shoulders and savagely pulling her hair. No response. I would fake injury or, in extreme circumstances, actually hurt myself, but she would not come out of her trances to notice.

Eventually, I learned the hard lesson we all learned: No child is perpetually the center of anyone's world but his own. Ma would return to me, often more loving than before, more playful with tongue and teeth, more patient and exuberant. It was as though, unable physically to escape, she had found a way to leave me that I could not stop. It was even truer now than then.

Since nothing I could say or do would be sufficient to rouse her, I immersed myself in the task of extricating from the jumble above the rafters items we would need for the trip. It had long been my responsibility to supervise the packing up and putting away, and every spring I expended considerable time and energy devising and implementing new improved systems for keeping things up there organized—wasted time and energy, for every fall the chaos was worse. I suspected mischief makers, vandals, saboteurs. The loft was almost emptied now, and numerous resting and hiding places had been revealed. I wished I could rest and hide.

A loop of frayed rope and one last tarpaulin had been stored too far back under the eaves to be reached without contortion. I had certainly not directed that they be put there. Swearing and sweating, I flattened myself on the dusty boards and stretched, and then my fingertips encountered something soft.

Assuming it was a work glove left there since last spring by some careless man, I would not have bothered with it if I had not wanted to avoid my entranced mother. I grasped a pliable protrusion that I thought was its empty finger, and the thing came out easily, on its way to the trash bag slung over the edge of the rafters. Fleetingly, then, I thought it was a flimsy rubber mask, and then I saw that it was a dead rabbit.

Not just dead. Gutted. Drained. What I was holding was an ear—empty, indeed, as the finger of a handless glove. The hollowed body cavity had collapsed in a dozen places, somehow the more disgusting because there were also places where it had not collapsed. Gashes in the neck—toothmarks—gaped wide and gray, and the fur around them had been sucked clean of blood. Between the ears, across the top of the small skull, were holes as if punched by a knitting needle.

"Look at this," I called to my mother below. "Somebody's been indulging himself." Rory, I was sure.

I used my teeth to hold on to the rabbit carcass so both hands were free to tug at the rope and tarp. They were wedged tightly under the roof slope, and dislodging them turned out to require the use of my feet, too. All of this contorting had rendered me dusty, sore, and more than a little irritable by the time I got everything down. I dropped the bloodless rabbit. Its aftertaste in my mouth was dusty.

"Would you look at this?" I demanded again.

She already was. She had crouched on the floor, a black cone-shape with her webs and cloak billowing and then folding and settling around her, and her long fingers were poking at the flask of skin and bone. "I don't like this," she observed. "We don't take more than we need. Such lack of self-control. Such sadism." She shook her head.

I left her brooding there while I took a load out to the pickup. It seemed to me that, old and female and my mother though she was, she could help. The petulant thought was mostly habitual and warranted no attention or expression.

When I came back into the garage, Ma was gone. She had left the drained rabbit carcass for me to dispose of, which I did. I was getting tired. Although I did not look forward to most aspects of the southern migration, it was always a relief to regain some strength and stamina, if only for a season.

On my next trip out to the truck, absurdly loaded down in order to decrease as much as possible the number of passages back and forth, I caught sight of Mitchell and Stockard dozing in the shade in the corner of the courtyard, flabby arms folded like wings over their bellies. I shouted at them to help me. They both stirred, though with not nearly so much alacrity as they should have. Lazy. Not overly bright, either.

Mitchell waved in what I assumed was acquiescence, and they both got to their feet and started rather desultorily in my direction. By this time, my muscles were trembling under the excessive weight, and the strain was making me a little nauseous, so I did not wait for my cousins to catch up. When they were nowhere to be seen by the time I had unloaded myself and returned to the garage, I was frustrated to the point of fury.

Determined to insist that they fulfill their obligations to me and to society, I wasted a good half hour looking for them. At last, one of the women chanced to inform me that they had been sent, along with Rory, to collect the last of the produce from the gardens.

Sullenly I finished loading the things in the garage by myself, rather fervently indulging in a little masochistic fantasy about working so hard that I would collapse, injured and exhausted, and that my need for medical care would delay the start of the trip. Accordingly, I actually did fill both the dolly and my scoop too full, and I strained various muscles, but not enough. Limping and indignant, I trudged through the late-night chill back to the house.

On the porch I sat on the glider and tried to

decide what to do next. My mind refused to stay with its own lists, and I allowed myself a few risky moments of worry. There was plenty to worry about. For one thing, I was beginning to have intimations of the autumn not long hence when I would no longer be able to withstand migration. Men who were forced by infirmity to stay in Tallus all winter almost never were alive to greet the returning migrators in the spring.

There was a suggestion now of dawn. Dully, I was hungry. The clouds of insects around the porch lights were noticeably thinner now than even a week ago, and many fewer rodents and snakes populated the cooling grasses. Every autumn I was stirred by what must have been a primordial panic that we would all starve to death before the next spring.

I pushed at the porch floor a few times with one foot, to get the glider moving, then gave it up as too much trouble. The sun rose. It hurt my eyes. I would have to rouse myself now if I wanted to eat. That seemed like too much trouble, too.

CHAPTER 5

Delays mounted. Just before dawn one night, the air prickled with the first snow.

Several women besides Alexis had had trouble falling asleep. I had assigned crews to take down and rebuild the white-noise apparatus in each of the three hibernaculum trucks. That had solved the problem for everybody but my sister, who seldom slept deeply anyway, no matter what we did.

Then there had been a glitch with the nursery, not technically within my purview but certainly affecting the discharge of my own duties. Nobody was ever especially comfortable leaving the infants in the charge of prepubescent child care workers while the adults and teenagers either slept or played. Conventional wisdom had it that this awkward system was an adaptation left over from the days of maternity colonies separate from single-sex migration; if so, I reflected sourly, it was time for the next evolutionary step.

The trip itself was hard on the babies, too. Every year I was bitterly amazed when we made it back to Tallus in the springtime having buried only a few infants along the way, having forced only a few mothers to wake up suddenly and forever bereaved, only a few fathers to settle down to living the rest of their lives with what they called the ultimate loss. Only a few tragedies every season. As though only a few, because they were inevitable, were also acceptable.

So it was legitimate cause for alarm, as well as for heightened frustration at the continued disruption of my schedule, when I was suddenly informed, at what should have been the last minute, that we had less than a full complement of nursery staff. I did not ask why, whether the supervisor had miscounted babies or misassigned workers, or whether there were special needs that had not been factored in, or what. "Fix it," I growled, and stalked off, aware that it was probably managerial stupidity to entrust the solution of so major a problem to the very people whose incompetence had caused it in the first place. So frustrated I was shaking, I tried to take care of other things on my list about which I had some idea what to do.

Unwillingly, I overheard some of the frantic brainstorming among the first- and second-line supervisors. "Why can't Meredith help us out?" That was Stockard. "She's not hibernating yet, is she?"

"She'll throw a fit. Alexis will throw a fit," predicted Ramsey, and he was right.

We were treated to a mother-daughter temper tantrum. They threw things and broke things that someone else would have to clean up, since they certainly would not. Wearily I added that to my list, which seemed to be growing rather than shrinking.

Meredith threatened to hitchhike south by herself. Alexis threatened to put an adult male on nursery duty all winter. She was not impressed by the argument—true, if self-serving—that depriving a male of his seasonal R&R at Ambergen could have physical and social consequences as dire as depriving a female of her winter sleep. Perry, who was advancing the theory, was talking through his hat. He had no way of knowing whether there was any truth to it, but it sounded good.

Eventually, Stockard or someone did come up with some other solution to the problem. Again, I did not ask the details; at that point, all I wanted to know was that it was solved. Altogether, that little fiasco cost us the better part of forty-eight hours.

During that unwelcome downtime, I went to talk to my mother. Ostensibly and officially, I was checking on her hibernation status, as we routinely checked on all the sleepers throughout the autumn and winter, the elderly ones more often and more thoroughly than the young and middle-aged. This did not, of course, include the really ancient hibernators, the Old Women, who were, as far as I knew, left completely on their own. I never had understood how they lived. I had no idea whether they were, in fact, alive in any sense with which I was familiar. Even if I had had the courage to enter their dens, hedgelike and burrowlike structures at the far back of the Tallus property and the far back of Ambergen; even if I had known how to get in and how to get out; even if I had had the time—I would not have known a dead Old Woman from a live one, or what to do if I knew they were dead.

When my mother was in hibernation, she was as good as dead to me. That seems terribly solipsistic to me now. I knew no male who could really think of women other than in relation to himself. We were so dependent on them, individually and collectively, for sustenance, order, and meaning that it was hard to regard them as anything other than our exalted functionaries; they regarded us in the same way, though in rather less respectful terms. On this issue, all of us differed from Sebastian—and, for that matter, Rory—only in degree: Everyone who wasn't *me* wasn't quite real.

I was telling my mother a bedtime story of sorts. This was such a peculiar thing to do, and had the dangerous potential to affect me so deeply, that I held myself apart from it even as it was taking place. I did not think about distancing myself; I would have had to think about *not* doing so, so habitual was it by then to participate in an event of alleged significance without actually coming into contact with it.

Obviously, though, the images associated with my mother falling asleep that year, with me crouching beside her and spinning out another bogus version of The Dream like a lullaby, entered my consciousness despite all my best efforts to keep them out. Embellished and vivified by all that has happened since—and by that very refusal to engage fully at the time—the memories have come to mean more to me than did the incident itself.

I eased open the door to the hibernaculum and encountered my sister, tossing and turning as she tried to fall asleep, struggling to relax. Even when she did manage to sleep, she never achieved much peacefulness. After weeks suspended in the sleeping position, her tension somehow defied the smoothing pull of gravity and her muscles stayed taut. Her hands stayed clenched, fingers wrapped around thumbs or unfolded just enough to turn fists into claws. The slightest change in her microclimate disturbed her; no matter what we did, we could not keep the environment stable and quiet enough for her. We found ourselves constantly shushing the youngsters, and her own were the worst: "Quiet! Your mother's trying to sleep! Don't you care about your mother's health?"

Meredith would—deliberately, it seemed—run on her heels, so that her footsteps boomed, or slam into a wall, giggling hysterically, because she'd tried to stop or turn at the last second. Rory's music was never louder than when he had been cautioned not to wake his mother. Sebastian would sit in the crook of a tree and throw pebbles at the wall of the hibernaculum with a compulsive regularity that drove me crazy, let alone Alexis; we would take his rocks away, and discover he had hoarded more, or physically remove him, dead weight and stiff as a board, and he would be back in his place before we had turned around.

The trip south was even worse. While most of the sleepers were lulled by the motion and engine noise of their trucks, Alexis could hardly sleep at all. Not entirely awake, either, she would crawl out of the trailer into the cab and insist on riding there, perched on the wheel well or squatting on the floor behind the seat, making the male drivers and passengers more than a little self-conscious as their energy levels rose and their inhibitions faded. Not to mention that she was an inveterate backseat driver.

Poor David was especially affected by his wife's chronic insomnia. Going south made him feel better, although he never reached normal male levels of health and activity anymore. His invalidism persisted in direct proportion to Alexis's wakefulness, and lately there had been years when he'd had only a few days of relative well-being.

I knew Ma worried about my sister's wakefulness. From what I had gleaned about the physiological and sociological functions of hibernation, she had reason to worry. Cyclical profound sleep conserved a woman's physical energy. The altered state of consciousness conserved her mental and, some said, spiritual energy. Although seasonal migration had a vaguely comparable effect for men, because of our differing metabolic patterns between winter in the south and summer up north, migration had turned out to be not nearly so effective an evolutionary adaptation as hibernation. On the whole, females of our species lived much longer than men, and they developed greater stamina, discipline, creativity, productivity, and all-around class.

Whenever a woman's sleep was disturbed, an inordinate—and dangerous—amount of her stored energy was expended. I had read that being awake for only a few midwinter hours could deplete thirty days' worth of reserves, and there were stories of virtually mythological proportions of females starving to death in their sleep.

Indeed, that had happened to us once, when I was a child. The details had become hazy to me; I had been too young and too frightened then to inquire, too reticent since. But I remembered that there had been some sort of trouble on the spring trip north, an accident or car trouble or something, and by the time they got home every single female in that hibernaculum truck had died.

My mother had contended that the community never would recover from such an immense loss. Certainly my mother never recovered, for my older sister Chloe had died in that truck. Chloe had been twenty-two years older than I, and I hardly remembered her. But Ma used to tell me stories about how much Chloe had loved me, how much time she had spent with me, how she had tended me in the nursery long after she'd passed puberty and hadn't had to anymore.

Given the female sensitivity to environmental change during sleep, and the potentially drastic consequences of such disturbance, our annual migration had come to seem to me a quite maladaptive species characteristic. It was, of course, much harder to keep the ambient environment stable and unintrusive when we were traveling than if we had stayed in one place. Any of an infinite array of glitches could occur: Detours. Roughness in the road or in the driving. Mechanical breakdown of the specially equipped moving vans we used these days to transport the slumbering women south—their walls as if fur-lined once they were fully loaded. To put an even finer point on it, in this category of mechanical failure alone there were infinite possibilities for disaster: engine breakdown, problems with the elaborate climate control systems, an exhaust or a cold air leak into the trailers. Virtually anything could happen.

So why had we developed a social system, not to mention a physiology, that depended on both female hibernation and male migration? Either alone would have been complex enough to manage, and most other societies I knew anything about maintained one or the other, or neither. Of what possible use was our reliance on both? There were numerous other questions like that, equally unanswerable.

What, for instance, could possibly be the evolutionary value of our species' stubborn refusal to accept mortality? Surely we all had always known we would all die. Surely there could be no disputing the even more dreaded corollary: In one way or another, we would all lose everyone we loved. With a few alleged exceptions, the veracity of which enjoyed far from universal acceptance, everyone ever born had died.

So what was the point in continuing to regard death as an enemy? My aunt Jeannette was one hundred thirty-three years old when she died. In the last weeks of her life she was terrified and sorrowful and furious, never passing through any stages of any kind, never coming close to acceptance. She railed that it wasn't fair. She wept that she didn't want to die. She insisted that it was too soon, that she wasn't ready, that she still had things to do.

And why did loss—even the threat of loss, even the *imagined* threat of loss—cause so much pain and panic? Why, that is, was I so terrified that my mother would die? Of course she would.

In any event, I took my female-tending responsibilities very seriously. Partly this was a personal commitment, though admittedly one without much passion; I cared about my mother, and there were other women of whom I was fond, though it would have been presumptuous to call them my friends. Partly it was habitual, perhaps even instinctive. And there was also a relentless conviction that the entire social order depended on our successfully bringing the females through the winter.

Put that way, and from my vantage point now, the power inherent in the masculine caretaking role is obvious, disconcerting, even a bit thrilling. But for most of my adult life, and as a child observing adult males, it was the drudgery of the job that was most apparent.

Naturally, men had developed numerous ways to escape it without rebelling in any public way. Chronic illness or other physical incapacitation was effective; David patently could not take care of hibernating women or of anything else, and so was left alone. Simple waywardness worked; my grandfather's seasonlong debaucheries were legendary, as were his seasonlong hangovers. Mental disability would do; Miles had never been held accountable for much of anything, and Sebastian could not even be asked. Then there was utter lack of character; surely even Alexis knew not to entrust Rory with anything.

I worried occasionally, in a mild and quite ineffectual way, about the upcoming generations. It was, at the very least, ludicrous to think of Rory and Sebastian tending their sister Meredith now that she would be beginning her winter sleeps; at worst, and far more likely, it would be disastrous. My nephews were probably the worst of the lot, but in truth I did not know of anyone among the current crop of boys and young men to whom I would feel confident turning over my various stewardships. My doleful assessment was that my gender, of dubious quality to begin with, was inexorably weakening as the generations progressed. Sometimes I would wonder why, but then I dismissed the question as absurd and the answer as self-evident; men were men.

I wanted to recount to my sleeping mother more of the fabricated Dream, but so far I had been able to come up with nothing new, and I was just sitting there. From the fluttering of her eyelids, the small fluctuations in her body heat, and her erratic low-pitched muttering, less audible than tactile, I guessed that she herself was dreaming now. She had told me that during the most profound part of hibernation, when her mind had truly stilled, she did not dream at all, as if she had sunk beneath dreams.

"I had The Dream again," I began, and then stopped. I had thought of nothing sufficiently elegant or dramatic to say next.

Her breathing slowed perceptibly, a longer pause between this breath and the next than between this breath and the last. Each time, waiting, I tried with limited success to prepare myself for the possibility that she would never breathe again. Each time, I understood that death had been averted, just barely, by the infinitesimal passage of a minuscule column of air.

I did not touch her for fear of interrupting the process—and also for fear of the intimacy such a gesture would imply—but I leaned over her to be close to her quieting. Her heart slowed with each beat. The fluttering pulse in her throat flickered and faded, nearly vanished. By the deepest part of the winter, a hibernator's heartbeat was virtually imperceptible, and, unless there was reason to suspect a medical trauma, the anticipated springtime awakening was almost entirely a matter of faith until it happened.

Her body temperature fell. I could feel the steady retraction of her radiant heat, and, absurdly, it was as if she were withholding something precious from me. She would continue to cool until her body was only a degree or so warmer than the ambient temperature, at which point it would be easy for her to freeze to death, so attuned was she to her environment. A single degree between life and death.

"This time I was flying through a fierce snowstorm," I went on. If I procrastinated much longer, she would not be able to hear me. I was not sure she could hear me now, but at best this was my last chance. "It was midwinter, and somehow I'd been left behind. I was very far north, much farther north than Tallus, and I was alone."

My mother stirred, perhaps or perhaps not in response to my words. I was both gratified and alarmed; I wanted her to notice me, but I did not want to be responsible for awakening her. I hesitated, thinking I ought to stop talking and go away and let her be. But the grim thought persisted that this might well be the last chance I would ever have to tell my mother The Dream.

In a burst of creativity born of desperation, I went on. "I was cold, colder than I'd ever imagined, certainly colder than I've ever been awake. I longed to find a nice warm hibernaculum but I knew there was none for me, and I knew that if I stopped moving I would die. I didn't want to die.

"The blizzard made it impossible for me to either hear or see. I was completely lost; I had no idea where I was or where I was trying to get to, only that I had to keep flying. There was snow in my hair, and I kept thinking, in that very clear and at the same time very confused way your mind works in dreams, that this snow was making my hair thicker and so it should be keeping me warm, but instead it was making me colder." Rather proud of that image, I paused to savor it, wondering if Ma was aware of it at all. "My feet were stiff from cold. There was ice on my wings.

"Then I was flying close along a cliff face, searching for a cave, I think, or some sheltered place. I couldn't see the top of the cliff or the bottom or either end, and it was brilliant red through the snow and completely featureless, no caves, no indentations, no ledges. I flew for an impossibly long time, and yet I didn't seem to be traveling any distance and time didn't seem to be passing. You know how time telescopes and twists back on itself in dreams." That was a nice touch.

"Then all of a sudden I saw marks on the cliff.

Although I was still beating my wings hard and had the sensation of flying, the marks stayed where they were in relation to me, and I didn't seem to be moving past them. They were higher than I was tall, wider by far than my wingspread, and it took me quite a while to recognize them as letters. It was an inscription in the rock. A message to me. But I couldn't make out what it said."

I stopped then, not so much for dramatic effect, although there was that, as because I had the equivalent of writer's block, no idea in the world what this portentous inscription might be made to say. My mother was clearly beyond me now anyway; she was soundly asleep, very still, very cool. The temptation was strong to touch her, to kiss her, to say something so vivid and important that it would capture her attention from wherever it had gone, to rouse her one last time. I turned away. It was not an easy thing to do.

My niece Meredith was standing in the hibernaculum behind me. Apparently she had been there for some time. "Liar," she said.

She was right, of course. I pushed past her and left the garage, and from lifelong practice had shifted my attention to more concrete and manageable problems by the time I reached the house: specifically, dinner.

Male appetites and energy levels were noticeably increasing. There was a general masculine muttering about being hungry. I was hungry myself. Every year it took a while to adjust to this seasonal change; the personal experience, though I doubted it would be supported by physiological analysis, was that overnight we went from a condition of extreme disinterest in food, eating only because it was physically and socially required, to a state of constant and insatiable obsession with food that would heighten, along with other hedonistic tendencies, the farther south we went.

But male hunger paled beside the female version. At this time of year, women consumed several times their own weight in food every night, and their feeding forays lasted virtually from dusk to dawn. Once they fell asleep and the convoy started south, tomorrow or the next day, they would have no more meals for months, so I supposed there was some rationale for their gorging. Still, I was offended by it. Such extravagant self-indulgence. Such lack of discipline.

All last night and all today, women had been leaving the house to go eat and coming back satiated, though not for long. They staggered around the house and yard, so full they might have been drunk. They dropped in their tracks to rest, sometimes half covering their faces with their arms and fancying themselves sheltered, sometimes spreading their long membranous fingers like umbrellas over their heads. Then they were off again, stumbling at first and bleary, but rapidly picking up speed, steadiness, and aim as the hunger reasserted itself.

When the sun had set behind the ragged black peaks in the northwest and the twilight was deepening toward opalescence, I sat on the porch and listened to the women feeding in the neighborhood. Careful as we were always supposed to be, I could not believe that people did not find us at best odd and at worst skin-crawling, and every fall I perched on an increasingly sharp cusp of anxiety, praying we would get out of there before somebody completely forgot social graces and did something so outrageous that the neighbors organized a vigilante posse to exterminate us.

Directly across the courtyard from where I sat, on the other side of the back buildings and up a rise, was a sparse pasture, and there Theresa had found our neighbor's big black bull. The animal was asleep. Theresa tiptoed up to it, feather-light although she was not a small woman, very careful and quiet although I could pick up her anticipatory trembling and labored breathing.

She touched the bull's back leg. It kicked. Her nose mere centimeters from the surface of its hide, she scanned rapidly for a pooling of blood heat close to the surface, and found a good one near the massive testicles and the penis as stout as her arm. She collected herself, lunged, and sank her teeth in.

The bull twitched its skin as though trying to

dislodge a pesky fly. Theresa's upper body jerked, but she was not much disturbed. She would be able to get a goodly amount of blood from an animal this size. My mouth was watering. Half awake now, the bull shook its head with the great curved horns and stomped its heavy foot. Theresa held on.

When she was full, which took no more than a few minutes, she withdrew her teeth from the bull's flesh and wiped her mouth across its prickly hide as though a napkin had been spread out there for her personal convenience. The bull snorted and shifted its weight, but now, as far as it was concerned, the minor discomfort was gone, and it sank back into unconsciousness.

Theresa made her way back to the house, belching and holding her distended belly. She heaved herself up the porch steps and collapsed into the lawn chair next to me, which crackled under her weight. "God, that was *good*!" she moaned, and then subsided into a bloated silence. She would stay that way until her digestive system had processed and stored enough of the meal that there was room for more.

In the creamy autumn dusk, there was hardly a living thing that some female or mass of females did not consider edible—apples, marigolds and asters, gnats, toads, field mice, barn swallows. So it would not be hard for all of them to find something to eat, albeit a much less satisfying meal than Theresa had enjoyed.

It took several nights for all the women to be full enough for hibernation. It seemed to me that this obsessive step in their preparation was taking longer than it usually did, and the weather was getting cooler earlier than normal, and we ought to be on the road. But there was nothing I could do about that except fret, which was of no practical help but did serve to make it clear that I, at least, was aware that things were not right.

It snowed again. The snow did not stick, but its presence made me nervous, and it interfered with the feeding on the night it fell. On what Alexis promised was her last night awake, she insisted—perversely as far as I was concerned—that I go out with her. I was a most reluctant and not even especially welcome dinner companion. I presumed the purpose was to give me last-minute instructions, or maybe to show off.

I was unaccustomed to spending all night hunting, pursuing, searching for food. Once we reached Ambergen we might eat all night, it was true, but food there was so plentiful and rich that we scarcely had to think about it; it virtually came to us, offered itself.

Alexis had also talked David into coming with us instead of waiting at home for food to be brought back. "It's nice that you can go out with us, honey." Misty-eyed, she clung to his arm.

"I feel like shit," he announced, without any particular emphasis. He even laughed disparagingly, as though allowing his listeners the option to discount everything he said. We already did.

Alexis hugged him. "Poor baby," she cooed, without a trace of sarcasm. "And on my last night, too."

"Sorry," David said automatically, though he was not.

It could be said that Alexis treated her husband more civilly than she treated any other man; she was kinder to him, less snide, less demanding. In truth, though, that was an indication of how she did not take him seriously. She treated men generally better than women. Her expectations of her daughter were far higher than of either son, impossibly high.

By now we had left the colony behind and were approaching the next farm. An unspectacular sunset had left the sky aglow, the halogen lights around the neighbor's outbuildings had just come on, and a nearly full moon had already risen. There was a fair amount of light. David's oversized eyes might actually have been of some use to him that evening, if they had not stopped functioning altogether.

As it was, he stumbled along on his wife's arm, wholly dependent on her to keep his balance and guide him in the right direction. It crossed my mind that the temptation must sometimes be strong to deliberately lead him astray, to get him good and lost and just leave him somewhere.

His long head bobbed and tilted almost as if he were listening for echoes to orient himself, but in actuality his hearing never had been especially good. He held his nose up as if smelling or heat-detecting blood, but he did not have the requisite organ and, in any case, he was a strict vegetarian, his diet more and more ludicrously limited even as his health continued to decline. For the past few years, as he became steadily weaker and more and more of his body parts stopped functioning, he had been subsisting largely on honeysuckle nectar, most of which, in northern summer or southern winter, had to be imported at considerable expense and enormous inconvenience.

As we came up on the neighbor's smaller barn, I hung back from the others, the best I could do to maintain my separation from them. When my mother was awake I could, at least, talk to her. Until next spring, there was nobody with whom I cared to interact.

The flying insects had been so thinned by the cooling weather that it was nearly possible to think of them as discrete creatures, for they could no longer rightly be called swarms or clouds. I knew that alarmed my sister. I just found it frustrating, and I was hungrier than I had been in a while. If for no other reason than the easy availability of unlimited food, it would be a relief to be at Ambergen again.

I knew Alexis was also worrying about her sons, as she did all the time and with particular tenacity every autumn. If she could have carried either one of them on her back or in her pouch she would have, but even if they had been small enough, Rory would have fought her and Sebastian would not hang on.

If she could have taken them with her into hibernation, she would have, too. As it was, she left strict written instructions about Sebastian's care, and in the days and weeks leading up to her sleep she talked to me obsessively about Rory, as if there were anything I could or cared to do with him.

Now, as the sky darkened around the gibbous moon, Alexis knew better than to touch Sebastian, but she left his side only long enough to chase down a hapless rabbit. She flitted back with it and passed it to Sebastian, though she should have eaten it herself for she would require a great deal more sustenance in the upcoming months than he would, and she would be out here tonight—meaning that the house could not be closed up and I, for one, could not go to sleep—until she got the sustenance she needed.

The boy looked at the rabbit blankly. He pulled it apart as if it were made of Legos, absently stuck one leg in his mouth, and let the rest of the carcass drop. Alexis screeched a scolding protest and went back for it herself, keeping an anxious eye on Sebastian, who had not altered his pace, which was made up of tiny overlapping circles and which carried him in the desired direction only because he happened to have been pointed that way.

During this little domestic drama, Rory slipped into the seam of deep darkness between the garage and the barn. *Good riddance,* I thought. The odds had just increased exponentially for an evening meal if not pleasant, at least free of open hostility that interfered with both finding food and digesting it.

I did not think Alexis had noticed his defection, and when she made one of her famous right-angle veers to follow him I still was not sure her intent was more than simple foraging. "Joel, watch Sebastian," she called back to me. I was grudgingly and fleetingly appeased that her mouth was obviously full; for the moment, at least, she was attending to business. Without waiting for my assent, or even to be sure I had heard—though how could I avoid receiving her orders, so shrill in the quiet twilight?—she took off between the buildings where the echoes set up by her movement were distorted or blocked.

Ma had often commented, with a lugubrious sigh and a shake of the head, that life expected a lot of Alexis, as though by comparison life expected little of me. No woman had it easy, of course, but Alexis was especially burdened, what with a handicapped son, a delinquent son, and a sick husband to take care of and only one daughter to help. She had never quite said it, at least not to me, but the rest of the message was clear: The more males in a woman's life, the harder her lot would be.

For me to be pressed without input into Alexis's service like that was hardly unusual, so my resentment was a bit surprising and certainly pointless. Scowling, I dutifully positioned myself so that Sebastian was more or less in my line of hearing. He was going round and round in his neither widening nor diminishing circles, stuck, perseverating, and not for the first time I rather envied his ability to shut out the bewildering world and stimulate himself.

I wondered whether the imprint of this intensely repetitive motion was in his body only, or whether there were also circles in his mind, interlocking, spinning, creating echoes wider on the outside edge of the curves than on the inside. Or whether his mind was blank. Or whether it teemed and swelled with tangled sounds, thoughts, images, heat sensations, his own sensory impressions that I couldn't name and probably wouldn't even recognize.

I did not dare let myself get bogged down trying to understand anyone else's perspective on the world, least of all Sebastian's. I was hungry and bored. I wanted to eat and be done with it.

Alexis reappeared carrying food. Her echoes telegraphed anxiety nearing frenzy, distracting me again. She never stopped moving, even while her mouth was pressed over her son's in a prolonged, nourishing kiss that would have seemed tender had the recipient been an infant but was slightly grotesque with a ten-year-old. This sort of thing went on all night.

By midnight, when the others went home, I was restless and exhausted. By three in the morning I was sufficiently worried about all the things I had planned to get done and cross off my list that night that I considered going home whether Alexis wanted me to or not; I was afraid, though, that if she got upset she never would get to sleep, and that would just cause more trouble for me.

Alexis found and took nourishment from, I swore, every warm-blooded animal in a fifty-mile radius. Horses, cattle, sheep, a spitting llama, dogs, cats, a pot-bellied pig—most of them were not even aware of the contribution they were making to my sister's life, specifically to the reservoir of brown fat that would get her through the winter. None of them, as far as any of us knew, felt much pain. None of them lost enough blood to her to cause any damage. The ballooning of the hump of adipose tissue between her shoulders was discernible. But her movements never slowed. Her nervous energy did not dissipate. I could not detect any evidence that my sister was any more satisfied than ever. This hunger and the doomed attempt to take the edge off it could, I reflected sourly, go on forever.

We were on the far edge of the county neighboring ours, and there was still no light in the sky signaling that we could go home and go to bed and call it a night, when we passed a house with an open window and someone sleeping right inside. Alexis commanded, "Stop," and I stopped the car, both it and I protesting. She said, "Oh, shut up," and we sat there for a while amid the gauze of late-night sounds and smells and tactile sensations, which included the breath, body odor, heartbeat, body heat of the woman asleep not ten feet away.

It might have passed for companionable silence if Alexis had been less agitated and I had been less nervous. She was going to do something I wouldn't like. She was going to create some kind of mess that I would have to clean up. At the very least, she was going to keep me out here, when I needed to be at home packing and resting for the trip. "I need your opinion, big brother," she said, and I listened as closely as I could, hoping to detect where the trap was, what setup she was maneuvering me into. But she said quietly, "I'm worried about the kids, and I don't know what to do," and she seemed genuinely not to know what to do.

Warily I asked, "What are you worried about?" Certainly I had my own list, but if they weren't the same things Alexis was thinking about I did not dare say them aloud.

She sighed. "Rory is so hateful, all the time now. I'm scared, Joel. I'm actually scared of my own son."

"Maybe it's a phase," I suggested, wincing at the sarcastic tone that crept into my words.

Alexis, for once, did not react to it. "That's what I've been saying, but it's only getting worse. He's eighteen. When do you stop saying it's a phase and say, 'This is who he is'? I'm afraid he's going to hurt somebody." She hesitated. "Or already has."

I could think of nothing remotely helpful to say. I heard the woman on the other side of the open window move in her sleep. Alexis heard it, too; I felt her rise toward the motion, then subside.

"And Sebastian." Her voice broke. "My poor baby. What happens to boys in our society, Joel, do you have any explanation? Why is it so hard for men to function in this world?"

The buzz of resentment I felt when she asked that was dulled by fatigue, which came not just from this long night but from my whole life. I did not want to talk about men, and most particularly not with Alexis. So I asked, with interest not entirely feigned, "What about Meredith? She seems to be doing okay, doesn't she?"

Alexis smiled a little. "I can't tell. She's secretive. She doesn't tell me things."

"She's fourteen," I pointed out.

My sister gave a sad laugh. "Damn kids. You do everything for them and then they grow up and have their own lives. Who do they think they are?"

I snorted, to show appreciation of the irony if not from actual amusement. The trials of parenthood were of little interest to me then, and I had no reason to think they ever would be. "I like Meredith," I offered, which was, albeit vaguely, the truth.

Alexis said, "I'm scared to go to sleep, Joel. I'm scared something will happen to my kids while I'm asleep, and I'll wake up to some terrible disaster."

"David's awake," I said lamely, and of course that angered her.

"Stupid shit," she hissed, an all-purpose epithet. "He's worse than no help. He doesn't think about anybody but himself, and he just makes more trouble." The woman in the bedroom stirred again, and Alexis stirred again in response, this time not subsiding. My own adrenaline rose. Alexis took a deep breath and gathered herself, but before she moved out of the car she turned to face me and asked directly, "Joel, will you promise me you'll wake me up if anything serious happens to my kids?"

I hesitated. It was tempting, because then handling whatever crisis would be her responsibility and not any man's. "Isn't that awfully hard on you?" I felt compelled to inquire.

"I don't sleep all that deeply anyway," she said.

"And it's hurting your health."

"My choice," she snapped. "Will you promise me? Because if you won't, I won't go into hibernation at all, and you'll have to put up with me conscious the whole season." I saw the flash of her grin, mean and sharp in the darkness.

It did not take much for me to give in. "Okay," I conceded, and she nodded once, then opened the door. "Alexis," I called in a sudden whisper. "I wish you wouldn't do this. This is really risky."

"Don't be such a wuss," she threw back aloud. "I'm not going to hurt her or anything. She won't even know."

I sat in the car then, helplessly, and with grudging admiration watched my sister as she let herself in the partially open window, lowered herself over the sleeping woman, and drank her fill. Unless Alexis was a carrier of something communicable, which I doubted, it was true that her victim would not be hurt beyond a few small puncture wounds that might take longer than normal to stop bleeding. The amount of the woman's blood Alexis required to fill herself, for this moment, was minuscule, and the access holes would not even scar. But if the woman awoke while Alexis was at her, there would be hell to pay, and I really did not think I had the energy to deal with that.

In less than ten minutes, Alexis finished. She let herself out the window, opened and shut the car door with hardly a sound, and sank back against the seat. "Let's get out of here," she murmured, although she needn't have; we were already pulling back onto the road. Alexis was asleep before we got home, and I found myself carrying her into the hibernaculum and settling her into her place, an action so risky and so tender that it took all my own reserves to accomplish it.

Then I went to bed, too, but only for the day. We would leave for Ambergen as soon as the sun went down.

CHAPTER 6

There were certain rules of the road: We never stayed in towns where there was only one motel; when the route and schedule allowed, in fact, we tried for the cities and midsize towns, of which there were a few but at awkward intervals for a rushed journey like this, hoping to be less conspicuous. We were, of course, still quite conspicuous. Every year one of my mounting worries about which I could do absolutely nothing was that surely this time, in this town, somebody would get in our way.

In all my years traveling back and forth along these several routes, no one ever had. It was a source of constant amazement to me, and constant anxiety. There were apocryphal stories about clashes between townspeople and migrators generations ago, when we were flying, when we were taking so much blood. But we were different now; we had, most of us, evolved.

Now we migrated in a giant convoy: hibernaculum eighteen-wheelers, passenger cars, minivans, pickups, even motorcycles for the particularly reckless among us. Traveling across the country through nighttime landscapes, we were bound to attract attention. I did not understand why we hadn't, and almost wished we would—then bit back the thought.

Rory and his cohorts presented a real threat, but I didn't dare regard it as more than a nuisance because there wasn't anything I could do to bring them under control. I could only hope they'd hold off on their various orgies until we got where we were going.

Usually there were four nights on the road to worry about; the trucks were slow. This year, because of the delay in getting started, we would put in longer nights driving and make it in three.

My father used to tell a story about when he was young and foolish—although it had always been apparent that he rather admired that reckless young man he had once been. Some of them had made the entire trip south in a day and a half, for no reason other than the hell of it. One of his companions had, in fact, not made it. I knew this from my mother; he never mentioned that part of the tale.

We had set off in a giddy spirit of adventure, which even I had found infectious. Pete rode with me in the cab of the lead truck, and I found myself actually enjoying his company. We argued amiably over what radio station to listen to, finally agreeing to alternate between all-night talk radio, which I found vastly irritating since I cared not a whit for what the person-on-the-street opined about anything, and country music, the whinier the better, which I liked only on the way to Ambergen and to which both Pete and I sang along, although he didn't mean any of it—broken hearts, wander- and every other kind of lust, finding oneself in a world that didn't help—and I was sure I meant every throaty word.

Sometime after midnight, Pete remarked, "Where are the others?" and I realized they were not behind us. Behind us stretched the dark and quiet highway, empty as the highway ahead, and on either side there was not a sound, no pools of warmth or light.

"Shit," I said, and started to pull over.

Pete cocked his head to listen to the speedometer. "Jesus, Joel, how fast were you going?"

"Fast enough to lose them, I guess." I had slowed down considerably by the time my tires hit the gravel on the berm, but they still spun and spat.

I killed the engine and got out. The night air was cool. I heard Pete's door slam as he got out, too, and we met by the side of the road.

We were partway up a graded hill. Ahead of us, the highway continued to rise, not steeply. In the middle distance I heard a car approaching, but saw no headlights yet.

Behind us, though, I both heard and saw the rest of our party. Down the hill, which was considerably steeper in that direction, and strung out around it like a honking and growling flock of animals, the stragglers were not moving very fast, and, though their headlights and tail lights marked the route for miles like red-and-white spoor, there did not seem to be enough of them.

"Cops," said Pete, and as he spoke I heard the siren. My blood chilled.

We waited while the rest of the convoy caught up to us. One after another, vehicles large and small lined the side of the highway. There was no surer way to call attention to ourselves than to all congregate in one place like this, and the fact that I no longer heard the police siren made me more rather than less uneasy.

I had been sure the missing driver would be Rory or one of the other young men, but it turned out to be Mitchell, on Rory's motorcycle. Rory was pleased to relate what had happened. "Fucker was playing chicken with us. Should have known not to trust an old man."

"What do you mean?"

"You know," Rory said, voice narrowing like his eyes. "Chicken."

"The term 'chicken' covers a multitude of juvenile games, most of them life-threatening, all of them moronic."

Rory screeched with laughter. Pete said grimly, "Three or four of them lie down in the middle of the road and the one on the bike maneuvers around them and over them. You get points for coming close without hitting anybody. Ramsey and Josh play it. One of the growing list of things I wish I didn't know about my sons."

"You get fucking *millions* of points if you draw blood," exulted Rory.

"And Mitchell was playing this game? Mitchell's a grown man."

"Hey, it's fucking winter, almost. Anyway, he wiped out."

I was not, finally, the only one interrogating him. Stockard demanded, "Is he hurt?" at the same time that Perry said, "Oh, shit, he's dead."

Rory was still the only one answering anything, although Josh and Ramsey, at least, obviously had been involved. They stood back well away from their father and behind the cars, and they were quiet. "How the hell should I know?" Rory snapped. "Cop was right there, right on top of us. Must have been hiding on some side road or something. Fucking sneak attack. We didn't hang around to see what went down."

"We can't, either," Pete said to me. "We can't wait."

Ted said, "We can't just go off and leave him."

From the backseat of Ted's car, where he had been stretched out under a blanket, David called weakly. "I can't take much of this traveling. Mitchell knows we have to keep going. For the good of the group."

"What do you want to do?" Perry asked Ted. "Go to the police station after him? Or the hospital?"

"We have to get going," Pete said again.

"You drive," I said, and threw him the keys.

A thick cloud cover had settled in, which absorbed both sound and light. We traveled along the highway, cooled now from the heat of sunshine and the friction of tires, under the low sky, through it in hollows where fog gathered like shed fur. Pete had not turned the radio back on, and I didn't, either.

I thought about Mitchell, of course, although I tried not to. It was true that we could not afford to wait for him, much less rescue him, and it was true that he should have known better than to play before we got to Ambergen. But I did not like just driving off and leaving him. Perhaps it was migratory loosening up or the fondness that comes in the wake of sudden tragedy, but I decided I had been rather fond of Mitchell. Mitchell had been a good guy. I would have preferred losing any of a number of the others. Rory. I would not have missed Rory, though I would not have relished informing Alexis of what had befallen her son. David. Pete, even, now that he was whistling nonstop between his teeth and drumming his bulbous knuckles on the dashboard and the window and the seat between us. I gritted my teeth, told myself that at least Mitchell had not been driving a hibernaculum and given the state patrol cause to look inside, and tried to send my mind elsewhere.

We drove through several little towns, some with no sign of wakeful life and some, disconcertingly, with lights ablaze and noise—a hammer and drill in one place, people arguing in two houses in a row in another. The travel sounds of our convoy must have reached those people, who were up later than they had any right to be, and I imagined them interrupting their argument and their construction to rush to the window and look. By the time they took us in, we would be gone.

The towns got larger and closer together. Our pickup would be entering one of them before the last car had left the previous one behind. The sun was not yet perceptible over the horizon, although the predawn change in the land and the air had taken place, when we came to the midsize city where we would spend the day. Nervously I hoped none of the designated drivers had lost the reservation information.

Pete, at least, knew where we were going. He pulled into our motel without being told, and for a minute I was afraid Perry had lost track and booked us into the same place we had used last fall, which would have been unwise. But this place was brand new. A few vehicles pulled into the parking lot after us, and the rest went on, as they were supposed to do.

I was more exhausted and stressed than hungry and would have been content to make do with room service, but we stayed at the cheapest motels possible and were lucky to have a shower and more than one thin towel. At that early hour of daylight, it was worth the chance that we could escape notice. Stockard, Pete, and a couple of the other men whom I knew were unlikely to want to party went with me in the Honda, out to one of the feedlots that ringed the city and contributed its thick, almost sweet permeating odor. I assured myself that there was no reason this should take very long, and, mercifully, it didn't.

The city was awakening as we staggered back into our motel room, meaning that a hundred thousand potential enemies were regaining consciousness, presumably refreshed and ready for a new day. I spared a thought for Mitchell, shuddered, collapsed on one of the lumpy beds that were not full size no matter what the brochure promised, and was asleep before the sun came up.

The next night I drove alone. I was disappointed not to have company, not least because it would be harder to keep my mind on driving. But Pete had started a word game with his sons, I assumed for the purpose of preventing them from repeating the stupidity of yesterday; I considered it nothing more than paternal wishful thinking, and laughable at that, even though the game did have rather creative obscene puns and palindromes as its basis. Grudgingly, I thought I should do something of the same with Rory, although he would be a harder sell. I was taken aback to discover that he and Sebastian were riding with their father in the backseat of the car Pete was driving, with Josh and Ramsey in the front. I was a little offended to be thus left out, although I would have scrambled to make up excuses if I had been expected to participate.

I took one of the hibernacula that night, because that would leave only one vacant passenger seat, and in the hope that the necessity of coaxing along the clunky old truck would force me to stay alert. Fortunately, the hibernaculum radios could pick up stations from all over the country. I was definitely in the mood for a spate of songs about loneliness, or about the forever-unavailable dark romantic stranger at the truck stop around the next bend.

Driving the hibernaculum put me in the middle of the convoy. So when, not long after we had started for the night, I began to suspect something was wrong with the truck and eventually pulled over to check, I thought drivers ahead of and behind me would notice and stop, too. But the gap my truck left in the procession simply closed, they all kept going without so much as a honk of support, and I was left alone with a truck full of hibernating women in a landscape that would have sinister potential whether it was empty of other wakeful life-forms or not.

The unusual vibration I had felt in the cab had seemed to originate in the trailer, which made me think about the climate controls. I had some minimal mechanical ability and could make simple repairs or readjustments, but if there was a significant malfunction I would be in trouble. Ramsey and Ted were the mechanics, and they had gone blithely on their way. I could not, of course, wait for the auto shop in the next town to open in the morning; even if they knew anything about hibernation mechanics, which was not likely, I could not exactly just pull in with a truck full of sleeping, expiring females and announce, "I've got a little problem here."

I jumped down from the cab. The air was noticeably more humid and warmer than it had been even last night, and I had the sudden sick premonition that I would not make it to Ambergen after all, would come so close only to fail. The dials on the outside of the truck appeared to be functioning. I unlocked the door and went in, gasping at the unpleasant wet cold and at a virulent unfamiliar odor, feeling very much the alien intruder that I was, and resenting that, for without men like me these women would all die in their sleep.

The dials and gauges inside, including the big calibrated master control, seemed fine. There were no palpable system failures in the microclimate. But there was a noise I could not identify, the vibration I had heard and felt in the cab, pervasive now, a loud low buzz.

I stood still, held my breath, and listened. Though my ear muscles were opening and closing adequately, I could not pinpoint the source of the sound. I moved haphazardly around the hibernaculum, checking sleepers; they all seemed as they should be. But the whole truck was trembling, through the soles of my feet where they supported my weight against the floor, then through my lungs and pores when I lifted off and hovered.

I was seriously tempted to get back behind the wheel and hope the problem would take care of itself. Sometimes that happened—rarely, but often enough to be an intermittent reinforcement, the most potent kind, for irresponsible behavior. With great annoyance and trepidation, I instead undertook a detailed investigation, feeling positively noble because I knew I would earn no points with any of my compatriots.

Theresa was all right. I made a minute adjustment in her curtains. Becky, Maryanne, and Louise were all right. I made my way slowly along the first aisle, carefully checking every sleeper in all three tiers. Everybody was fine. I found no breaks in the ambient atmosphere, no loose pieces that could account for the steady and insinuating vibration, nothing amiss.

But as I rounded the end of the first bank of tiers and started up the second, I detected something. A concentrated presence like an absence. An inversion of radiant heat and consciousness like what I imagined a collapsed star to be. The force of it sucked me around the corner, bringing me face-to-face with an Old Woman.

I tried to pull away and could not. She would not allow it. I tried to close my ears and eyes, tried to shield my heat detectors, but was given no choice but to perceive her in awful, intimate detail.

Even now it is tempting to turn away, to demur that I cannot and should not attempt to describe the indescribable, that to do so would be to trivialize, to give a misleading picture, even in some way to be heretical. But:

Vibration like a cosmic explosion distilled into a space smaller than that occupied by my own body. Rancid odor, not of death but of pure life. Radiant heat a flame very hot and very far away, under layers of ferocious cold.

Tissue-thin skin. I touched it, not wanting to,

and fissures opened, but there was no blood and the creature did not react. Tissue-thin breath, and no detectable heartbeat at all.

Yet she could not be said to be asleep. This was not hibernation in the usual sense, but another kind of consciousness altogether. She was aware of me. She engaged me. I did not think she heard or detected or saw me in any ordinary sense, but I was the focus of her full attention, a laser of frigid and entirely personal malevolence.

Bloated. Recognizably still one of us, but distorted: Still four limbs and tail with scoop, but all the appendages were distended beyond any functional use, hard to the touch but with a certain gruesome give. The hair on the swollen torso had a thick silkiness to it that activated an impulse to bury my hands in it, my face, and the flesh visible at jawline, pubis, armpit was a mottled, lustrous gray.

From every orifice of the Old Woman's head, something oozed. Viscous saliva ran between her bared teeth, marking the floor under her—and my forearm, when I did not move it quickly enough—with mercurial highlights. Inchoate sounds, suggestive not of a foreign language but of metalanguage, drooled, too, and sticky clicks and whistles. From her ears came a chunky drainage that matted the fur, and tears streamed slowly from her eyes.

She was buzzing. I could not determine what

organ or body part was trembling to cause the vibration, but it was clearly emanating from her. It set my teeth on edge, caused my fingernails and toenails to itch, rang in my ears and my throat. Whether it was doing any damage to the other hibernators, I could not tell.

Abruptly, I could not stay in the company of this Old Woman one more second. Retching and dizzy, I staggered out of the truck into the night, which was balmy and friendly by comparison, fumbled to get the door locked, and climbed back into the cab. Barely able to manage the suddenly complex tasks of driving, I got the truck back onto the highway and gunned the engine, desperate now to catch up with the others.

CHAPTER 7

Afraid to go even the speed limit, although a state trooper likely would take no more interest in the Old Woman than in the rest of the truckful of hibernating females, I drove with excruciating caution. At every intersection I came to a complete stop, whether or not I was supposed to yield and even when there were no other vehicles anywhere around. I used my turn signals conscientiously, every time I changed lanes or made a turn or pulled off the road to relieve myself in the increasingly lush vegetation. The vibration subsided. Maybe I was just getting used to it.

As latitude decreased, so did altitude, and pressure mounted in all the sinuses of my skull. My head ached and my ears rang. I was trembling, perhaps from the insidious vibration I could no longer consciously feel. My stomach cramped and lurched, and the longer the night wore on, the more often I was forced to stop.

Whenever I got out of the truck and made my way into some field or copse or glade, for the purpose of defiling it with my excrement which would shortly be transformed by natural processes and alteration of perspective into fertilizer, I was acutely aware of the presence in the trailer. She shared the expansive night with me, a companionship far more unnerving than loneliness, although I felt loneliness acutely, too.

I could not fathom why she was there; I had never heard of an Old Woman leaving the dens at all, much less traveling all the way to Ambergen in this motley company. I could not come up with a reasonable scenario to explain how she had got there. And I did not know how to regard her presence, whether it was dangerous, whether I should do something about it and if so, what and how.

I never did overtake the others. All night long I encountered two other vehicles on the road: another eighteen-wheeler, whose driver pulled his horn with a squawk like a jaunty elephant as though we were comrades, and a speeding van, shocking in the silence of the night; I thought of murderers fleeing the scene of the crime, and watched their tail lights disappear in my rearview mirror, my uneasiness not assuaged by the knowledge that they would still be nearby when I could not see them.

Flora began to close in, the pillowed sounds and sickly sweet aroma of green growing things. After we had been in the south for a while, I would feel cocooned rather than suffocated, the environment lush and ripe instead of on the verge of decay. The relative emptiness of the landscape around Tallus, which I was now remembering nostalgically as clean open space, would gradually over the winter come to seem barren, and I would be reluctant to go north again in the spring. But at the moment I was finding it hard to breathe.

When I finally reached the motel listed on the itinerary, the sky was already pale and too many of our vehicles were in the lot. We should be more thinly distributed among more motels than this, and we all should have been asleep by then. When I found them, crammed into too few rooms because, Pete informed me, there had been a screw-up with the reservations and nobody had wanted to cause a fuss, Perry's jovial "Thought we'd lost you" was the only acknowledgment that I had not been traveling with them the whole night.

There were so few rooms available that I had to share a very small one with Pete and David. Daylong exposure to David's complaints and Pete's snoring would doubtless afford me precious little sleep. I was working myself into a fine snit that gave me some thin pleasure, however much it contributed to my overall agitation. I would have to talk to someone about my horrific cargo, but I found myself unable to bring up the subject amid the hubbub of all the men trying to get themselves fed and settled down for the day.

David started the minute I carried my bags into the room, whose drapes were, not surprisingly, only translucent and not the opaque that would allow real rest. From the place he had claimed on one of the two narrow beds, he sighed heavily and declared, "I'm hungry."

"We'll go get something and bring it back," Pete said amiably. I could hardly remember the last time anybody had expected David to get his own food. As far as I knew, he could not even make a sandwich. In the northern summertime his wife or daughter brought him his meals as if he were an infant. During the winters at Ambergen, the men responsible for stocking the larders always made sure there was enough food sufficiently processed that David could eat it without much help. Even at that, he sometimes had difficulty opening a box.

Legend had it that in our youth David and I had been friends. Alexis was fond of reiterating, to her bored children in dreamy tones or as a means of describing herself to total strangers, "Ah, yes, and I married my big brother's best friend." Somehow, once again, she was using me to her advantage; while I did not quite understand how the mechanism worked, I resented the appropriation.

Ma liked the fable, too, and also used it for her own purposes. Watching for my reaction, taking my measure, she would assert, "David's your oldest friend, Joel. It's really sad that you two have lost touch." Denying it would have called too much attention to myself, but the regret was hers and not at all mine.

We had had some foolish fun, David and I; thirty-five years later he still wanted to look back on those days as the best time of our lives. We had not been friends. I had never been any good at relationships; I did not have friends.

I was supposed to, naturally; I was male. Infants of both sexes signaled their food-bearing mothers to them in the teeming nurseries with their own distinctive piping, which mothers and not usually fathers could identify as the voice of their own child among the multitudes. But boys engaged their mothers more, looked them in the eye, held on tight, while girls accepted the food for its nutritional value and tended not to imbue it with more subtle and convoluted meanings: "She loves me. If she ever stops loving me I'll starve to death. I have to be good or she'll stop loving me." I remembered that my mother had taken me along at night when I hadn't wanted to go; I did not remember, but it was another family legend, that more than once I had let go of her back and had to be rescued in midfall.

Studies had shown that boys learned to play and work in concert with each other far earlier than girls; for girls, the parallel play of toddlers developed directly into competitiveness early on. Myself, I had always been a loner, not especially competitive but not much involved, either, simply disinterested; my chosen approach to the world was the adult equivalent of parallel play.

My irritation with David far exceeded the specifics of his admittedly pitiable if largely self-induced circumstances. For me, he was a symbol of masculinity. His chronic ill health, disabilities, and disproportionate helplessness were not generally regarded as out of the ordinary, except perhaps in degree: All men were weak, dependent, impoverished in both physical strength and character. David was only a bit more extreme than most.

Pete had gone out to eat. David had fallen asleep sprawled across the other bed so Pete would be sharing with me. If I had any hope of sleep today, I'd better take advantage of this time when I had chosen fatigue over hunger as the need to meet and Pete apparently the converse.

I flipped on the remote control for the TV high in the corner, but David stirred and I hastily shut the set off again. I picked up one of Pete's sports magazines, could find nothing interesting enough to read even if it would put me to sleep, turned off the light, and lay down.

The room was nowhere near dark enough. David complained even in his sleep, no words but whining noises. The image of the Old Woman kept coming to me; now that I knew she was there, just outside the door, I could not escape the feeling of being unable to escape. I tossed. I put the pillow over my head, instantly felt claustrophobic, jerked it off again. From one or more of the other rooms, water hissed in the pipes as diurnal people got themselves ready for the day. Cranky from the growing conviction that I would get no sleep at all that day, I was not aware of drifting off.

The expanse of red rock showed itself to be a tombstone. On it were engraved my name and date of birth, in letters and numerals as tall and half again as wide as I was.

I had the impression of flying very fast, but the inscription changed its position relative to me very slowly. I was flying close to the rock face but could not seem to touch it. The air was cold and roughened by snow and ice, and it had a palpable quality of alienness, as though it were not air at all but some other medium, neither breathable nor capable of supporting flight.

Now came a deep depression at least the length of my body. A hyphen, I guessed. It made a ledge

—a climber's handhold, a horizontal surface to which hardy lichen could attach; a roost. Following the hyphen indentation was a longer and wider trough that, presumably, held the numerals of my death date; I glimpsed their outlines but could not read them.

Underneath were three grooves of varying length but similar width and depth. I understood that this was my epitaph, already carved in stone, but it, too, was obscured. The lines cut across the cliff face for quite some distance, and I flew along them, powerless to change direction or to land.

I awoke to the unsettling realization that I'd just, in fact, dreamed a fragment of The Dream. This was something of a shock, and would have been easier to make sense of if I had been able to tell my mother about it. But she, in the proximate company of the other hibernators and of the Old Woman, was sound asleep and quite unavailable to me. Of course, I would not really have been able to talk to her about it anyway, since she was under the impression—carefully calculated and nurtured by me—that I had been having The Dream regularly for some time.

The Dream as it had actually presented itself to me was, in many ways, considerably less real than The Dream I had concocted; certainly it contained less imaginative detail, less plot, fewer narrative hooks.

I kept plummeting into sleep and soaring back

into wakefulness. Every time, I broke through into a miasma of satiation and nausea; every time, Pete was snoring and David was whimpering or hacking or making loud disgusting noises in the bathroom, and the instant he noticed me conscious he would start to detail his current discomfort in a whisper louder than many people's speaking voices.

Finally, in desperation, I came to the surly decision that being thoroughly awake was less annoying and less tiring than flitting back and forth between agitated dreams and agitated consciousness, and I got up. How I would drive safely the next night, which was still hours away, remained to be seen.

Despite the too-bright hour, I needed to stretch my legs and get some air, which, redolent of decaying plant life and animal excrement, could not exactly be termed fresh. I could not bear the prospect of getting back behind the wheel until I had to, and especially I did not want to drive the hibernaculum again.

The motel was at the edge, rather blurred, of this sprawling city, and it did not take long, even under my own power, to reach farmland. Many nocturnal creatures had already taken to their burrows for the day, and many diurnal beasts weren't awake yet, but soon my ears picked up a cacophony of promising echoes, rapidly sorted through them and focused on one.

Medium sized, I thought, and slow-moving, probably asleep. Nearby. There. Warm-blooded, mammalian.

My series of clicks and squeaks was short because I already knew more or less where the prey was and all I needed to know about what it was. Quickly I constricted the muscles in my ears so I could concentrate on the echo. A stray memory of how hard that had been to learn, before it became second nature, nearly cost me my dinner, but I managed to retrieve my concentration and started to home in.

Human. Not old, but decrepit. Not sick, as far as I could detect, and not drunk or otherwise high, which was fortunate since I did not have the patience to suffer through a contact high today. But worn out. A rural version of a homeless man, sleeping against the rough barn wall.

Swiftly I crept up to his sprawled form, making little noise that he would have heard even if he had been conscious. He smelled foul, and he was filthy. I took pains not to touch him yet, but I had to lower my face closer to his disgusting flesh than I wanted to in order for my heat detector to work, and I was not pleased to determine that the best place for this one would be the tip of the nose. His nose was running.

I held my breath, curled my tongue into the back of my mouth, retracted my lips as far as they would go off my teeth. As I gingerly lowered over the slimy, bulbous protuberance, I had a flash of what I would look like to him if he happened to wake up at this precise moment. Dracula in miniature, I thought, and almost laughed, which surely would have roused him and led to all sorts of trouble.

But I was in and out in a matter of seconds; except, perhaps, for an upsurge of weird imagery in his dreams, or maybe no more than a stinging sensation that his dreams attributed to something more or less fanciful than its actual cause, the guy never knew I was there. When he woke up, he might discover a tiny, pronged wound, already healing over.

Leaving the still-sleeping drifter as soon as I could, I sailed over the corral fence. I was invigorated even though I knew that wouldn't last the day. I was also feeling more than a little self-righteous, because of the demonstrable fact that we were able to sustain ourselves without harming any other living creature, a metabolic peculiarity that put us in a definite minority among the world's species.

Some of the others had come out, too, and they had all gone on ahead. This time, it would not be hard to catch up. Numerous other groups, pairs, individuals were out in what was now dawn. From all sides and from above and below I heard their clicks, squeaks, laughter and protestations, calls to each other—such a commotion that, though most of the sounds I made would be inaudible to both locals and prey, I worried that someone would hear us.

A stronger possibility, actually, was that they would see us, but it was unnatural for me to think in visual terms. They would see a swarm of us black as smoke against the lightening sky, soft contours among sharp angles, dangling feet and arced scoops and fanned ears. Or, alone, high-stepping or prancing, each according to his personal style, jerking like the windblown branch of a leafless tree among all these trees that never lost their leaves, still as a terrified mouse without wings.

I flattened myself against a thick, scaly trunk, up under a branch bigger around than I was, where light from the setting moon, the rising sun, and the farmyard spotlight, all very nearly the same shade of warm saffron, made a pocket of deeper shadow. I settled myself and concentrated on my breath.

From just this pale and pitiable mimicry of hibernation, the best any male could hope for, there was a noticeable calming effect. Whether my heart actually slowed, whether there was a measurable drop in my body temperature and respiration rate, I could achieve a few imperfect moments of what I had come to think of as the converse of a buzz. A hush, maybe.

But my ear muscles would not stay shut without a conscious, escalating, and intrusive effort, and it wasn't long before a different sort of noise pierced my fragile trance. This was not an echo, but a direct, assaultive clamor, announcing "Prey!" and, with equal vehemence "Predator!"

It was both. It was Rory, and he was attacking a young girl.

The information came to me in a split second, and before I was even aware of processing it I was in motion. Later I would realize that, at that moment, it was unclear whether I was rescuer or conjoint attacker; heady adrenaline propelled me, clenched my fists and bared my fangs to fight, engorged my penis and brought the taste of blood into my mouth.

They were not hard to find. They were rolling and thrashing in the narrow strip of remaining darkness between the barn and the garage, and they were both making a great deal of noise that would, I was sure, be audible to anyone. Rory was grunting and panting in a manner that would have been comical under other circumstances, and the girl was bellowing in fury, shrieking in pain, shouting vivid obscenities in a shrill child's voice.

I reached between them. I pinched the girl's breast, pulled her hair. I grabbed my nephew by the collar membrane at the back of his exposed neck and wrenched it hard. The element of surprise more than counterbalanced his youth and greater strength, so that I was able to pull him off the girl with a single sharp tug. He tumbled sideways, actually hissing and growling. The dark skin of his intended victim picked up stray light and glinted red, and she exuded an acrid, arousing fragrance.

Mostly I heard her: the sharp intake of breath when she saw me, another strange male creature looming over her. The scrabble and shoosh of her body across the ground as she scrambled to her hands and knees and then to her feet. She was Meredith's age, maybe younger.

She was bleeding from mouth, rectum, vagina, and various lacerations all over her body, and I knew Rory had been indulging himself with her in numerous ways. She raised her fists and advanced on me, then swerved toward Rory. "I'll kill you! You fucking son of a bitch!"

I put out a hand and stopped her, shoved her a little. Though the force was necessary, I was gratified by it, too, and that caused me to hold back, so she did not stumble as completely out of Rory's reach—and mine—as I had intended. "Get out of here." I made my voice as angry and mean as I could, which wasn't hard since I was incensed with both of them.

I was ready for a struggle, but after only a brief hesitation she obeyed. She did not run or turn her back on us. With measured backward steps, she eased around the corner of the garage and was gone.

"Motherfucker." That was my nephew, uttering what was without doubt my least favorite epithet.

Flying over to him, I clawed the front of his already-torn shirt into a fistful of tatters and yanked him to his knees. He hadn't bothered to zip up his fly, and his cock was still erect; it was all I could do to restrain myself from hurting it specifically. I was sputtering, unable to think of anything sufficiently outraged and articulate to say to him.

He, however, was never at a loss for words. "What'd you stop me for, Uncle Fag? That's what spics are for."

The content of his ranting was quite beyond any response I could think to make. I hissed, "You stupid little shit."

He pulled away from me, laughing, and made a show of being in no hurry to get out of my way. I went back to the motel and waited. David was still hungry and still saying so. It was some time before I could round up all the men and convince them that we'd have to drive on, through daylight too bright and too transparent for us to be out in, because Rory's brutal little encounter with the local girl had made this town an unsafe place for us to stay even a few more hours.

There was much grumbling, and Rory almost refused to get in a vehicle. I would have been delighted to leave him there. I was wondering with a certain savagery whether I could get away with explaining next fall to his mother and grandmother, "It was his choice. I don't know what got into him," when he flung himself into the cab of the hibernaculum I had been driving last night, slammed the door, and turned the radio up loud, a disco station that I could not believe he liked any better than I did. Imagining the tinkly noise permeating back into the trailer and into the Old Woman's trance, I was practically gleeful. She and Rory deserved each other.

I strode toward the driver's door. My uncle Perry stepped into my path. "Don't do it, Joel," he warned.

"I'm just going to drive," I said through my teeth.

"You're not safe to drive. You'll kill him and yourself, too."

"Fine," I snarled. "Perfect." But already my anger was subsiding into a parody of itself.

"I'll drive the truck," Perry said firmly. "You go ride with Pete and the boys."

CHAPTER 8

Pete glanced over at me from where he sat behind the wheel. "Kid really got to you, didn't he?"

"That girl is who he really got to." I shuddered, passed a hand over my face and temples.

"Probably wasn't as bad as it seemed."

"Probably liked it," offered Ramsey from the backseat.

Josh said, "Yeah. They're into fucking a hell of a lot more than our girls are, you know. They don't have, like, seasons, you know. They can get it on anytime, anyplace." Both boys laughed.

Their father did not laugh, but he also did not object. Neither did I.

Pete was driving with two fingers of one hand and all but lounging in the seat, while I hunched my shoulders toward the dashboard and pressed both feet hard against the floor, as though I could help to get us there. Somewhere in my primal social consciousness had lodged the idea that once we had made it to Ambergen, we would have averted or avoided some terrible disaster.

"Rory's a hard one," Pete admitted. "Not that any male child that age is easy." He made a face, more exasperated in a fond sort of way than seriously concerned, meant to indicate his progeny.

"Little turd," I said. From the backseat Josh and Ramsey chuckled.

"He is that."

"I think he's more than that. I think he's disturbed and dangerous."

"Oh, come on. We were all a little nuts at his age. We've turned out okay."

Adults often said that, I had noticed, particularly those whom I would not agree had turned out okay. I was spared having to invent a noncommital response or rev myself up for a conflict with Pete by a nasty little automotive drama.

The white Jeep that had been charting an erratic course ahead of, behind, and beside us for some miles now abruptly shot across three empty lanes and, with nary a signal, cut in front of us. I sank farther in my seat and stomped on my imaginary brake. Pete swore. Josh rolled down his window and yelled. The Jeep blinked its brake lights impudently at us, then took off at what must have been close to a hundred miles an hour along the curvilinear, wooded, rain-slick highway.

I could tell that Pete was sorely tempted to give chase, and his sons were urging him on. It was my turn to warn him, "Don't do it, Pete." He didn't, but it took admirable restraint.

We rode again for a while without saying anything—not exactly in silence, since the boys were hooting and talking in stage whispers and the radio talk show host was baiting callers. I was debating whether I should bring up the Old Woman stowaway, to Pete at all and particularly within earshot of his sons, when Pete advised, "Don't waste your time worrying about Rory. There's nothing you can do, and it's autumn, and we're almost to Ambergen. Give yourself a break, Joel."

His advice struck me as cavalier. Instead of providing me comfort or relief, it evoked dread.

One of the most seductive forms of magical thinking was this: If I could worry in sufficient detail and with sufficient energy about a particular trouble, it would not happen. It never worked, of course; or, more precisely, there was no way to ascertain whether it worked or not. The world being chock full of troubles, no one could ever think of them all. Frequently enough, I was surprised, in one way or another: What I had been conscientiously worrying about turned out, when it did come, to have a slightly different size, shape, texture, so maybe it was something different. Far worse than I had imagined, or not nearly so bad.

We all knew perfectly well that magical thinking was ineffective. But in our tiny arsenal of weapons and defenses, it was often the best we could do against the slings and arrows of fortune that could, indeed, be outrageous. I did not want to give it up.

"What do you know about the Old Women?" Even as I instantly regretted having brought up the subject, I held my breath to hear what he would say.

Pete's ears flared. He hesitated, then said cautiously, "What do you mean, what do I know? I know the same things everybody else does. Why?"

"Have any of them ever migrated?"

"I don't think so. They're so self-sufficient they don't need any tending. As far as I know, they've never been out of the dens. Not in living male memory, at least." He drew a breath and exhaled it raggedly. "Suits me fine. They should just stay in there."

"What do they do in there, anyway?"

"Sleep, I guess."

"Sleep?"

"Well, hibernate."

"Hibernate, like the other women?"

"Well, not hibernate, exactly. Some other thing." He had put both hands on the wheel and his knuckles were white, although the highway had stretched uneventfully since the Jeep had disappeared. "Not our business, Joel. Leave it alone."

"They have to eat. Who feeds them, do you think? And what do they eat?"

"Shit, man, why are you talking about this? What do you care about the Old Women?"

The boys in the backseat were still chatting between themselves, but there was an artificial quality to their conversation that let me know they were listening. "Later," I said to their father, and he was only too happy to let me shut up.

Nineteen hours later, we pulled into the town where we would spend our last day on the road. We found our motels, located optimally in far-flung parts of the city. But all of them belonged to the same chain, which caused me to fantasize uneasily about the conversation at the next staff meeting.

Too wired to sleep right away but too exhausted and nervous to care anything about eating, I tried to settle down. I had a room to myself this time, and I turned on daytime TV. The mindless drone of soaps and talk shows and feminine hygiene commercials gradually eased my taut mind.

Sometime later, there was a pounding at my door. It took me a while to understand what it was, and longer to convince myself that I had to get up and see what was going on. Groggily I checked my watch; it was still afternoon. I had trouble keeping my balance and heading in a straight line when I finally went to the door.

My uncle Perry stood in bright sunlight that stabbed my unwary eyes. I backed up hastily to let him enter. I shut the door and reluctantly turned to face him. He was breathing heavily. I waited. He said nothing to explain this interruption of my rest.

Enormously irritated, I stalked the short distance across the room and urinated without shutting the bathroom door. Over the noise of the toilet flushing, I finally demanded, "What's wrong?"

"We lost one," he said.

Whatever he was talking about, this was bad news. I came around the thin partition between the toilet and the bed. "One what?"

"A baby. Maryanne's baby. Stockard found him when he made rounds."

I inhaled sharply. "Do we know what happened?" We almost never knew what happened. We counted ourselves lucky if only a few infants succumbed to migratory crib death every year. But I had to ask. There was paperwork to be completed, and Maryanne, of course, would need an explanation.

Perry said, "No. Ted and I double-checked all the systems in the nursery after Stockard finished. Everything is functioning fine." He shook his head and sighed. "Shit just happens, I guess."

I did not yet need to think about who would tell Maryanne her son had died, or how she would be told. We had all winter to decide that, and she might well not be the only recipient of the tragic news. I went back into the bathroom, splashed cold water on my face, and said through the towel, "Did you guys take care of him?"

"Yes."

Perry stayed in the room then until it was time to hit the road. We said nothing more about the dead baby, but the fact that we also did not talk about anything else was as much a tribute to him as we knew how to pay. We just lay on the beds and dozed off and on, and when the light was low enough through the bent slats of the blinds, we got up and got ready for the night's travel.

The news had spread among the men, of course, and everybody but David and Rory seemed subdued as we got ready to leave. David was going on about how badly he had slept ever since leaving Tallus. Rory was on a tirade about the "Mexican faggots in their goddamn cute little cowboy shirts and their high-heeled boots and their jeans tight so you can see how they're hung"; apparently he had not even been in his room for more than an hour or so.

I could have let somebody else drive again, and probably should have. My nerves were buzzing from several days of insufficient sleep; I was light-headed from lack of food, although still not hungry; the death of Maryanne's son, on top of everything else, had seriously rattled me. But I was determined to be at the wheel when we pulled into Ambergen.

The last night of the journey was uneventful, except for the not at all gradual appearance of palm trees along the sides of the road. This was the sign: Every year, we would come over that particular rise and down into this humid, tepid, thick-grown valley, and there would be rows and groves of palm trees where there had been none before, and that meant we would reach Ambergen within the hour.

My stomach lurched with excitement. Stockard said, "We're here."

I braced myself back against the seat. "Not yet," I admonished him. Anything could happen in an hour.

Ambergen was green. It smelled green. It tasted green, felt green on my skin and hair. It sounded green, wet, thick with life just this side of rot. A long green driveway, shaded in the globular moonlight, up to a green mound, green pillow, green womb of a house, with green grass; green woods so dense there might not have been individual trees or individual leaves; green roof, green walls, tinted picture windows reflecting green and curtained pale and dark green.

As soon as I pulled the pickup into the cul-de-sac, the rest of the convoy behind us was obscured. I killed the engine and sat back in the seat to absorb the sensory bombardment that arriving at Ambergen always set off. There was a thrill of relief so intense that it might well be called joy.

As the rest of our family—cars, bikes, pickups, vans, and the big hibernacula—emerged from the Ambergen woods to nudge up against the base of the interconnecting domes of the Ambergen compound, Stockard said again, "We're here." This time I didn't caution him against saying it; I said it, too.

CHAPTER 9

Sometimes I went in and out of the hibernacula without taking any particular notice, just doing my job. At other times, such as now, I would be assaulted by such hyperawareness that every move I made, however prescribed and routine, suddenly took on a rarefied quality, and I was both actor and audience. Sometimes, in fact, the entire sequence of actions, which had become virtually autonomic, would palpably shift in my perception. Then I'd find myself frozen with my fingers wrapped around the lever on the side door or skimming through the crowded interior, as I'd done countless times before, suddenly so aware of the alienness of this hermetic world that—for a beat or two, till I could corral my stampeding thoughts—I couldn't think what to do next.

I roused myself now, slipped through the side door—whose opening, to protect the inside climate, was barely wider than my body turned sideways—and closed it quickly. The seal made a faint, elongated *pop*. The hibernaculum was cool, cold to me now that my body had adapted to the south, and I shivered through my down jacket.

The clouds of my breath were considerably warmer and denser than the combined exhalations of all the sleeping women, because in this state their oxygen needs were far lower than normal and their used carbon dioxide correspondingly decreased, while I was virtually panting.

The gray walls might have been draped with fur blankets, flesh blankets, leathery blankets where arm membranes were wrapped around certain sleepers like corn husks around tamales, cabbage leaves around halupky, newspapers around derelicts, shrouds around corpses. The effect was of a mottled quilt, glittering here and there with the silvery hoarfrost that filmed the hair of those at the outer edges where the atmosphere was even cooler than in the rest of the room.

As befit her age and rank, Ma's spot was near the center of the preternaturally quiet mob, where her own energy would be augmented by the clustering of the others around her. I'd settled her there myself and it wasn't hard to find her. I made my way through the vertical tiers of women, all of whom were as close to death as it was possible for a living creature to be. They weren't actively giving off cold, the way a dead body does—or the way the Old Woman in the other hibernaculum had done when I'd discovered her on the migration. But they weren't radiating any heat, either; almost exactly, they matched the ambient temperature in the room.

Something about that in particular brought me up short, as though I had never noticed it before. Taking care not to come into contact with any of them, I wended my way among them. My hair stood on end, in horror and wonder, reverence and dread.

Ma's little feet, in fluffy yellow slippers and thermal socks, were at the level of my shoulders. Her head, cocooned in a plaid babushka with red plush earmuffs, didn't reach the floor. If I'd dared to wrap my arms around her middle, I could easily have clasped my own forearms. She was so small, so old, and so still.

I knew that things were moving inside her body, albeit sluggishly; her heart was beating, her blood was flowing, her thoughts and dreams were taking shape and then dissolving again. But from the outside, where I had always been exiled, she appeared absolutely motionless.

I was seized by the conviction that she was dead. She'd eased across that permeable boundary between life and not-life. She hadn't said good-bye, and I hadn't known when she left.

So swiftly and certainly did this notion lodge

itself in my mind that I was already in the throes of grief, already frantically listing ways I might cope without her and crossing them off as they showed themselves one after another to be ineffective, by the time I realized that the data did not support such a conclusion. My mother was not dead. Not yet. Someday, though, she would be; my relief, though enormous, was tempered by the knowledge that I wouldn't always be entitled to it.

As unobtrusively as I could, grateful for long phalanges and flexible knuckles, I inserted my fingers inside her layers of clothing and swaddling to take her pulse. It was, as it should be, barely perceptible, and for several minutes my own thundering, racing heartbeat obscured it completely. But then my fingertips registered the very faint flickering at the base of her throat, buried under the folds of her flesh and skin. I counted. In five full minutes by my watch, there were six beats.

I held my palm up to her inverted mouth, which in her sleep felt vulnerable even though it was studded with perfectly respectable teeth, including intact fangs. For quite some time I felt nothing, then just the barest stirring of air. I myself was short of breath and light-headed, as my quickening male metabolism demanded more oxygen than was available in here.

I wouldn't be able to stay much longer. The 93

percent humidity was also affecting me, making me clammy and giddy. I was shivering seriously now. Obviously I didn't need to check the climate controls in order to know they were working. I checked them anyway.

Then, against procedure and against my own professional judgment, I bent and laid my head against the spongy hump of brown fat between my mother's shoulder blades. By the time its embedded mitochondria had heated up like the coils of an electric blanket to signal through the padding of her unconsciousness that it was time to wake up in the spring, this mass would have dwindled, used to sustain her during the months when she consumed no new food or drink. Though I understood this process perfectly well, had studied it in training and worked with it for most of my adult life, there were still times when it seemed nothing less than magic.

Still early in the season, the hump was cool, springy, substantial as a firm pillow. I rested my face very lightly against it and murmured, "Ma."

My voice was much too loud, even though the sound waves were thoroughly and almost immediately absorbed by all those soft, somnolent bodies. I flinched, and there was a general sighing and swaying, as if of protest, from the sleepers. One or two of them shook their heads slightly, as if beginning the ascent toward wakefulness, which could be as explosive as the launching of a rocket; I'd known body temperatures to shoot up sixty degrees in minutes, heartbeats to accelerate from barely perceptible to five hundred per minute, all of which was wearing on the body and psyche of the waking female and on the nerves of the responsible male.

Thankfully, they all subsided again. My mother didn't react at all. I was relieved, but I was also disappointed, and there was a strong temptation to call her again, more loudly and in her ear, or to shake her awake. She was, as she'd always been, quite beyond my reach.

Then The Dream was in my head. Was I dreaming? I wasn't asleep. It was my mother who was asleep. Was my mother dreaming?

I was flying along beside the red cliff. My muscles ached and I was exhausted. I'd been flying for a long time. My ears fanned. My eyes strained. My detectors were picking up no heat of any kind from anywhere. I was alone.

The cliff went so high that I couldn't sense the sky, so low that I couldn't sense the ground, and very deep. I was possessed of a dreamer's certainty that there was nothing on the other side of it, that there was no other side.

My name carved in the cliff had been unfurling beside me all along; I became aware of it. The J was much taller than I was, the D so much wider that it took a long time to travel all the way across its bulge.

The trenches for my epitaph were empty. It made lugubrious sense to my dreaming self that there should be nothing worth saying about me. Here was my birth date, followed by the hyphen, which made either a chasm or a ledge depending on which way you looked at it. Here was the crater designed to hold my date of death. As I soared endlessly over it, I had to struggle not only to keep moving but also against some strange magnetism that threatened to pull me into it, like the almost sexual urge to jump off a high bridge. At the same time, numerals pushed up toward me out of the soft red rock. The first two numbers were those of the month and day I'd been born. The last two represented this year.

I was abruptly roused then by movement and a voice behind me, too loud. As though I'd been in a trance, my adrenaline shot up. There was also the strong feeling of having been found out, a mixture of dread, embarrassment, and defiance. Belatedly, I backed away from my mother and called further attention to myself by foolishly trying to pretend I had been doing nothing out of the ordinary. I made as if to check her pulse and temperature again, did the same with my great-aunt Ione who slept next to her, and then turned, indignant, to face the intruder. I was frowning and shushing before I saw who it was. "Quiet! What are you doing in here?"

When I saw it was Rory, I knew the risks were

greater than mere disturbance of the hibernating women. This troubled young man, for all that he was my nephew and I harbored a certain fondness for him, was capable of doing real harm. Now I really would be forced to run through the entire climate control and security systems again, in all three hibernaculum trucks. I was livid.

Rory fixed me with a glare so animated with what I took to be hostility that it was as though another living creature were in the room with the two of us and with the sleepers who could be considered either barely or profoundly alive. His bark of laughter was deliberately raucous and utterly without mirth. "Go fuck yourself," he told me.

"Tell me something." I shouldn't have been talking, but I could not stop myself. "Why are so many words that have to do with sex used to mean something violent or at least negative? Fuck, screw, suck—"

"Motherfucker," he said.

I bared my teeth. "Get out."

"She's my grandmother," he snarled. "You don't own her."

I caught the odd plaintive tone in his voice but ignored it. "Get out of here." I was whispering, but so furiously that every syllable was an explosive sibilant. "You'll wake her. You'll kill her."

"I just wanted to talk to her." Though he was

now whispering, too, his voice broke. He left. I went after him.

Outside it was a muggy autumn evening, positively sticky in contrast to the atmosphere inside the truck. I made sure the doors shut and sealed properly.

Rory hadn't gone far. He had crumpled onto the ground like a much younger child, legs straight out in front of him, shoulders hunched. I didn't want to deal with this. At Ambergen we weren't supposed to have to deal with problems. I stopped in front of him. "What's the matter with you?" He didn't answer, of course. I sighed, crouched, and asked more gently, "What's wrong, son?"

He looked up at me with an expression of despair on his triangular face. I was suspicious; Rory could fake any emotion that he thought would serve his purposes. But he sounded genuinely distraught when he wailed, "What *is* wrong with me, Uncle Joel?"

"Why?" I asked warily. "Are you sick?"

He nodded miserably. "I think so. I think I'm really sick."

I reached to touch his shoulder and he cringed. I said, "Have you talked to your mother about this?"

He snorted sadly. "I talked to my dad."

I managed not to say anything snide, expecting that he would. But he stayed quiet for a while, then stormed away, inexplicably angry again. Shaken by how close we might have come to real contact, I was both relieved and saddened that his familiar, nasty bravado was back in place.

I closed up the hibernaculum and went on to the next. Everything was functioning as it ought to be. My pulse was racing uncomfortably as I prepared to check the last one, which was the truck where the Old Woman had been.

She wasn't there now. I went to the spot where she had been, and there was no sign of the pulpy, misshapen creature, no gooey residue of any of her secretions, no extraordinary vibration. Gingerly I proceeded up and down the aisles, up and down the hibernation tiers. Everybody was sleeping peacefully and profoundly. There was no sign of anything amiss. I checked again.

Finally I let myself out of the truck and closed and locked it. I stood in the chilly garage, hands pulled up inside my sleeves and head retracted into my turned-up collar. I didn't know how to think about the vanishing of the Old Woman any better than I'd known how to think about her presence, and so, eventually, I simply did not.

I went on into the house, where a group of us had been ensconced in the den all day, eating and drinking and watching television. During my inconvenient upsurge of responsibility, everyone else had left the room, too, except David. He was surrounded by debris: pyramids of empty beer cans exuding a vague sour-grain odor, popcorn kernels scattered like broken teeth across the red rug, sections of newspaper stacked between his feet as though he'd been reading them, which he couldn't. If my sister were awake, she would read him the whole newspaper; of his three children, only Meredith would ever do that, and supposedly she was asleep, too.

I settled myself back into the rocking chair. David said, "I'm going to be a grandfather."

He'd been watching wrestling. I loved wrestling. I told myself that I didn't take it seriously, that its sheer ludicrousness was what made it so entertaining.

The Molester had just slammed Emil the Earless into the mat. Emil didn't even try to make his grunting and groaning realistic and the crowd's howl of indignation and glee made me laugh, even though I was indignant and gleeful myself. I reached for a cold beer from the cooler on the floor and chugged half of it. I was having fun.

The house was wrapped in a thick layer of continuous noise, like night in a city, except that here, Ambergen, it was the noise of unbroken partying. Instead of traffic, sirens, and highway construction, this cacophony was made up of laughter from all points on the auditory spectrum, music of any sort that people could dance to or use as backdrop, and the occasional scream of delight or outrage. We kept the windows open to let some of the party sounds in; even though much of the time I preferred not to be in the midst of it, I didn't want to be shut out, either. Vegetation oozed in through the windows, too, smelling too sweet, causing my head to reel at first giddily and then unpleasantly if I breathed deeply.

Emil the Earless was up on his enormous knees, with his enormous butt sticking up into the air and the Molester standing over him looking mean. The crowd roar swelled. I was laughing, but there was a real anger, too, a little surge of savagery and blood lust. "Get him," I said to the Molester, leaning forward and pointing. "Kick the son of a bitch in the balls."

David expanded on what he had said before. He would keep on with any subject until, in self-defense, his trapped listener made some small response, which reinforced him to talk more. "Meredith got herself knocked up. Did you hear me? I'm going to be a grandfather."

I was forced to acknowledge that I'd heard him the first time. But the mildness of his tone threw me off. As when the oncologist remarks, "You have a tumor," or the structural engineer observes conversationally, "the foundation of your house is collapsing." There was a cognitive dissonance between the content of David's statement and the manner in which it was delivered, and because of that, I found it difficult at first to evaluate the seriousness of the information. In fact, I watched the end of the wrestling match, in which the Molester bested Emil by grabbing his allegedly earless head as if there were ears and flinging him onto the mat, before I actually thought about the implications of what David was saying, which were numerous.

I finished my beer, discovered that the cooler was empty, got up to get another one, came back into the room dominated by the thirty-five-inch picture and surround sound of the large-screen TV, flipped through the channels until I had one college football game on the main picture and another on the little window picture in the upper left corner. In the summertime I am thoroughly bored by sports, televised or participatory; baseball, in particular, utterly fails to move me. But in the winter at Ambergen, I can get fanatical about football, and there are enough pro and college games on to keep my adrenaline happily, although vicariously, heightened for months at a time.

After I'd figured out the scores and the circumstances of both games—one was a blowout, but the other had CU down by one point in the second quarter and the new young quarterback had just thrown a Hail Mary pass—I said curtly to David, "What do you mean?"

It was a mistake to encourage him; David

would talk through an entire game even if half a dozen people told him not to. He was regarding me with the neglected-invalid expression he'd all but perfected. *"I'd* like a beer," he said, and his voice was even more of a whine than usual.

"You can't," I said wearily.

"Don't tell me what to do."

"I'm not. The doctor does."

"I want a beer."

CU made the extra point. The crowd erupted, and the camera lovingly panned the delirious faces of the fans, as if this were something important, a moment we should all remember. I was on my feet, too, cheering and waving my newly opened beer, feeling only a little silly to be the only one. In the middle of the jubilation David complained, "You treat me like shit."

"You want a beer, get it yourself," I told him, resettling myself, a little out of breath.

"You know I can't see well enough to do that."

"You know," I said, turning on him, "I bet when Helen Keller wanted a beer from the refrigerator, she got it herself."

"Joel! Please?"

Both games were at halftime. Such thoughtlessness in the networks' scheduling annoyed me; you'd think they'd stagger the games so there wouldn't be any empty spaces. I turned the sound down. "What's this about Meredith?"

Sullenly, coyly, David said, "Get me a beer and I'll tell you."

I did. I opened it for him and held it out. He didn't raise his hand. Seething, I touched the back of his hand with the can. Then he deigned to take the beer, raised it to his mouth, and took a long sip. I sat down and waited. Eventually he said, "Apparently that's why she had such a hard time falling asleep. She's awake now. Has been all day. Says the baby's due this winter."

This wasn't right. Babies were born in the spring. Women controlled the fertilization and release of their ova so the babies were always born at the optimum time. What did any of us know about childbirth or the care of a newborn? "Does Alexis know?"

David grinned. "Nope."

So both David's children were telling him things they hadn't told anyone else, most notably their mother. All of this—Rory's worries about his health, the mysterious appearance and disappearance of the Old Woman, Meredith's pregnancy—was too much for me to take in while I was drinking and watching football. I turned the sound back up for the halftime shows.

CHAPTER 10

There was a story, really an instructive folktale, about a man so eager to migrate that he'd started off alone in the middle of an early blizzard. When the weather cleared and his family began migration, they'd discovered his frozen body along the way. The story never specified why he'd been willing to take such a risk.

I had fallen into fitful sleep for perhaps the dozenth time and was dreaming vaguely about flying, or about not being able to fly, when I was jolted awake—adrenaline geysering, heart palpitating painfully, intense anxiety having abruptly congealed into outright panic. What had brought me to full nightmarish consciousness was the sudden awareness that someone was too close, someone was *touching* me while I slept.

From my infancy I distinctly remembered the primordial teeming of the nursery. All those squealing and squirming little bodies, smelling wet and milky. Like inverted cattails. Like bunches of soft brown chili peppers, mewling. Like nothing, really, except what they were, a whole season's worth of babies, myself among them, a mass of infancy whose individuals were virtually inseparable even to themselves. And every part of my body—which, though tiny and incompletely formed, was all I had—*touched* by some other body.

My mother had touched me, too. Memories of being in intimate contact with her had a more complex feel to them: deep comfort, the sure knowledge that I was loved shot through by the surer knowledge that I would not always be, and pain. I did not understand the pain. I did not understand why the memory of being caressed by my mother was always associated with the memory of the nursery, dangerous where it should have been protective, painful where it should have been nourishing.

That infantile population density had evolved because it was efficient for feeding, of course, and was also purported to make both mothers and babies feel secure. I had felt claustrophobic, couldn't get enough oxygen, couldn't move without rubbing against somebody else. At the time I wasn't able to think of any alternatives—and, in fact, probably there weren't any—nor had I understood what was causing me such acute discomfort.

But when I got old enough not to have to wait for Ma to find me with dinner, when I could go out and come back by myself, the sense of expansiveness had been exhilarating. It had also been largely symbolic and short-lived, since a man's life could hardly be termed free.

That dread of being closed in had stayed with me, and, ever since what I thought of as my release from the nursery, I'd determinedly slept alone. My room up under the eaves of the main house was as private as it was possible to get. On the infrequent occasions when I'd spent the day with a woman, either she'd left or I had before we fell asleep. I could not bear the thought of inadvertently coming into contact with somebody else while I was not conscious.

So I was wide awake now, and agitated. My first thought was that the intruder was the Old Woman. I was only slightly less distressed to discover that it was Meredith.

Incredibly, she'd been massaging the places under my shoulder blades where the muscles always ached, and her lower body was curled so snugly around mine that her scoop actually prodded between my legs from behind. I crawled hastily away from her to crouch in the dusty space where the ceiling sloped nearly to the floor. Dust swirled in the shaft of nectar-colored sunlight that came in the single slitlike window.

I'd righted myself too quickly; vertigo made me

hold my head in my hands. I propped my elbows on my knees, shrank the membranes under my arms till they were snug and firm, and sputtered at her, "What the hell are you doing awake?"

"Couldn't sleep."

"What are you doing in my room?" My niece laughed and shrugged.

With clumsy but alarmingly effective licentiousness, she slowly wrapped herself in some sort of nightshirt that, though tight and short and low-cut, did cover most of her. I did not want to be noticing that. Airily, she instructed me, "Oh, Uncle Joel, chill."

"Where's your mother?" I demanded, stupidly. Alexis ought to be in the hibernaculum, sound asleep. Meredith stretched, exposing the contours of her body, which were both childlike and womanly. She was, without a doubt, quite pregnant.

She yawned as if she herself had just awakened, causing me to wonder in considerable alarm how long she'd been here, whether we had in fact slept together. The very idea made my skin crawl, for more reasons than one. "I guess she's out looking for my-brother-the-asshole."

"Why?"

"Because he's *not here,*" she informed me sarcastically. "Because he's *gone.* Which, if you ask me, is, like, he did us all a humongous favor. One less guy to put up with, you know? And he's *such* a prick." Meredith moved her hands in an elaborate gesture of dismissal, and unwillingly I noticed how long and evenly jointed her fingers were, how tapered her wrists. Her hands were like fancy fans. "But Sebastian's here," she added with false cheer, and laughed again.

The sun was too bright, and everything was blurred, so I could see less than usual. There was a faint *skritch* and, now that I listened for it, the sound of mammalian breathing in addition to Meredith's and mine.

Sebastian's body heat was so impacted that it hardly radiated. But when my sensor passed over it, there was a discernible jolt. If he'd been prey, he'd have been easy to miss in the general landscape, protected by his own odd kind of camouflage; but once detected, he'd have been easy to home in on, easy to capture.

He was squatting by the door, not as if he were on his way out but rather as if he'd only barely entered and then stopped in his tracks. Sebastian did that a lot, never evidencing any sense of direction or purpose. The thought of him lighting like that in my sleeping space and perching there for who knew how long, while I'd been, however shallowly, unconscious, was even more unnerving than discovering his sister there.

The planes and angles of Sebastian's body were struck oddly by shimmering light and sound waves, so that they sounded and looked deformed, almost alien, even more deformed and alien than he really was. There seemed to be folds along his sides where there shouldn't have been, and the angles of his knees and elbows, fingers and toes were wrong.

There was eerie metronomic motion and that *skritch*ing noise as, with a persistence that appeared methodical but undoubtedly wasn't, he pulled out strands and clumps of his own hair. I exclaimed, "Sebastian!" but of course he paid no attention to me. "Meredith," I appealed. "He's hurting himself."

"So what else is new?" But she did wriggle down, rather more suggestively than necessary, landing lithely on her flexed toes, and she did go to him, albeit with much sighing and rolling of eyes. She crouched in front of him, not touching. Her young knees peaked higher than her strong young shoulders. Her hands tented over her knees. She was gawky, lanky, and altogether lovely. I looked away and did not listen.

But I could not help thinking how much she reminded me of her mother when Alexis was her age, even though I would have been hard-pressed to point out the specific similarities. I found myself wondering whether she would remind anyone of me.

Our family was nothing if not a motley bunch; it would have been as hard for someone observing our physical characteristics to suspect we were related as for someone who knew intimately our personality quirks and character traits. We mirrored in microcosm the diversity of our extended clan, which some touted as evidence of adaptability and others considered dangerous cultural and genetic confusion, not to say bastardization.

Meredith was the one who could be said to resemble every other one of us in some way. She had the pug nose and undershot jaw that her mother and I had inherited from our father's side of the family, but combined with her father David's large eyes and ears. Although she and her brothers hardly looked alike at all, she and Sebastian had the same velvety hair that never grew more than half an inch long. In some lights, in fact, they looked bald. Meredith's hair was so light in color that it could be called white or even silver. She had the same thick, protruding lips that Rory had, though his had achieved a remarkable level of pouty arrogance that hers, so far, only implied.

For all that, Meredith's overall physical appearance was well blended and attractive, even or especially now that she was pregnant. Her personality, though, had the distinct air of having been inexpertly cobbled together. She was both whiny and passive like her father and abrasive like her mother. She'd taken on, to a lesser degree, both Sebastian's compulsive need to self-stimulate and Rory's free-floating outward-directed hostility.

There was also, though, a real sweetness about her, and the breathless anticipation that she could be any of a number of things in her life, that she could do not so much whatever she wanted to do but whatever presented itself to her.

Clearly, Meredith didn't know who she was. This wasn't unusual in a fourteen-year-old, of course—for that matter, it wasn't unusual in adults, either—but she was more wildly at loose ends than anyone else I knew. Alexis had been counting on puberty and the onset of sleep cycles to meld all the disparate aspects of her troubled daughter into some sort of harmonious whole. I had had my doubts. Maybe pregnancy would do it, though bearing a child at the wrong time of year and the wrong time of life was a high price to pay.

Intent on her younger brother now, she began to trill from the back of her throat, like a mother calling for her baby. Even I found the sound soothing, and even Sebastian responded before long. He looked indirectly at her and cocked his head. He uncurled, a little at a time. He pulled out one last fistful of hair from the back of his forearm, as if for good measure, and then stopped.

"Good," Meredith pronounced, nodding exaggeratedly. "That's a good boy." It struck me that her ultra-competent, patronizing, controlling manner toward him differed only in degree from the manner most females assumed toward most males most of the time. "Come on," she told him. "Let's go get breakfast and leave Uncle Joel alone." Then, without any further complication, they both went out of the room, leaving me to wonder, irritably and worriedly, what that had all been about.

Rory was gone all night. Alexis was in and out all night, slamming doors, ranting and haranguing, enlisting anyone she could nab in pointless brainstorming about where her wayward son might be. The phrase we used to use to describe a state like hers was "strung out," and, to my knowledge, contemporary vernacular hadn't supplied an adequate replacement; Alexis was definitely strung out.

Her habitual method of movement was not walking or flying or running, but flitting. She was in constant motion, making stops so abrupt you'd have sworn some obstacle had been thrown up in front of her, executing precipitious turns without regard to anyone who might be behind her. She flitted from one topic of conversation to another, too, seldom finishing a thought, even more seldom waiting for what anyone else might have to say.

Now, sleep deprivation and worry about her children, amassed on her basic far-from-mellow personality, had made her even harder to get along with than usual. She was edgy to the point of explosiveness. Her eyes were hollow. Her body temperature vacillated between feverish and chilled, causing those whose sensors passed over it to shiver and sweat themselves. Her appendages trembled. She collided with objects and people, not noticing or not caring, as she flew in and out of the houses, in and out of the woods surrounding the houses, in and out of neighbors' barns, attics, basements, garages—not so much searching for her son as expending and generating random energy.

She was putting herself in jeopardy; she couldn't go on much longer like this. She was putting us all in jeopardy. Her agitation was dangerously contagious and wearing, and it wasn't inconceivable that she'd wake up Ma, either carelessly or deliberately.

Stockard and Pete got into a shouting match over American foreign policy, which quickly, not to say eagerly, escalated into a fistfight. Nobody interceded, because the brawl was providing entertainment and release for audience as well as contenders. There was some egging on, and I myself was aware of disappointment when—out of common sense or self-restraint or simple fatigue —they stopped before they did each other serious harm. Emmett watched talk shows in front of the big-screen TV and masturbated openly, casually, and, I might add, unproductively.

David very nearly lost it with Sebastian. David was never the most patient or involved father with any of his children under the best of circumstances, and of course Sebastian was particularly trying. The boy was rocking, as he was wont to do, and emitting one simultaneously high-pitched and guttural noise from his vast repertoire of annoying, repetitive sounds. David kept remonstrating, more and more loudly, "Sebastian, stop! Knock it off! Do you hear me? I'm not a well man!" Those four phrases, repeated endlessly, till I was actively considering decking them both.

I managed not to by leaving their presence, but the house was crowded, the energy level crazy, the atmosphere charged like a tropical storm coming up. The vine-thickened trees and flowering bushes that layered the house writhed in the maelstrom. Rain hadn't coalesced outside the dome or in, and perhaps would not, but drops beaded on my hair and clothes.

Ambergen was not surrounded by woods but had grown in them. Tendrils had worked their way through the porous walls, more of them every season, every moment, so that the interior of the domes was a mass of tangled vegetation, still leafing and blooming and sending down roots, only slightly less active than the exterior. I couldn't escape the sensation of being touched everywhere, on every surface, by inchoate, undifferentiated life, and at the far circumference arc of the farthest dome room, I quite literally stumbled over Rory.

I did not want to be the one who found him, because then I'd have to deal with him. Pretending distraction, I started on past. But he breathed, "Yo, Uncle Joel," and I was trapped.

He was not alone. He was also not clothed. Supine in the stippled light, his body glittered as if spangled under stagelights. Another young man —dark-skinned, dreadlocked—was on his knees with his head bent over Rory's crotch and, presumably, Rory's penis in his mouth. There was the tumescent odor of sex.

My nephew grinned at my reaction. "Get in line," he suggested, a bit short of breath. "He's good."

Rory's racism was exceeded only by his homophobia. I didn't understand what this liaison meant, but it had a strong aura of sinister obscenity about it. The black kid had not acknowledged my presence. His muscled shoulders heaved. I said, sounding pompous even to myself, "I don't have time for this, Rory."

"Sure you do. What else have you got to do with your time?"

Despite myself, I was embarrassed. "Who's

your friend?" I asked, inadvertently sounding lascivious and embarrassing myself further.

"Ernie. But he ain't my friend, he's my *slave.* My *loooooove slave."* Then both boys stiffened and Rory cried out, and I made my escape, livid with helplessness and disgust and with worry coalescing like the rain.

CHAPTER 11

This room was curved all around, the ceiling domed, the floor sunken, the walls a single circular wall. The air was gauzy with fragrant steam, on the verge of being unbreathable but so pleasant in the nose and throat and lungs. Heat vapors from the tubs buoyed us like thermals.

Naked, hair glistening and odoriferous, Josh, Ramsey, many of the younger men, and not a few of the older ones lay back in the warm bubbling water and passed around a bong considerably more elaborate than sheer function required. The fine smoke of the burning weed, filtered through water and through the oxygen-rich air that the dense flora exhaled into the room, made my head swim, pleasantly but with an edge of uneasiness. I was not entirely relaxed, but much of my tension was soaking away.

"Where's Rory?" somebody asked, and someone else replied drowsily, "With that kid. That Ernie. Off somewhere."

There was a pause, and then Perry said, "He can't do this."

"What's he hurting?" Josh demanded, voice strained as he held the cannabis smoke in his lungs. "He's just having a little fun. That's why we're here, right?"

"The kid's human," Mitchell said.

"What's the matter?" Ramsey's truculence, never more than a pale imitation of Rory's, was further blurred by the fact that he was quite stoned. But he made another attempt. "What's the matter, you prejudiced against humans or something?" He gave a little laugh, three or four high-pitched hoots quite separate from one another, and subsided.

"It's a security risk," Mitchell insisted.

"He can't do this," Perry said again.

"Somebody needs to do something," agreed Stockard.

I asked hopefully, "Where's Alexis?"

"She went back to sleep."

This anxiety was insufficient to rouse me from my torpor. I had had a toke or two myself, and wine, and I moved back and forth between sleep and consciousness as if through a thoroughly permeable boundary. I could taste blood against the roof of my mouth, tiny globules bursting like candy with a liquid center. Saliva pooled, ready to inhibit the clotting of the sweet liquid for as long as I needed to drink. I could take as much or as little as I wanted; whether my victim died, or merely sustained a minuscule double puncture wound on, say, the tip of its nose or the tender inside of its knee, was entirely up to me. I fell asleep dreaming of hunger and power, satiation and guilt.

I awoke to screams.

Instantly wide awake, I dropped to an upright position but otherwise stayed where I was. Many of the men and boys had left the sauna, and those still there were, like me, stirring groggily.

I'm not proud to report that I tried my best not to get involved with whatever was going on. I stayed still and made myself small, hoping the disturbance would resolve itself or somebody else would take care of it. I should have concerned myself with keeping somebody from getting hurt. I should at least have been motivated to find out what new danger or thrill this eruption signified. Instead, my overriding emotions were a sullen resentment that my relaxation had been disturbed, confusion induced by drugged sleep and oversatiation, and a determination never to deal with any more trouble ever again in my life.

The clamor escalated. The warm, humid, overgrown peace of the room was disturbed by shouting, squeaking, the squishing of feet on layers of vegetation, the thumping of bodies together, the wet *pop* of squashed fruit and the creaking of thin-trunked fruit trees bumped into. The odor of struggle cut through the cloy of the orchard and the stale aromas of the sauna room which would have to be cleaned and aired before it could be used again.

Sighing and swearing, I unfolded myself and managed to get minimally dressed. No one else was making any move to investigate, but I pushed through the fibrous door and went outside. After the sauna, the tropical climate seemed almost chilly, and I shivered resentfully as I slogged toward the melee.

I picked up two darting images and a relatively stationary one, and then I realized that the principals in motion were Meredith and Sebastian, the figure moving only slightly and infrequently was their father.

I went through a junglelike tangle and over a little rise, and sound waves struck my fanned ears directly like flung swords. I flinched.

David was at the center of it, his children wildly circling him. They dipped and swooped as though flying, although they were not. They scrabbled, danced, spun. They poked at him with their strong young fingers, springy knuckled phalanges, and long curved nails. They drew his blood. They came at him ferociously, banking steeply at the last possible second, so close that they repeatedly grazed his neck and cheeks with their blood-teeth.

My niece and nephew were emitting most of the noise. The only sound from David, a peculiar one under the circumstances, was the steady clicking of his tongue. If he was helping his frenetic children to home in on him, then this must be some sort of game. But it was impossible not to be aware of the sinister, bizarre overtones.

Sebastian was *laughing*. Both of them were laughing. Meredith sounded close to hysterical. But Sebastian's humorless staccato cackle elicited in me a distinct frisson of horror.

Rather more slowly than was called for, on the chance that whatever was going on would play itself out before I got there and I'd yet be spared direct confrontation, I made my way toward them. The kids dispersed, whether because of my approach I couldn't tell; I'd have been surprised to have even that much influence.

Meredith circled behind her father, pretending to leave, but I knew by the cant of her body and the rhythms of her steps and wingbeats that she wasn't done. David, who surely knew that, too, didn't even look at her. Meredith feinted once or twice, bulbous lips pulled back away from her teeth in a leer that would have been ludicrous if there hadn't been real menace in it. Then she began creeping, as though her father were prey.

I shouted, "Meredith!" but she ignored me. I

shouted, "David!" and he did look up, blearily, but not at his daughter. He couldn't have seen her anyway, of course, but something about the absence of such a commonplace gesture gave me the creeps. From quite some distance Meredith leaped, and I was impressed by the strength of her thigh muscles, especially considering her advanced pregnancy.

When her hurtling body made contact with her father's stationary one, the noise of it shocked me, and I found myself suddenly worrying about the safety of the baby. I saw her fangs pierce the back of David's neck. I heard her suck twice. I smelled the welling warmth of blood brought to the surface. David winced and whimpered but did nothing to defend himself, didn't even shudder to shake the kid off. Then Meredith threw back her head, produced a long sound that was half chortle and half gurgling swallow, and sped off.

Sebastian, meanwhile, had dropped in place. He was still emitting that harsh sound that might once have passed for laughter, but now he was simply perseverating on both the vocal production and the body movements that went with it. He wagged his head. His tongue flicked in and out between his teeth. His shoulders flexed and relaxed compulsively, so thin, and the avial lumps quivered pointlessly. The noise went on, utterly rhythmic, with no variation in tone or volume or pacing. I couldn't tell that he even took a breath. "Sebastian," I said, but he was as oblivious to me as to everything else external to himself. "David," I tried. "Are you all right?"

He was bleeding from several cuts and scratches and from the pair of puncture wounds on the back of his neck. He gave the impression of being even more weak and sickly than usual. But what he said was "I feel fine." It was not like David to downplay somatic or psychological complaints, so I was ready to believe that he did, in fact, feel fine. A shudder passed through me; this wasn't right.

"What was that all about?"

David didn't answer. He was staring off into space, eyes glazed and face drawn into an expression that could be called either dreamy or stunned. I sighed, took him into the house, and tended to his wounds. They were not serious. Even the puncture wounds on his neck were shallow and clean, and the trickle of blood had already stopped.

David was too weak and lethargic to do anything but lie on the couch. He wasn't the only one. The couches and beds throughout the house were, more often than not, occupied by men in various states of consciousness, undress, and hedonistic activity. David's listlessness didn't seem out of place, except for the impression of sickness that he chronically exuded.

I made sure he was settled, and as safe as it was possible for him to be, and then I left him. I wandered through the house, halfheartedly looking for Meredith and Sebastian, but mostly looking for something fun to do. The night was young.

Finally, though, I settled on duty over fun, and went grudgingly out to run through the required nightly inspection of the hibernaculum trucks. Although this job was conducted with increasingly dulled attention to detail as the season wore on, I couldn't avoid the discovery that one of the sleepers had been injured.

It was Theresa. She had a gash in her shoulder, where she'd apparently swung against something in her sleep. The wound wasn't bleeding because her blood was flowing so slowly. I managed to clean it without disturbing her and to assure myself that, however unexpected and upsetting, it wasn't dangerous to her health. With any luck, it would heal by the time she woke up, there wouldn't be a scar, and she'd never know she'd been injured.

But just in case I had something to answer for in the spring, I surveyed the area to determine what the cause of the injury could have been. My crews had, of course, prepared it according to routine and specification, had thoroughly cleared and cleaned and repaired and refinished, as they always did, and I'd inspected their work myself, as I always did. Then and now, I found nothing amiss. They'd overlooked no sharp objects, uneven surfaces, protuberances, or rough edges anywhere near Theresa or, for that matter, in the entire sleeping compartment.

I supposed it was conceivable that the normal stirrings of Theresa and her neighbors could have pushed her against someone else's claw. But I couldn't imagine there being sufficient force in such minimal contact to account for the long deep scratch and the surrounding patch of shorn skin; also, the angle seemed wrong.

I puzzled over the situation for a few minutes. Then I gave that up as pointless and decided just to hope it wouldn't happen again and nobody would notice. But it was another thing that wasn't right.

In one of Ambergen's numerous bedrooms I found Rory. Sprawled with Ernie on the king-size bed that was made positively enormous by all the rumpled bedclothes, he seemed both innocent and derelict. He was snoring softly. Ernie, however, was wide awake, and he grinned.

"You can't stay here," I whispered fiercely.

"Why not?" he asked aloud, sweetly. "Rory wants me to."

"Nobody but family can stay here."

"Rory says I'm family." He giggled.

"We're—not the same as you."

"No shit. But it's cool. Really cool."

The air in the closed little room was syrupy with the odors of sex, alcohol, and marijuana. Rory moaned, turned over, flung his arm hard across Ernie's neck, and sank into heavy unconsciousness again.

Ernie said, "I am a trifle hungry, though."

Thinking to get him away from Rory, I said, "Would you like some breakfast?"

Ernie made a face and rested his hands on his flat stomach. "Don't mention *food,* man. I can't stand no talk of food. Anyway, it's night. Time for dinner, not no breakfast."

"Coffee, then?"

"Hey, cool. Coffee. Black. Strong and black. As black as you can get it." He grinned.

I assumed this was both a racial and a sexual reference and was slightly embarrassed by it. "Follow me."

We wended our way, myself in the lead and Ernie following with many a noisy stretch and luxuriating sigh to the main kitchen. Pete and Ramsey were sitting at the table eating some kind of hot cereal whose very appearance made me slightly queasy. Behind me, Ernie made a noise of discomfort.

Pete was noticeably nonplussed by Ernie's presence. Ramsey affected a knowing air. Ernie settled backward onto one of the kitchen chairs, long legs spread and incompletely covered by his satin robe, and seemed to be the only one of us completely at ease.

I poured his mug of coffee—not strong or black enough to suit him, I guessed sourly—and set it in front of him. I poured my own and leaned against the counter to drink it, though there were empty chairs at the table. I wondered how we would get rid of him. I tried to think whether there were really any family secrets with which he could not be allowed to escape.

It wasn't long before Ernie and Ramsey were chatting and laughing together like old friends, making allusions to things that I, at least, didn't know about. Pete got up and brought the empty bowls, crusted with greenish remnants of the cereal, to the sink. Not quite under his breath, he said to me, "Nothing like youth to make you feel old, huh?" We both laughed without much mirth. Pete said to his son, "If we're going to get to that game, we'd better leave," and Ramsey left the kitchen with him, high-fiving Ernie on the way past. That left Ernie and me alone.

"You have to leave," I told him.

His unnaturally wide, unnaturally bright eyes teared up, tears also unnatural. "Where would I go?" he wailed. "I don't have nowhere to go!"

"What about your family? Won't they be looking for you by now?" I hadn't thought of that until I said it. Now the image of a rescue party tracking Ernie to Ambergen set my teeth on edge.

"My family don't give a shit about me." This seemed to restore some of his affected good humor; he seemed practically cheerful again. "Haven't seen them in a loooong time."

"Why not?"

He rolled his eyes. "They are so boring. You can't imagine."

Meredith came in, and Ernie's gaze swiveled toward her and locked there. Not just his gaze: His entire body leaned toward her, and tension sprang between them. I thought that her heat detectors must be working at full bore. I wondered what Ernie used instead of heat detectors, and told myself I didn't want to know.

Meredith nodded to me without diverting any of her focus from Ernie, who said silkily, "Well, good morning. Aren't you supposed to be asleep?"

She smiled. There was something between them that I didn't understand. Thinking "This isn't right," I set my coffee cup down and left the kitchen to find a less risky way to spend the night.

CHAPTER 12

BECAUSE OF HIS PASSING

I was not dreaming. I was not asleep, either—I had not slept, in fact, for close to thirty-six hours. We were immersed in one of those virtually endless card games that developed once or twice every season at Ambergen, high stakes and not exactly fun.

I also was not fabricating The Dream. I had not, in fact, added anything to it since Ma had gone into hibernation. This phrase, though, was new.

BECAUSE OF HIS PASSING

People talked a great deal about their dreams at Ambergen. Scarcely an evening went by without someone wanting to go on about his dreams of the day before, and there were spats over dueling interpretations, the more bizarre and less personal the better. There were, I swore, dream competitions: If, say, Josh announced at breakfast that he'd had a dream about turning into a mouse, Ramsey would hardly be able to contain himself, having just remembered that he had dreamed about turning into a kangaroo.

Like the others, I was aware of more dream activity down here than up in Tallus. But they were free-associative, fragmentary, mostly nonsensical dreams that burst like bubbles the moment I awoke and left only the impression of sensory vividness, no messages, no storylines or cryptic clues.

The phrase presented itself whole and uninterpreted to my mind's ear, a waking auditory vision of sorts. I rubbed my ears. On the other side of the octagonal poker table, across the mounds and trails of chips, Ted scowled and admonished me, "For Chrissake, Joel, play."

"Yeah, yeah." I saw his bid and raised him another fifty, by no means confident that either my hand or my skill at bluffing would support such a move.

Stockard exclaimed, with rather more vehemence than I would have been able or willing to muster, "Shit!" and folded. He sat back in his chair with his hands on his belly and his eyes closed.

BECAUSE OF HIS PASSING

I was not hearing an actual voice or even the facsimile of one. Rather, the phrase was forming itself in my mind in a way I could only call meta-auditory. It was most distracting.

Emmett had just told a long, rambling joke. I had missed the setup, but the punch line was: "BOOBY trap!" delivered with great gusto. Ted and Stockard had apparently heard the gag before, for they joined in the shout and in the resultant hilarity. It was entirely possible that I had heard it before, too. I grinned with some jocularity of my own, laid down my cards, and swept up their money, laughing aloud at their howls.

BECAUSE OF HIS PASSING

For a split second this time, I had seen the words, grooved into a red cliff. The cryptic nature of the—what? exhortation? koan? riddle?—was annoying. I did not want to play guessing games. Whose passing? And to what did "passing" refer—his death, or his passing by or through something, such as life? And what was the sentence to which this clause was subordinate?

On the next hand I folded, though I probably didn't have to, and left the game. Sleeplessness and prolonged concentration on the game, which had little context outside itself, had rendered my mind murky, and I was stiff from sitting still for so long. Aimlessly I moved around.

Men were asleep or semiconscious all over the place. Every hammock and cot and futon and bed was occupied by at least one body. The floors were littered with people, resembling not piles of old clothes as the cliché would have it, but of flashy new garments carelessly discarded after one wearing. Not a few were naked, or had collapsed tangled in their own or others' clothes in such a way that both garments and body parts looked rent and wrinkled.

One or two of them stirred. I noticed in passing that Mitchell was among them; I hadn't been aware that he'd been sprung by the state patrol and showed up here, and I was mildly relieved. I really did not want a conversation. Even more, I did not want to have to take care of a hung-over partier; already there were messes in corners and on stairs that someone would have to clean up. Not me.

I stepped over and around all obstacles, and kept going. With any luck, my loft up under the eaves would be unoccupied. The very thought of some relative in there made my hackles rise.

Rory sprawled naked on his back near the front door with his arm spread and slightly curved as if holding a phantom lover or victim. Astonishingly, his penis was engorged and nearly vertical, like a flagpole. He actually opened his eyes, groaned some generic expletive, and thudded back into unconsciousness.

For lack of anything better to do, I went to check on David. He was the same as he'd been since Meredith and Sebastian had attacked him —in fun, she'd insisted almost nonchalantly;

David had offered no explanation. Indeed, David hadn't spoken, to me or to anybody else I'd heard of, in the days since. He'd been lying in bed as he was now, quiet, ashen, limp. I wasn't sure he was ill, not sure enough to risk taking him to a doctor in town, and definitely not sure enough to wake Alexis. She'd made me promise to arouse her if anything serious happened to one of her children, but she hadn't mentioned her husband, and in any case I was not at all convinced that this malaise of his would fit her definition of "serious."

He could move all parts of his body that were necessary to move in order to get around; he could walk from the bed to the bathroom with no more assistance than usual. He ate. He excreted. He slept and woke. He did not appear to be in any pain, and the wounds, minor in the first place, were healing. But it was as if one more of his few remaining connections to the rest of the world had snapped. I did not like it. This was not right. But it didn't seem to require intervention, which was fortunate since I could think of none that would not make things worse.

I did ask him, "Can I get you anything?"

He made no response, verbal or otherwise. His blankness suddenly pissed me off.

Foolishly, I repeated, much more firmly as though I could simply insist on civilized behavior, "David. Answer me. Is there anything I can bring you?"

Predictably, he still did not respond. I had to admit that this uncharacteristic silence was a relief from his endlessly recycled and elaborated complaints, which were, like the repetitive noises a child makes—like Sebastian's repetitive noises, for that matter—annoying to a grown-up in direct proportion to how gratifying they are to the child.

I heard that he was breathing regularly, and that his heartbeat was neither remarkably fast nor extraordinarily slow. He just didn't seem to be in this world anymore. I sighed and left him.

The stairway up to my room was impassable, without maneuvering around draped bodies and puddles, both dried and slippery, of various body fluids. Disgusted and very tired, I turned the other way and went outside. That was a mistake. I could hardly see for the sunshine. I could hardly hear for the cacophony that never stopped down here, hardly could be said even to subside. The heat, already intense, and humidity clogged my senses, and the dense vegetation swallowed up virtually all usable echoes as if converting them to its own rampant purposes.

At the cusp between nighttime and daytime, either twilight or dawn, I always felt most alienated. Grimly I thought about food. Far too tired to be hungry, I knew I needed something nourishing. For the last couple of nights and days, I had gorged myself on junk food, fruit and vegetables and potato chips, beer and soda pop. None of this had the least nutritional value, though the sheer mass of it managed to deceive the stomach into believing itself full.

I headed for the veranda. Maybe, with a minimal expenditure of energy, I could pick up blips and buzzes of heat from the multitude of nocturnal life-forms as they scuttled away and diurnal life-forms as they emerged. With any luck, some of them would be logey, too.

I was stumbling through the living room, where half a dozen men were watching yet another Schwarzenegger movie on the VCR, when something hit the floor-to-ceiling picture window covered over with leaves. It made one loud thump and then a series of smaller ones, like a skipping stone hard flung.

The object—soft, I determined; maybe half as large as I was—slid down the expanse of glass, catching on stems and branches on the way down, and disappeared from my hearing range into the thick flowering bushes along the foundations of the house. Then it struggled back up the sticky pane until it was at my eye level, its feet pressed into a lighter color and a flatter shape.

My first thought was that it was a bird or maybe a gecko. I would have been pleased not to have to go any farther than a few feet ahead of the window to snack, never mind that birds or reptiles weren't really of much more dietary use than apples or pomegranates.

But it was not food. It was more trouble. It was Sebastian. He was crouched on all fours like a gargoyle, staring in through the bushes and the window pane at us. Most likely, though, he was seeing nothing more external to himself than his segmented and overlapping reflections in the glass. From my vantage point, inside the brightly lighted house that was dimming as the outside sky lit up, I made broken reflections of my own.

The boy hung there on the glass, inches away, in an eerie parody of awful intimacy and utter separation. As I watched, transfixed, Sebastian's suction grip on the glass loosened, or he let go on purpose. He slid down out of range again, disappearing into the mass of rubbery leaves and blossoms as big as his head. The trail of moisture he left glistened vaguely in the rising light, but I could not smell or feel it from where I stood, and so could not tell whether it was his blood or some other excretory slime.

I was certain that he must be badly injured. He had hit the glass with considerable force, and some kind of fluid was oozing out of him. Wondering somewhat frantically, as well as pointlessly, what had possessed him to run full tilt into a plate-glass window, I raced out the door and around the side of the house.

Fighting my way through the under- and overgrowth, I found him crumpled on the ground, tinted rosy by the dawn and limned by the rising morning sounds. He was not hard to find; from him emanated spurts of such heat and then such cold that my sensors throbbed from the strain of trying to keep up. But he was quite still. I was sure he was dead.

I knelt beside him. I hesitated, then forced myself to lay my hands on him, opened my ears and kept them open. He was still alive, breathing, warm, but barely. I felt the unnatural escape of heat from under his chin, heard something seeping, touched with the tips of my fingers the series of puncture wounds under his neck and was seized with a terrible urge to insert my own teeth there.

Desperate not to acknowledge that impulse, I noted that he had a perforation of such wounds all the way around his neck, none of which in and of itself was particularly serious but all of which taken together had nearly severed his head. Out of no single hole had Sebastian lost much blood, but out of the entire choker of them he'd lost a great deal even though the anticoagulant in the saliva of the attacker had worn off and all of them were now drying.

I was stooping to lift Sebastian in my arms, finding him surprisingly heavy and especially awkward because for some reason I was squeamish about getting his blood on my clothes, when his father appeared, wraithlike, beside me. He gasped when he realized the extent of his son's injuries, and I assumed he would help me get the child into the house where we could tend to his wounds. But David backed off, put his hands over his mouth as if he were about to vomit, and moaned, "Oh, God, why do such terrible things have to happen to me? What have I done to deserve all this trouble and grief?"

I managed to get his son into my arms and straighten up with him. The boy's head lolled against my shoulder, and I felt an unexpected surge of affection for him. "Where's Rory?" I demanded of David, as if he would know.

He was vomiting now, and I was struck by a glancing sympathy for him. For whatever complex of reasons, his life truly was difficult. This was a quite unwelcome perception, complicating as it did my handy habitual way of dismissing David. I ought to go to his aid, as well, but I didn't want to, and I had the excuse—no less true for being convenient—that I could rescue only one person at a time, and Sebastian had first dibs.

The sun was bright at my back and glinting uncomfortably off the polished painted wood, hurting my eyes, which had already been aching from lack of sleep, when I kicked open the door and carried my nephew inside. Men who'd fallen asleep on couches and chairs and pillows on the floor of the front room stirred unhappily and muttered as our noisy entrance disturbed them. The door stayed open behind me until somebody got up and pulled it shut, and through it we could all hear the sounds of David being sick.

I put Sebastian in the bedroom and the bed his father had vacated. I intended no unkindness toward David, despite what I knew he would think. I intended nothing toward him at all, actually. It was just the first place I came to where I could safely deposit Sebastian. Small and thin as he was, he was heavy.

I was not disappointed, though, when David took it personally, as I had known he would. When he came in, staggering and wiping his mouth with the bony back of his hand, he complained bitterly. "I'm sick, Joel. I'm not a well man." He leaned heavily, dramatically, against the wall.

Bending over Sebastian, trying to focus my mounting panic enough that I could ascertain the extent of his injuries and figure out what to do, I didn't answer David. I scanned Sebastian, noting the breaks and tears in his body heat and the particular amalgam of sounds and smells emanating from him. Finally David pushed himself away from the wall and came up beside me. I tensed, ready for the first indication that he would get in my way. Looking down at his son, he inhaled with a sharp, sad whistle and was actually silent for a while. As I finished my examination, as much as I knew to do, David said quietly, "I'll get Alexis."

I did not know whether that was the right thing to do. I didn't know whether Sebastian was seriously hurt, whether we could take care of him ourselves or not. I shrugged. David hurried away. I called after him, "Don't wake anybody else," and he waved as though he had already thought of that.

I sat down on the bed beside Sebastian and took his hand. It was the first time in years that he had allowed more than the most cursory contact, physical or otherwise. Feeling oddly that I was taking advantage of his helplessness, I held his hand and found myself murmuring, "You're going to be all right, Sebastian. We'll take care of you. That's what families are for."

I did not realize Ernie had come into the room until he spoke. "Whooo-eee," he said, almost under his breath.

As though he'd inquired, I explained. "He's hurt. He's been attacked. Somebody took way too much."

Ernie came close and stopped. I did not know what he was planning to do until he had reached out, very tenderly and rested his glittering fingernails on Sebastian's cheek. "This sucks," he announced, and then giggled too loudly. I winced. "I mean, this ain't right. You know?"

I did not trust this kid and was trying to be vigilant. He had no business being here at all, and I knew I should be more appalled than I was by his participation in such a mysterious and private family event as this. Cautiously, I said, "I know."

I struggled to follow Sebastian's breath, and focused so intently to discern the infinitesimal inhalations and exhalations that the effect was of being eased into a meditative trance.

Ernie had bent his face very close to Sebastian's and was staring with his huge eyes into the boy's narrow ones. It made me decidedly nervous, though not for any definable reason. I wished Alexis would get here, and dreaded her arrival. I started to move between my nephew and Ernie, started to say something. Ernie sighed, almost dreamily, and backed away. He reached with his rainbow nails toward me but did not finish the gesture. He shook his head, making his braids and their ribbons flash. "I'm sorry," he said. Then he left the room, and I heard him singing softly—to himself, maybe to Sebastian, maybe to me—as he wandered through the house.

CHAPTER 13

"What else could go wrong this winter?" Stockard moaned, and I cringed. People were always fabricating methods to foretell whether troubles were over for the time being: The groundhog saw or didn't see his shadow. Deaths came in threes. Lightning never struck twice in the same place. Everything had gone wrong that could go wrong. Less than a week later, Meredith went into premature labor.

Alexis, who'd been sleeping only a few hours a day so that she could keep vigil at Sebastian's bedside, now flew back and forth between the two rooms, the two beds on which her two children lay, both perhaps in mortal danger, or perhaps not. She was frantic, and harsh with everybody except Meredith and Sebastian, and her orders often didn't make sense or were contradictory. Men groused. Many just left the house and found someplace else to do their partying, which was not a smart idea.

Rory hung around, and Ernie with him. Ernie sang or hummed as much as he spoke, like a character in an operetta. He had a good voice. He told me he had taken private voice lessons all through school. I wished he wouldn't squander the talent and the training on being silly. He and Rory got on my nerves, but Alexis seemed glad for their company, and Meredith actually asked for Ernie to stay in the room with her.

It was beyond me. Sullen and worried, I contented myself, as best I could, with running errands. I brought towels and hot water to Meredith's room. I brought cool compresses and a fan and more blankets and fresh bandages to Sebastian's. I served dinner to David, who was sitting up in the living room staring at the TV, which he had not turned on.

The house was eerily quiet. The unremitting melee of people at play still seeped in the open windows on the balmy breezes, but it sounded distant now, tinny, like a radio turned down low. I heard almost nothing from Meredith's room, no screams, not even any heavy breathing, and Sebastian was completely still. Deathly still, I kept thinking, and kept pushing the thought out of my mind.

The evening was still early, and for some time now there had been little for me to do. Alexis shuttled back and forth across the hall between her daughter and her son, and seemed already to have established routines and procedures; my sister had always been better in a crisis than when things were calm.

Alexis had said, "Joel, you're in my way," one too many times. I went outside and stood on the porch, prepared to sulk. The night air was sticky with humidity and pleasingly full of food. I paced. As I reached one end of the long curved porch, I grabbed a fuzzy miller moth out of the air, and then let it go, uninteresting and therefore unconsumed.

Pointlessly I started back the other direction through the white noise and plaited odors of the night, none of which had much to do with me. Rory leaped at me from the shoulder-high railing. He didn't yell "Boo," but he might as well have. I swore and batted at him, struck his shoulder, and managed thereby to knock myself off balance without affecting him in the least.

My long-simmering fury with him erupted. "Get the hell out of my way!" I said between my teeth. "Haven't you caused enough trouble around here?"

I saw his teeth, felt the heat spitting out of his long mouth. "What'd I do?" When I didn't answer, he demanded again, as if he really wanted to know what I meant, "What'd I do? Huh? You blame me for everything that goes wrong around here, don't you?"

I stopped. I turned to face him. "I don't know exactly what you did to Sebastian, but don't think I don't know you had something to do with it."

"I didn't do shit to him. Give me a goddamn break."

"You've always hated him."

"You're full of shit."

"You were jealous of him from the minute he was born."

He guffawed. "Jealous? Of Sebastian? Right."

" 'He oughta be dead,' " I mimicked him. " 'Fucking freak like that, what kind of life has he got? Just a drain on everybody else.' " I hadn't realized I'd stored away such a cache of overheard comments. There were many more. I took a breath to go on.

"You don't know what you're fucking talking about. He's my little brother. I love him." There were tears in his eyes.

This was more than I could take from Rory. This kid had gone to an enormous amount of trouble constructing an image of himself as a buffoon and a thug. I could not now be expected to believe this profession of affection and innocence.

A doubt did cross my mind, though: Rory had never tried to conceal his misdeeds. In fact, he had made sure every one of them was duly added to his persona. I'd have expected him to claim credit for harming Sebastian even if he had had nothing to do with it, rather than the other way around.

Suddenly, melodramatically, I was convinced that I couldn't stand to be in the same world with Rory, let alone the same family. There was nothing to be done about either of those associations; Rory and I were, like it or not, in a lifelong relationship. The best I could do was leave the house altogether, a patently unwise decision since Alexis might well need me. But I told myself, only once, that David or Rory could damn well help her take care of things for a change.

I jumped off the veranda and hastened toward the hibernacula garages before I said or did something to Rory that I would later regret, although I couldn't imagine that I would regret anything except, perhaps, doing what I was doing.

The moist air had become saturated and was now exuding rain. I hurried through it, feeling it bead my skin and hair and hearing my footsteps squish through the layers of vegetation alive and rotted. The sky was pearly. Experimentally I sent out a short series of clicks, and they came right back to me, blunted, blurred.

At first I was just wandering, my only aim to get away from Rory and everybody else. Somewhere, Ernie was singing; because it had become virtually incessant and had a self-stimulating quality not unlike Sebastian's repetitive noises, his melodies had gone from sweet to shrill, from pleasing to grating, without changing any intrinsic qualities. Now his voice soared over the noise of the Ambergen night and plunged beneath it, in a song I did not recognize that might have been of his own composition, and I longed for him to just shut the hell up.

To escape Ernie's singing more than anything else, I let myself into the first garage. When I locked the heavy door behind me, the voice was all but shut out. The fact that I could still hear it at all had to mean he was quite close by, closer than he should have been. I stood still and listened hard but could not locate him.

Although I did not think he could have gained access to the hibernacula themselves, it was not impossible that he, probably in devilish partnership with Rory, had figured out a way into the garage. Or that he was hanging around right outside, for nefarious purposes I could only guess at. I knew I should find him, flush him out, maybe take the opportunity to run him off our property altogether. Trespassing would have been a legitimate excuse for banishment where endless singing would not.

But it was so quiet in there. Not silent, for there were innumerable little noises from the hibernating women and the machinery that controlled their environment. But the peacefulness was profound and seductive. Telling myself I was only doing an inspection slightly more detailed than usual, I was drawn into it.

In order to get close enough to the sleepers on the top tier, I had to stretch and contort until I might have literally been clinging upside down to the wall. To get close enough to the sleepers on the bottom tier, I got down on my haunches, on my belly, actually crawled. Even then, I couldn't seem to get close enough, to be sure enough, to intrude far enough. The farther I went with this examination, the farther I yearned to go, the more urgent became my need to peer and prod and guess.

Alexis's empty spot, immediately inside the door of the first truck, looked both immense and pitiable. Meredith's, directly under it, showed few signs of having been slept in at all. I passed by them hastily; they had nothing to offer me.

Some of these women I had known all my life, a few rather well and most from a familial distance. Many of the younger ones I had known all of their lives, although there were virtual strangers among them, too, women whose names I might well not have known if there hadn't been name tags, and about whom I certainly knew few, if any, personal details. Until this moment that had been perfectly fine with me. Now, suddenly, I yearned to access them, especially while their altered state of consciousness could be construed as making them more vulnerable to my prying.

I could detect a fair amount about their internal systems—heart rate, respiration, oxygen levels, density of brown fat reservoir. But no matter what instrumentation or intuition was at my disposal, I could not detect their dreams.

And so when I came to Theresa, I lay down beside her and took her in my arms. This was a most peculiar thing to do, and the sensations it evoked for me—sexual, proprietary, even violent—were decidedly weird, especially considering what I had left behind in the house. Indeed, the proximity of birth, death, and danger made my need for Theresa, unspecified as it was, even more intense.

Astonished by what I found myself doing, I made a deliberate decision not to suppress any of it. I distinctly remember the rush of freedom that came with this decision; even the memory exhilarates and frightens me, and is associated with the intimate recognition of mortality that comes and goes, apparently unsustainable through day-to-day life no matter what we know in our hearts and souls.

I held the sleeping Theresa for quite a long time. One of the myriad risks I was taking was that my body heat would rouse her and thus do her harm. Nevertheless, I wrapped my arms around her, then my legs.

She did not respond. It was not unlike embracing someone dead, notwithstanding the tiny and far-separated breaths that occasionally moved her chest and the pulse I could just barely feel.

We'd been aware of each other all our lives; though I had virtually no memories of Theresa when we were children, and I doubted whether she had any of me, the truth was that we'd in some however minimal sense shared a childhood, an adolescence, a young adulthood, and now a middle age, and this fact alone stirred up intimations of intimacy though it hardly justified them. The idea of making love to her lodged in my mind, but it would have been at the very least rape and perilously close to necrophilia. By thus labeling the act I did manage to restrain myself from committing it.

I ran my fingers over her, then my lips, just barely grazing. With pleasure I noted how the texture of her graying hair differed from that which still had its melanin. I noted how her hips had broadened with the years and her breasts fallen, and how those changes made her so much more attractive to me now than she had ever been. The rume of hoarfrost on the tips of her hair tingled like carbonation against my lips and tongue. Among the regrets I had accumulated thus far in my life, keen among them was regret that I had not loved Theresa.

I left her then, which was not easy to do, and continued my survey of the hibernacula. If not for the driving need to avoid going back to the house, where Sebastian might be dying and Meredith was giving birth and Ernie was singing and all sorts of other incomprehensible events were going on, it might have passed for a routine check. The various dials on the inside wall of the truck droned and buzzed normally, as had those on the outside. Things felt the way my long experience told me they should: temperature and humidity in the optimum range, white noise sufficiently white, microenvironment intact. The women were sleeping as profoundly as they were supposed to be. I could feel the small but sturdy heat pulses of life from deep within each of them, a personal perception of life inside life like Chinese boxes, their stacking and inserting, rotating and sliding and fitting together producing a hypnotic effect.

I settled down beside my mother and quieted myself. I intoned, "Because of his passing," and waited, presumably for the rest of the phrase to emerge from my subconscious or Ma's.

My mother was dead.

I did not yet fully know it. I would not know it, but she was dead. She had died in her sleep. She had slipped through the barrier that is so permeable but that appears so solid to us.

We say, stunned, "She was so alive, it's hard to believe she's dead." Or, "I just saw him the day before he died," as if it shocks us that there is a final day, a final moment of life. We express the same notion when we shake our heads at the wonder of birth and comment on the magic of new life where there was none before.

In fact, it requires very little, certainly less than we might wish, for us to travel from one condition into the other. From a biological standpoint, perhaps from a religious perspective, there is a vast difference between life and not-life, in whichever direction a being is progressing; but in practical terms there's hardly a step.

"Ma," I said. Then, frantically, "Ma, listen, it's The Dream. Because of his passing . . ." But she was not interested in The Dream anymore, either, and she would not tell me what came next.

CHAPTER 14

Meredith had so badly wanted a son that she wouldn't even entertain the possibility that she might have a daughter. Like the child she was, she would say dreamily that it had to be a boy because she'd always wanted to name a baby Eli.

Meredith's labor was long and difficult. Although I hadn't paid much attention until now, dimly I had had the impression that childbirth was not usually an especially demanding task. As any mother would happily have pointed out, that was easy for me to say. But, really, I had never heard of a woman being in labor for more than an hour or so; this had been going on for days. I had never heard anything like this kind of crying and screaming, never seen a woman lose so much blood.

Maybe Meredith's youth was the problem, although her body looked perfectly womanly to me, to my sometime dismay. Maybe the difficulties came from being at Ambergen in the winter instead of at Tallus in the spring.

Or maybe I was wrong. Maybe childbirth was always like this. Maybe that was one hell of an hour.

I was awed by the sheer physical drama of it, the noise of it, by the blood and the pain, by the astonishing muscle contractions and bone expansions that without any decisions on anybody's part inched and flung the baby out into the world. I wondered if my mother had gone through this, if it had been worth it. Meredith, who had started whimpering with the first contraction, screamed now and roared. She also laughed in loud delight and her cries of "My baby! My baby!" rang periodically through the emptied house.

Alexis was almost as loud, yelling at her daughter and at her approaching grandchild. She knelt on the bed over Meredith, laughing and crying with her. The room was redolent with odors of fluids from female orifices: blood, tears, excrement, amniotic fluid. Warmer even than the very warm night, it shimmered.

This was, of course, a commonplace event. In our community alone, every springtime saw a vast crop of new infants, and there had never seemed about it any more mystery or magic than effort. But the night that Eli was born, I was almost overwhelmed by a sudden comprehension, heightened and sharpened as mundane things can sometimes be, that everyone had started life in just this way.

As had I. My mother, who had just left this world by a pathway still unknown to me, had provided the pathway for me to come into it. She had given me birth—a curious and evocative idiom, now that I thought about it.

Even that night, caught in the dual magnetic forces of birth and death, I was not so solipsistic as to imagine that my birth had been some sort of personal gift from my mother to me. My new-found awe was of a more existential kind: We had all been born. We would all die.

Naturally I had known that. But in what now seemed an odd and appalling ignorance, I'd never thought of it in any but the most abstract terms. I'd never seen a child born before; I'd had no reason to do so. It was a revelation to be in such close proximity when someone I loved, however distantly, suffered so vividly giving birth to someone I would love so much. For the birth of this child to follow so closely the death of my mother invited hyperbolic interpretation, which I only haltingly resisted.

Alexis said, "Wasn't it Yeats who wrote that line about the center cannot hold? Damn thing's going around in my mind all night, like when you can't get a piece of a song out of your head. Drives me crazy, you know?"

I said cautiously, "I haven't known where the center was for a long time."

She said, "Everything's falling apart. I'm scared all the time."

Hearing a woman, even my excitable sister, talk so openly about dread sent a chill through me. I tried, "We're going through a hard time right now. That's all. It'll pass."

She said, "I want my mother," and gave a short, hard chortle of disbelief.

I missed our mother, too, both acutely, as though I had just found her body, and with an ache that felt chronic, as if she'd been gone a very long time. Her body was still out in the hibernaculum, among all the others who were only slightly, but significantly, more alive. The microclimate there would keep her body till we could bury it up north in the spring, when the other women were awake to perform the rituals and supervise the manual labor, which would have been too much for me even if it had not been my mother. Fleetingly, I thought that it might be possible for me to think of her as only asleep until then.

Alexis and I were in the hall between Sebastian's room and Meredith's. From open windows and skylights all over the house, the noise of the night flowed in, pooling in places, drizzling in others. It being a sultry winter evening, the ubiquitous wraparound party seemed to be completely surrounding the house like water around a sponge. Inside and outside, all around the town, was revelry.

I hadn't reveled much myself this season. Like those miniature worry dolls to whom problems can be given and then contained in lidded lacquered boxes, Tallus was supposed to stow the hassles of everyday life until spring. This year, everyday life had come with us, with a vengeance.

I never had been as much of a hedonist as men were expected to be, and I doubted whether this year, even if the southern season had progressed as it was supposed to, I'd have been doing anything very wild. Once a man started feeling his age, it seemed to advance exponentially. Most women, on the other hand, didn't seem to change much over the years, until, like my mother, they just stopped.

Anxiously I tried to detect, past my sister, any sound or movement from the bedroom—scene of many an orgy, copulatory and otherwise, now thoroughly transformed into a sickroom for Sebastian. I moved to one side to clear the way. Alexis moved again, whether deliberately or not I couldn't tell. She blocked any sound, heat, or motion waves there might have been. I shifted position in the other direction, and she moved, too.

Her facial expression gave no hint that we were engaged in any kind of struggle; I vowed that mine wouldn't, either. But I must at least have looked confused, because she grinned.

After a few seconds of this little dance, sinister or ludicrous or both, Alexis turned slightly and allowed me a straight shot into the room. I was relieved and grateful, though why I should need her approval, verbal or tacit, I didn't know.

There was a tiny sound, the rubbing together of light dry things. There was small, intensely rhythmic movement. There was heat, concentrated in one small island in a sea of heat repression very close to active cold. Just before his mother repositioned herself crosswise between us, I saw that Sebastian was rubbing the back of his head with his knuckles, as he had done when he was a baby, and I picked up the odor of fresh and old blood.

Then from Meredith's room came the buzzing noise that mothers used to locate their particular children in the nursery. My sister's eyes whitened and her ears stood out. Then there was a faint staccato squeaking, and Alexis darted into the room. Afraid to follow her and afraid not to, bewildered as to where my place might be in this family drama, I hovered in the doorway.

The baby's presence in the room was immense, although he himself was tiny. Where he was now and hadn't been before, there was a pocket, a bulge of heat and solidity that drew my senses and held them. I was astonished to hear myself saying, though probably not aloud, "Welcome, Eli."

Alexis crooned, "Oh, honey, he's beautiful!"

Meredith was laughing or crying, gulping and gasping, virtually out of control. She raised both hands to her face, long slender fingers like the ribs of a tent without canvas.

The baby lay on his side on the bed, curled like a little comma, uncovered and uncuddled. His grandmother went to him, scooped him up, and brought him to her breast. She could easily have held him in one spread hand. She kissed him; she nuzzled the folds of his neck and made comforting noises. Then she held him out to the hysterical girl on the bed. "Here's your son, Meredith. Here's Eli."

But Meredith wouldn't take the baby from her mother's arms. She had turned away. She moved as far away from him as she could in the bed.

Then she was up, and flying toward me, wild and crying, stumbling against the wall as she came. Not knowing whether to stop her or get out of her way, I trembled and froze.

"Shit." For a vertiginous split second Alexis appeared to have no more idea what to do than I did. But then she came at me, too, faster and surer than her daughter, and I had no hope of getting out of her way. She thrust the newborn into my arms, which had never held a baby before, and hissed, "Take him somewhere where she can't see him."

I stared at her, then at the flushed and wrinkled little triangle of a face nestled in the crook of my awkward arm. His ears stuck out from the sides of his head like wings. Against the underside of my forearm, his nascent avial bumps pressed sharply.

He had hair—fur, really—russet in color and as long as the first knuckle of my middle finger, thick on his head, silkiest at the small of his back and on his shoulders and thighs. I knew this was called laguno, a term that suggested something primitive and exotic, and that most of the time it disappeared in a few weeks, which made me oddly sad.

Alexis shoved me backward. "Get him out of here!" she all but shrieked, and took off, I presumed in pursuit of the child who in the last few minutes had, willingly or not, become Eli's mother.

The baby spasmed. Thinking he must be having some sort of seizure, I peered at him, but he was hiccoughing, and that made me laugh. I was more than a bit giddy. "Well, it's you and me, kid," I whispered to him, and in that instant felt myself attach to this child because, in that first moment of encounter that was to set the tone for all of our relationship, it was the two of us against the world.

Carrying Eli into the deserted living room, I settled us down onto one of the big pillowed couches. I was awkward and tense because I was so afraid of dropping him, even of putting him in a position he would, for some mysterious baby reason, not like. I started to emit cooing sounds I hadn't known were in my repertoire, stroking him with my fingertips and with the long backs of my fingers, my whole hand. The contours of his little body were nearly unbelievable to me. I alternately held my breath to listen for his breathing and tried to match my breath to his, and I was seized with emotions I'd had no idea existed: Protectiveness that hurt because I was already aware that it was significantly limited; even then, I had no doubt that the ways in which I could not protect this baby were myriad and would make themselves known in their own good time.

A precise and fierce sense of connectedness, of "this child is mine" that had little or nothing to do with lineage. Fear for him.

Pleasure in the details of him: the way his toes and fingers already held on to me, the softness and solidity of him, his long thin tongue protruding from his miniature mouth and then receding again, the cool hairless area around his sweet nose where his heat detectors were detecting me, already feeding him information he was not yet equipped to assimilate. He had come into the world knowing things he could not understand, and that cruel condition would persist for the rest of his life.

I loved him. I had not in the least expected this. So far as I knew, I had until that time loved only my mother, although I allowed for the possibility that the preverbal emotion I had felt for my father could be called love. Love doesn't exist in a pure state; it's always shot through with other emotion—shame, dependence, loss, the fear of loss—making it difficult to recognize for sure.

A dangerous sensation of peace was settling over me. The longer and closer I cradled the baby, the more at risk I was of being submerged. I didn't dare let myself be lulled, but it was so tempting just to lie there with Eli nestled against me and not think about anything else. I actually did that for a while. Eli, who had been wonderfully awake and alert, fell wonderfully, deeply asleep. I listened to him, soaked up the sweet soft warmth of him. For a few minutes, we were safe.

Someone was taking him away from me.

I started and clutched him. He took a few big gulps of air and began to cry. I hated my complicity in upsetting him.

"She's ready for him now," Alexis told me as she took Eli out of my arms. I forced myself to make no further move to hold on to him. He wasn't mine to hold.

As I lay there and unhappily listened to my sister carry the baby off down the hall, a terrible sense of loss swept over me. It took my breath away. It seemed totally out of proportion to the circumstances.

She must have been moving in her characteristic too-rapid, careless way, because it was only a matter of seconds before I heard the door to Meredith's room shut. The image of my niece giving her son her full breast and engorged nipple had almost no erotic associations.

I had nursed at Ma's teat. I had rolled her nipple between my milk teeth to make it give up what it held. I had felt her teeth.

Pummeling my head hard enough to make it ache, I got up hurriedly from the couch. I was shaken by the memory and a trifle dizzy, and I stood with my ears closed and my head lowered in an attempt to regain my bearings. A strain of music, part of a popular song, pierced clear and pure through the fuzz of warmth and dimness and emotion that had gathered in the house. The music was lovely, and strange although I'd probably heard it semiconsciously a hundred times. What was different this time, I realized, was Ernie's singing, a steady descant high above the melody line, that turned a simple song into something uncanny and beautiful.

All of a sudden it was reminding me of my mother. There was no reason for the association; she'd never sung that song, as far as I knew hadn't especially liked it or even, probably, paid any attention when it was played, however ubiquitously. But the song, which seemed to repeat the same phrase with variations and to go on for longer than it should, reminded me of her, and again I was swept by strong emotion unfamiliar and confused.

I wanted to see the baby, but Meredith's door was closed. Sebastian's was open. I went in.

The first thing I noticed—was assaulted by—was the absence of the odor of blood. Sebastian's room and this entire end of the hall had reeked coppery and damp ever since he'd been ensconced here, the good smell undercut by the threat of its source. Now the air was unladen. It was such a surprise that I could hardly breathe for a moment or two.

Then I detected the lack of body heat from the place on the bed where Sebastian lay. Such utter lack of heat that the sensation was of a black hole, sucking in heat from the room, sucking in mine and obliterating it. Stillness like that, too; absence of motion so total that it absorbed motion, and I was ashamed of the rapid beating of my heart.

Trying to imagine myself motionless, I approached Sebastian's body. It was so manifestly not Sebastian that I thought of the given metaphors, which now seemed not so much trite as inherently insufficient: the soul leaving. The shell of the body discarded. The spirit ascending.

I touched him. I gasped and drew my hand back from the profound chill and bloodlessness of his flesh. I said aloud, opening the quiet like a fresh wound, "Oh, Sebastian."

Meredith and Alexis burst into the room behind me, Meredith carrying her son. Alexis was wailing wordlessly; I wondered when she'd started, when she'd known her son was dead. Meredith was quiet. The baby was emitting a thin high cry that I hadn't heard him make before.

Alexis started circling the bed on which the emptied body of her child lay for the taking, in a peculiar fluttering dance of death—of grief, I supposed; of Godspeed. Rory leaped snarling down from a high corner, where he had apparently been suspended in the gloom, and landed on his sister's back. She hissed and flung out her arms, and without conscious deliberation I received the baby from her. He was limp, then unnaturally stiff. His odor had changed.

Ernie unfolded himself from his hiding place underneath Rory's higher perch. "Man, I have had enough of this shit!" He made for the door. "I ain't stupid. I know when I'm not wanted."

Rory and Meredith, a single bizarre creature, moved to stop him. Rubbery shadows unfurled, amid a whirlwind of flapping. Claws and fangs curved. The heat and smell of them melded and exploded. The three of them made a monstrous noise.

In my unaccustomed and ineffectual embrace, Eli still mewled. The sound tore at my heart.

CHAPTER 15

Ernie said softly, "Just you look at the back of his head, man. Look there at the, like, base of his skull."

Eli lay on his back where I'd placed him across my lap, and he mewled. The cry was thinner now, and had taken on a coagulated milky quality, but otherwise it hadn't changed, and it certainly hadn't stopped, since Meredith had carried him into this room.

I slid my hand under Eli's fuzzy head. Along the base of his skull I felt a row of mushy indentations. When I touched them he didn't wince or cry out above his constant small wail, but my fingers came away wet. I lifted my hand toward my nose. I did not recognize the rich, creamy odor. "What the hell is that? It's not blood."

"It ain't his blood they're after," Ernie told me. "It's his brain, man."

"How would you know that?"

"I know."

"You're not even one of us. You're a stranger. You're an alien."

"Ooh, an alien. Cool." I heard him lick his lips. "That's how I know."

Very gently and with great trepidation I turned the baby over. He stiffened in midturn, then went limp again, and his wail continued, muffled now against my knee.

Scanning his body, I found evidence of three puncture wounds under his skull, one under each ear, and at least one—the edges were blurred—through the soft spot at the top of his head. Most were oozing clear liquid whose smell was subtler than that of blood, more insidious. The brain fluid could not precisely be said to be warm, but it sang with energy, even in this dribbling and diluted form; I could only imagine the rush it would have carried in its first fresh spurts.

"His brain," I said dully. So this was what Rory had been building up to. The ultimate high. The ultimate savagery. The clues I had missed or ignored paraded across my mind like the life review of a person about to die, and now they made horrible sense.

I kept my palm on the baby's back and considered Ernie. From across the half-lighted room I could see only his form, but I heard his heavy breathing and the nervous tapping of his nails on a hard surface. "Hey, man," he objected softly, and laughed a little. "Like don't look at me. I ain't got nothing to do with this shit. I'm, like, a victim, too, you know?"

"You're with Rory," I said, then took a breath and said it directly. "You're Rory's lover."

"Oh, I am everybody's lover." His attempt at exaggerated salaciousness came off hollow and turned my stomach. "That's what I do, man, you know? Hey, I'll be yours if you want."

He was a pretty boy. We were alone in this locked bedroom with the baby and the body of Sebastian. I was shocked to find myself actually considering his offer, fleetingly wondering what such a thing might be like.

Ernie's laugh had obviously been practiced so that it would peal. It was out of place here, and startling. "I can do a lot of nice things. I came knowing a lot, and Rory's taught me a whole lot more."

"Rory?"

"Sure. This sucking shit, you know? It's, like, fuuuun." His voice swooned as he pulled a lascivious face.

I gathered Eli to me, buried my face in the baby smell of him, and demanded of Ernie, "What does Rory want from me?"

Ernie stood up. I noticed again how graceful his movements were, how radiant his heat. He stretched, and I was sure it was a deliberately languid and seductive motion, made very nearly obscene by the dire circumstances.

Although, in truth, I didn't know that the circumstances were dire. I had no real idea yet what was going on.

"Rory?" repeated the boy, mocking me. "How would I know, man? Hey, this is your crazy family, not mine. I'm just passing through, you know?"

I held the baby for a while. He cried. The wail was getting fainter and sounding more strangled, as if he were choking on his own voice. "What have they done to you, Eli?"

It was a rhetorical cry of anguish, but Ernie took it on himself to reply. "They done sucked his brain, man. Don't you know about that? They been doing it for years. Rory told me everybody around here knew about that."

I managed to shake my head. My ears were ringing as if from too much noise. Trembling violently, I was afraid I would drop the baby, and I curled him in against my chest. "They've gone too far. They've damaged him for life. If he can even live like this."

"They ain't looking to kill him, man. They, like, looove him, you know? They just want to use him." He gave an elaborate, pretty shrug. "There's worse things."

Meredith and Rory came into the room. Although I still did not entirely believe I was a prisoner, I did take strategic note of the fact that they didn't lock the door this time. The two of them sat down on the bed as if nothing were wrong, as if they were not virtually leaning against their brother's emptied corpse, as if Eli weren't draining brain fluid, as if we had not been locked in this room for hours. Meredith's face, under the garish makeup she had begun to affect this winter, was swollen and flushed, and I guessed she had been crying, which gave me some hope for her. Rory, though, just grinned evilly at us. Nobody said anything. Ernie began to hum, then stopped.

Finally I said, "Where's your mother?"

"Oh, she gave up," Meredith said, almost airily. "Said she'd had enough for one year. She went to get some sleep."

My heart sank. For all her emotional lability and frequent mean-spiritedness, my sister had always been able to find a way out of every mess. With our mother gone, I would have to look to Meredith now for leadership, for enough strength and sanity to withstand her brother and the others. She was not mature enough. She had had no womanly experience other than bearing this child, and she had been unable to protect him.

Rory crabbed over to the end of the bed and patted the narrow, snug space between him and Meredith. "Come here," he commanded Ernie.

"Gee, bro, thanks but no thanks. I don't think so."

Rory snarled, "I ain't asking. Get your black ass over here before I whip it for you."

Ernie giggled and said smoothly, "Oooo. What's this, a little s and m? Hmmm? Rory, love, I never would have guessed." But he didn't move.

Meredith said to me, in a tone much like her brother's, "Give me my baby."

So conditioned was I, still, to the belief that mothers could always take better care of their children than anyone else and had an inalienable right to do so, that I had started to hand him over before I caught myself and curled my arms inward again. Eli had stopped mewling, and there was no detectable motion from his body against my hands and arms anymore. "He's hurt," I told her foolishly.

Meredith and Rory looked at each other. Then, obviously having planned and rehearsed, they both got off the bed and advanced toward us.

Ernie gave a little shriek that sounded as much coy as alarmed. I turned my back to them so that the baby was protected, at least temporarily, by my body. The whirling motion made him cock his head and fan out his ears. I didn't think he would be focusing yet; doubtless he could not really hear me. But he was listening.

There was sudden harsh movement behind me and on both sides. Ernie shouted. Long segmented fingers with claws came around my waist and grasped at the baby. I bent over him and managed to pull him free. I was bewildered to discover that it was Meredith on Ernie and Rory on me.

We struggled. Desperate to keep Eli from more harm, I was ineffective at fending Rory off, but he also seemed less concerned with me than with the baby. Our battle had a peculiarly gentle cast.

From the abrupt change in energy and then from the sound and smell of them, Meredith and Ernie were having sex. I could hardly believe it, and was offended. Their arms were around each other. Their groins were locked. Her teeth were piercing his left nipple, his head thrown back in ecstatic pain.

"Let's get out of here," Rory growled.

For a long moment I did not understand.

With a mighty grunt and a string of curses, my nephew picked me up with his nephew in my arms and flung us toward the door, which was now standing ajar. "Get out, you stupid fag bastard!" he roared.

Meredith tried to extricate herself from Ernie, but they were too far into the mating act for her genitalia to relax. Frantically she stretched her upper body and long arms toward us, calling for her baby and cursing her double-crossing brother. As Ernie's penis was twisted sharply by Meredith's strong vaginal muscles, he cried out.

Shuddering, I paused, in a confused impulse to help him somehow. Later I would marvel at this entirely uncharacteristic reaction; it would have been far more culturally and personally predictable for me not even to consider that helping Ernie was my responsibility. In fact, I did not consider it for long.

Fairly howling in rage and frustration by now, Rory snatched Eli out of my grasp and was out the door with him. I followed, feet barely touching the floor.

We tore through the house, along the main corridor from which the rooms petaled outward as if from a thick stem. My ear muscles were opening and closing hard and fast, their clatter reverberating through my skull and allowing in data so dense that I could not have processed them under the best of circumstances.

I slipped on residue dropped from the overhanging plants and banged hard into an open door, misjudged the angle where the hall turned toward the front of the house and hit the wall hard enough to bounce back and lose my balance, then careened into the opposite wall. Ears ringing, hip throbbing and already getting stiff, I kept going.

A commotion spilled out into the far end of the hall behind me, and Meredith came flying. I thought I heard Ernie's voice, ululating so sadly and so beautifully that I actually slowed, though I had enough presence of mind not to stop. Meredith was clicking madly, her sound waves bouncing off me like knives. I could not have said precisely why, but I was afraid of her, although she was my niece and considerably smaller than I, and although I had never, until tonight, known I had reason to be.

Rory was holding the baby wildly above his head, now balanced precariously on the fingers of one hand, now upside down or by one foot. Eli was wailing again, but not nearly as emphatically as the situation warranted, and he was not struggling. I strained to catch up with them, but Rory easily maintained the distance between us, and I knew perfectly well that he could sprint ahead and disappear with Eli without much effort.

For some reason, he did not want to lose me. Of course I was leery. But I could not let him run off with Eli, and I could not allow Eli to be hurt any more than he already had been. Suspecting that I would feel the fool when this whole thing was over and dreading the public humiliation of discovering that I had got it all wrong and there was no danger, I nonetheless continued the mad chase through the house.

Suddenly Rory gave a cackle and shot up the attic stairs. I paused to catch my breath, and did not hear him up there, in my room or anywhere else. Meredith was coming up fast behind me and I tried to start moving again, though my side and hip hurt and I was still painfully short of breath. But she zoomed past me with hardly a glance or a blow and raced up the stairs after her brother and her son.

Then there was eerie silence. Leaning against the wall and doing my best not to slide down it to the floor, I tried to visualize what might be going on up there and could not. The attic stretched across the top of the entire huge house, and was full of nooks, crannies, alcoves, roosts, things in storage that we had not taken out this winter, things that had been in storage so long they had been forgotten. It would be easy for my niece and nephew to hide from me up there. It would be easy for them to ambush me. I decided that I had a very reasonable excuse for giving up, and I very nearly did.

But I thought of Eli. I thought of Sebastian and, even, of Miles. I thought of my mother, and what it would have taken to ameliorate the disappointment and condescension that had always edged her voice when she talked to me. I thought of the cryptic phrase from The Dream, my unfinished epitaph inscribed on a red cliff wall: BECAUSE OF HIS PASSING

I went up the stairs, as resentful as I was determined or fearful, reflecting that at least none of the other men was in the house to see this ridiculous scene. When it was all over, I'd be either a hero or a laughingstock. At that moment, I would have had no trouble deciding which outcome to bet on.

Cautiously I raised above the attic floor, already doing everything I knew to do to bring in information: cocking my head, clicking my tongue and working my ears, dilating my nostrils, attending to my heat detectors, straining my weak eyes. There were mice up here, and spiders and various insects. There had been, if there were not now, geckos and some kind of small bird. But I didn't find anything large and warm enough to be Rory, Meredith, or even Eli. I dug my nails into the soft wood floor and hoisted myself up.

Rory said, "They're over there. See for your fucking self." He was under the eaves not far to my left, wrapped small around himself, effectively concealed from my inexpert probing by a stack of boxes and a roll of carpet. I flinched away from him, scrabbled over to the other side of the stairway opening, and crouched, readying myself for his attack. Rory said in disgust, "Shit, I ain't gonna hurt you. I thought you were so fucking worried about the kid. Well, there he is."

Meredith was cross-legged in an armchair whose ragged back was turned in my direction to face the east window. Once I had located the top of her head and the points of her long knees sticking out on the sides, I circled around and she didn't try to hide. She appeared to take no notice of me at all, or of her brother. All her attention was fixed on her baby, who was stretched on his back across her lap, and they gave the impression of domestic tranquility, a little diorama of mother and son.

Welcome relief and unwelcome embarrassment began to tingle in the pit of my stomach; I had misinterpreted, been conned. But then Meredith bit into the top of Eli's head. I heard her begin to suck, and the fragrance I now recognized, with horror, as that of brain fluid was sharp in the dusty air.

I darted forward and had my hands around the baby before I'd had time to think. But I could not just yank him away while his mother's teeth were embedded in his skull.

I shouted, "Meredith, what are you doing?" and that was enough to cause her to raise her head. I had time to notice the glaze in her eyes and the viscous liquid drooling from the tips of her fangs, and then I had Eli and was across the attic and into the stairway with him. Meredith hissed and cried out and came after me. I heard Rory whooping as if cheering on the home team.

Clutching the limp infant, I missed the top step and fell backward. I managed to hold him on top of me so he was not hurt by the fall, but I was bruised and the wind was knocked out of me. I lay at the bottom of the stairs for only a second or two, but it was almost too long. Both Rory and Meredith were coming down.

I scrambled up, still hardly able to draw breath, and started through the house again. I had no clear idea where I should be taking the baby, only that this place was manifestly unsafe for us both.

David stood up from the couch in the living room like a gopher out of its hole. I had forgotten he was here. I yelled to him for help, but he went right past me, stumbling and holding on to things, and stepped in front of his daughter. He was saying "Meredith, honey, I need—" when she collided with him, and they fell with a muffled thump and clatter.

I was out the front door and into the woods then, now hoping nobody would return from the night's partying because I did not want their interference. I sped with the baby into the first shelter I could think of, the hibernaculum garages; the keys were in my pocket, and only Stockard and Pete had copies. I unlocked the big door of the first garage, hurried inside, and locked it again behind us. Now I could breathe, though my chest hurt, and I could rest and think.

Eli's wail, very thin now and punctuated by ragged, shallow breaths, hardly disturbed the overpowering silence of the hibernacula. Thinking that maybe I was holding him wrong, I hefted his small bulk so that he was resting against my shoulder. The sleeve of my shirt where he'd been lying was damp and sticky, and I could feel moisture gathering against my collar. I didn't know what to do with him. It was not clear to me whom or what we were hiding from; it was not clear how I would know when we were safe.

The door opened. I backed up, but not quickly enough to escape the blade of half-light that sliced across the floor. Rory came in quickly, shut the door behind him, and locked it. There was no sense pretending he didn't know we were there. I demanded, "Where'd you get the key?"

"What's it to you?"

"It's my responsibility—"

He advanced on us, musk and heat rippling. "You still don't get it, do you? It ain't me you ought to watch out for, it's them." He gestured broadly toward the trucks. Then, as if understanding hadn't already descended sickeningly upon me, he added, "It's the bitches."

Suddenly I craved details. "What do you mean?"

"Who do you think murdered Miles? Your girlfriend, Theresa!" He held his palms in the air as if announcing a winner. "Who do you think killed Sebastian?"

This time he didn't tell me, so I asked breathlessly, "Who?"

"His mother! My mother! Your sister!" he shouted in mock approbation. Palms still upraised, he added, "She didn't mean to. Of course not. She just went too far."

I could hardly speak. "How? Why?"

"They've been doing it to us all. They've been

draining us all. Why do you think men are such a fucking bunch of losers?"

"Ma—"

"Grandma, too. But they didn't want to kill us. They just wanted to use us. They just wanted to be able to say how fucked up we were and how the world would fall apart if it wasn't for them."

I shook my head. "You expect me to believe that the women have been damaging us for life just so they could feel good about themselves?"

"That, and for the rush. I mean, blood's one thing, but brain fluid—now that's something fucking else." He lowered his hands, which were now fists. "Believe me or don't believe me, I don't care. But the kid's got to get out of here. Maybe it's already too late for him, too."

"I'm going to take him away," I said, not having known until that moment that I had anything resembling a plan. "I'm going to take him to the caves." Instantly I regretted having told Rory that much, but I was almost certain he wouldn't know where the caves were, maybe not even what they were.

I was right. He snorted. "Caves? What the fuck are you talking about?"

But I knew better than to say any more. After a lifetime of believing that I understood both rules and roles, now nothing was clear, including my own motives and, certainly, Rory's. I turned away from him and began to arrange a pile of blankets and tarpaulins on a shoulder-high shelf, clutching Eli close to me with one hand while I fumbled with the other. Small night life scurried, but I was no threat to them, and Rory ignored them altogether.

"I'm out of here, too," he said. "I'm coming with you. To the caves." He laid on heavy sarcasm.

I was appalled. "What about Ernie?"

"Motherfucker's nothing but a human whore." Rory sneered unconvincingly. "I ain't risking my neck for him."

"We'll talk about that in the evening," I told him, stalling clumsily. "I'm tired. You're tired."

He laughed. "Shit, man, what makes you think I'm tired? I'll be flying high for a *long* time."

Rory was always stoned, I suspected, but most of the time I didn't know it. Knowing it now made me even more nervous. To get away from him, although I was sure he'd still be there when I got back, I said, "I'm going to go check on the sleepers. For the last time." To my amazement, the idea brought with it sadness and guilt.

I took Eli into the first hibernaculum. Infants and children were not allowed in here, for fear they'd disturb the sleepers or contaminate the environment. I carried him down the first aisle, past Theresa, and it occurred to me that she and I might have had sons, whose brains she would have consumed drop by drop. Or daughters, whom she would have taught to consume mine.

We paused for a long moment at the place where my mother lay; to someone oriented visually, she would have looked not much different from the others, but the feel of her was radically without life. I had no idea how to think about her now, or what I would tell Eli about her or any of his other foremothers when he was old enough to hear.

We retreated back up the second aisle. Softly I recited their names to him, checking their dials and gauges. The inspection didn't take long; I wasn't paying much attention to detail, I was keeping no records, and I could hardly stand to be in the company of all these regenerating women.

I carried Eli down the steps and was shutting the door when an impulse swept over me. The master control was in a locked compartment beside the door. The key was on my ring. I opened the hatch and gave the knob a massive turn counterclockwise, which would shut everything down. The hibernating women in that truck would be dead before the day was over.

I felt the satisfaction of revenge. I felt triumph, and the pleasure of having taken action. I also felt a gratifying sense of heroism: future generations of boys and men saved. I started toward the second truck, intent on following the same sequence. I would name all the names. I would touch them. I would introduce them to Eli, the heir to their accrued misanthropy. And then I would kill them all.

But I couldn't do it. Whether it was because my source of information was Rory, a kid whom I usually wouldn't have believed if he told me the time of night, or because, even in the first shock of discovery, I had an inkling that these individual women, like their foremothers, were as caught up in cultural and physiological imperatives as we men were—whatever the reason, I could not leave them all to die in their sleep. I returned to the first truck and turned the knob of the master control back to its proper position. Doubtless there would be some damage to some of the sleepers from even those few minutes of downtime. I would have to be content with that.

I settled into my makeshift nest with Eli. He seemed to sleep, although I was not sure I would know. I dozed fitfully. Rory roamed in erratic circles and arcs all day, and when evening fell and we began to talk specifically about our escape, he was even more wired and edgy. We would leave after midnight, we agreed, when most of the other men would be back in the house or elsewhere partying.

I had never been good with plot twists. Even after the obligatory scene in a mystery novel, in which the author sat the reader down and explained whodunit and why, I usually could not follow. But this time I managed a twist of my own, and surprised both myself and Rory, who had not thought me capable of such duplicity.

He agreed to go out for food for all of us. He left as soon as the twilight had turned the sky a misty indigo, and I waited only a few minutes before I gathered Eli, a diaper bag I had put together from odds and ends in the garage, and a bag of trail mix Miles had kept hidden out here for emergencies. Thanks, Miles, I thought sadly. Sorry, Miles.

I crept out of the interlocking domes of Ambergen and was on my way, circling wide around the noisiest areas where I knew men were coming home from hunting. It was not until I had completely left Ambergen behind and we were deep in the middle of the night that I started to think more about where we were going than where we had left.

CHAPTER 16

Eli was not reliable about holding on to me. Whether he was physically too weak or had been drained of the self-preservation instinct, I didn't know, and at the moment it didn't matter. It would matter for his future, of course, and mine; but since I could not now imagine the future anyway, beyond getting to a safe and private place, I didn't waste much time worrying about it yet.

I concentrated on carrying him in my scoop, which was the only way I could come up with to transport him when it became clear, nearly disastrously, that he could not hold on underneath and could not balance on my back. Not having been designed for this purpose, the appendage ached and trembled from his weight and angle. I wished for one of those baby carriers that fastened the child close and left the adult's hands free. As it was, I had to support Eli all the time with a hand under his bottom, or he would tip sideways or end over end right out of the scoop.

Periodically he would further startle me, and thus endanger us both, with a loud little eruption of clicks and squeaks, quite unlike any other sound I'd ever heard him produce. This odd behavior didn't seem to be in response to anything I did or did not do, or to anything in the passing environment, and the outbursts came at irregular intervals. Unpredictable and incomprehensible, they worried and agitated me, and I held myself tense—sometimes for hours, sometimes for only a few seconds at a time—waiting for the next raucous flurry.

The first day we spent in the dim but not especially cool sanctuary of a little adobe church that, for reasons obscure to me, was both open and empty. The sound inside it was thick and there were almost no echoes. Above the small plain altar was a stained glass window depicting the crucified Christ, all primary colors and primitive shapes; prismed through it came the unpleasant rays of the sun rising over the high plains.

We had eaten en route. It was not an easy thing for me to feed Eli the way in which he could eat; with my mouth pressed to his, the way I had seen and never really noticed dozens if not hundreds of mothers feed their babies, I tried without complete success to control the muscles and reflexes of regurgitation so that he got the right amount of partly digested food but I was not quite vomiting. Miles's trail mix had provided some relief from hunger, although I doubted anything in it would be usable by my body or, by extension, Eli's.

A herd of goats, wandering loose across the unfenced prairie and equally unfenced highway, had finally provided a full meal, and then I couldn't travel for a while. The delay made me nervous as dawn approached in this unsheltered place, but I would be too heavy and slow to get off the ground until I had digested what I needed and excreted the rest. Trying to hurry the process, I was bloated and sleepy by the time we found the church.

I decided on a place for us under a pew, the only shelter in the simple, not to say bare, sanctuary. From the diaper bag I had cobbled together in the hibernaculum garage, I took two rags—stained but not really dirty, I hoped—one for cleaning him and one to use as a clean diaper. Eli was the first baby whose diapers I had changed, and already I felt like a pro; the satisfaction this little competence gave me was keen. But Eli was excreting almost nothing, and that didn't seem normal to me. I changed him anyway.

I also changed the dressings on his wounds, deciding I could remove the turbanlike swaddling I had fashioned for his head. The punctures along the base of his skull and under his ears were already closed and virtually healed, as was typical of wounds we inflicted on our victims. But the hole in the top of his head looked to be still open. I halfway convinced myself that it was just the normal soft spot, the notion of which—a brain protected by only skin and flesh—had always slightly unnerved me.

Perhaps I was wrong to have taken him. What did I know about caring for an infant, particularly an injured one? Perhaps I should give up this ill-conceived rescue mission before I made things worse, and take him back to Ambergen, where people would know what to do.

The memory of Meredith's strong young teeth embedded in Eli's fontanel was enough to dissuade me from such an act of cowardice and contrition, then and later. But there were moments during that long journey when I was almost sure I must have misinterpreted, I could not really have perceived what I had, in fact, perceived.

I slept in long fitful spurts punctuated by anxiety. Several times Eli woke fussing and could not be comforted; guiltily drifting in and out of sleep, I held him until he wore himself out. Twice he gave forth with those loud squeaks and clicks so fast they blended into an abrasive buzz; I found it hard to go back to sleep after those episodes.

Once someone came into the back of the church; Eli stirred at the same moment I heard the intruder—although, of course, it was we who were the intruders—and I shushed him, even laid the flat of my hand over his mouth, frantically remembering those awful stories of parents suffocating their children whose crying threatened to expose their hiding place to the enemy. Someone had come to pray. A young man, silent, making no plea audible to anyone but himself and, presumably, to God. Above my shushing hand, Eli's eyes were very big, although I didn't think he saw much, and above my wrist and my fingertips his huge ears quivered. I was afraid that if I removed the gag of my hand he would emit some incriminating noise, if not a clicking outburst then a whimper or an infant sigh. I was afraid that it would be terribly easy to smother him without even realizing what I was doing.

The young man rose from his knees and stood in front of the plain little altar for another brief time, then turned and came back up the aisle, past our pew. Nothing about him gave me any hint about his reason for coming here or about what he would do if he found us; his stride, the expression on his face, his scent could have indicated anything. He left the church, and both Eli and I breathed more freely.

We made it through the first day, and as blue-pink dusk washed across the flat land, we started out again. Eli was considerably more active; I thought that might mean he was getting better, and I was pleased, but it made him much harder to carry. If I dropped him, he would be killed. If I dropped him, I would be released from this immense obligation I seemed to have taken on myself, and it could not really be construed as my fault, since I had never carried an infant any distance before and Eli would not hang on. Frightened, I pushed the awful fantasy away.

We hadn't traveled an enormous distance, but landscape and climate had altogether altered. Below us for much of that night the gray desert was perforated by darker pygmy pine trees. Bushes, really; and I wouldn't have thought to call this place a forest since it was neither dense nor tall. But I supposed that was what it was: trees gnarled by wind and aridity, each separated from its neighbors by open desert space, but together adding texture and design to the expanse of flat sand.

I was charmed. I was tempted to drop down among them, and decided that I would if we were still in the pygmy forest closer to daybreak. But the dwarf trees were behind us before the night was over, and we could not afford to waste any time on frivolous whims. Since this might well be our only chance to explore this country, I regretted the urgency that had brought us out here.

We passed a day in a shallow canyon and another in a puny grove of cottonwoods along a trickle of a river. It was cold, and too bright. The sunlight caused nausea, which was not helped by the cow's blood I consumed for both of us; the animal had been killed on the road, not long ago but its blood had already started to turn. Eli accepted the mildly disgusting stuff from my mouth without interest, and swallowed no more or less of it than of any other meal, which wasn't much.

I worried that he wasn't eating enough. I worried that he would get chilled, catch a cold. I had the uneasy impression that I was worrying about the wrong things, but it gave me a certain illusion of control that I saw no reason to surrender yet.

On what should have been the last day of the trip, I could find no shelter of any significance. We traveled far too late into the day. I was exhausted. Eli was alternately clamorous and alarmingly still. The landscape was quite flat and nothing grew in the arid soil higher than a few inches; the root systems, which I knew to be extensive in their search for underground water, would do us no good.

We came upon no rock outcroppings, no canyons or arroyos or even ditches, no buildings of any kind, no trees or bushes, pygmy or otherwise. I veered south a little, then north, but I was so disoriented by the daylight that I was afraid to stray very far off the route I only dimly and in the most general of outlines recalled.

It must have been close to noon when I finally

gave up on finding any semblance of shelter and sank onto an open field undifferentiated from the vast emptiness we had been traveling through for hours—open to raptors that rode the thermals making it clear that the high flat sky was truly three-dimensional, and occasionally, chillingly, flapped their wings; open to snakes whose jaws were wide enough to swallow a baby without even snapping unhinged; open to all manner of dangers I had not even heard of. I did my best to find a place for us among stones smaller than my hand and plants smaller than that. I was taking a fearful risk, but I saw no choice.

I wrapped Eli snugly and held him close to me, partially under me. He struggled, weakly but with clear intent to free himself, and I felt the vibrations of his attempts to squeak and click. It struck me how profoundly dependent an infant was on its caretakers, how impossible it was not to violate a baby's trust in countless necessary but probably hurtful little ways. Despite his obvious desires to the contrary, I kept him trapped in the paltry protection of my body, which was all I could do for him then, and tried to ignore his distress signals so I could rest if not actually sleep.

Eventually he quieted. Through the haze of fatigue and photophobia, I regretted the necessity of forcing him to give up. But I did sleep. I had to sleep, for both our sakes.

I woke up several times to uninterrupted sunshine and a sky of that vast and disturbing western blue. Then I woke up to a storm.

The brown land had turned to gray, mottled with darker gray. Its features, thrown into auditory and visual relief by the storm-light and charged air, were more distinct now than they had been in brighter light, so that I saw that the landscape was not at all empty. The electricity in the ground and the air made my nose and the heat-detecting area around it tingle. Small creatures were scurrying for cover; I could hear and smell them all around us. Rain fell hard as stones. The thick sky flashed with lightning and reverberated with immediate thunder.

Eli and I were both already drenched. He was shivering alarmingly and crying with all his might, squeaks and clicks melted into a heart-rending little wail, and it struck me as especially pathetic that I could scarcely hear his cries over the storm. I got to my feet and tried to scan the area close by us and farther away, but the storm made it impossible to know what I was detecting. In any case, there was no reason to think that shelter would have miraculously appeared now where none had been before. There was nothing to do but wait out the storm.

I had not been aware of the storm approaching, and while it was above us it seemed to have always been there. There was no sound but the sounds of the storm, no light but its gray-black and gray-yellow, no odor but those of the rain and the lightning.

I picked up no more signs of other life, and it seemed perfectly possible that Eli and I were the only creatures still alive. But that was nothing but self-aggrandizement. The storm did not last long. The center of it moved away toward what I thought was the east, and in the diminished violence, life began to show itself again. More life, in fact, than had been apparent before. Birds skittered among the glistening bitter-smelling grasses, bent on capturing a worm or bug or two while the tiny prey was forced above the saturated ground. Although this was the wrong season, it was not hard to imagine that legendary springtime moment when desert flowers bloomed.

But the storm had not been kind to Eli and me. He was pale, and his wails had a hoarse timbre that could not be healthy. I was shaking, and I would not be able to travel with the excess weight of rainwater in my clothes and in Eli's bag.

I was actually relieved when the sun came out. In the high, arid climate we were dry before long, but it took the rest of the day and all that night for either of us to calm down.

I managed to get us moving again shortly after night fell. Trying not to think about how precarious our situation had become—not that it had ever been secure—I headed more or less southwest and just kept going. There was a harvest moon that night, pink long after it rose, and the autumn wind was full of birds and insects which, rightly, paid no attention to us. It was conceivable that I would hunt for us tonight, but I could not waste energy on anything not mammalian.

Then I knew that we were there. I dismissed the very real possibility that I was arbitrarily deciding to end the journey because I could go no farther. This had to be the place. I closed in.

Here was a high red cliff. Here were openings in the striated rock, some horizontal slashes, some vaguely round, some vertical or slanted or crooked cracks that interrupted the flow of the strata and made a jagged pattern. Coolness seeped out of most of these fissures. Homing in on cold instead of on heat was confusing.

I missed the caves altogether on the first few passes. I had, after all, not been here since I was a child, and in those vacation trips Ma had found the way on rutted surface roads, a fair number of which were not on any map. The rest of us—Alexis and I, sometimes a friend or two, in earlier years my father—were consummate passive passengers, not paying much attention to where we were going or how. The trips had stopped when Alexis and I were teenagers and it became impossible for us to spend more than a few minutes together without bickering, at the least, and more often than not drawing blood.

Ma hadn't even mentioned the caves to me for at least thirty years. When I was a small boy, she used to tell us wonderful stories. Legends, really, embellished and expanded with each telling, about the origins of our species and of our family. These tales came, though, not from any collective unconscious but from my mother's imagination; I had never heard anyone else tell them. Whether this made them more true or less, in the mythical sense of truth, I could never decide.

In some of the stories, our ancestors had evolved in the dark underground chambers, and our emergence into the upper world was regarded as still incomplete, still incipient and even inchoate. Other tales involved mythic heroes, always female, who were our progenitors.

So I thought of the caves in a primal sort of way. I was not aware of having thought of them at all for most of my adult life, but now, when I was in great need, the image of them had appeared whole and alluring in my mind, and they were the only place I could think of to go.

I was gratified that I had been able to get us this far, but it would do no good if we just kept passing fruitlessly back and forth above the brown prairie and the red cliff. My memory of the cave entrance was vivid; I had been awed by it as a child, and I remembered the awe more than any detail that would help me now. But I thought there had been an enormous fissure in otherwise unremarkable terrain leading down into a complex labyrinth of perpetually dim, naturally climate-controlled rooms and corridors and antechambers.

The baby and our respective paraphernalia, his at least double mine, were heavy and growing heavier. He was already squirming and fussing, I presumed for food, his needs insatiable and often uninterpretable. An entire colony of adults could spend their entire lives tending to one child and still not come close to meeting all its needs. But now it was personal, a perpetual low-level feeling of inadequacy and defeat and, therefore, anxiety and resentment; like many a parent before me, never mind the circumstances under which that role had been visited upon any of us, I'd taken on an impossible and endless job.

Eli was screeching now. I was both hungry and tired, but mostly I was frustrated. I could not find our destination, which I was certain, without a shred of evidence, was within reach. And someone was following us.

The high dry prairies went on and on and the sky met it all around with no seam and virtually no features, like the flattened orb of a pocket watch snapped shut. I found myself longing for an outcropping of rock—not even for signs of life per se, but for some variation, some break in or thickening of the empty white noise that emanated from this empty landscape. I knew it wasn't really empty; I knew that plants and animals and people lived here, and that many, most, would not have been at home anywhere else. But what I was picking up was a relentless roar of emptiness, and I was almost grateful for the sensation—in the back of the roof of my mouth, just the faintest of impressions but steady now—of someone else in the night, pursuing.

Under me, Eli gathered his tiny body in a tremendous effort and let loose a terrible thin stream of noise, like a machine gun. As I curved my body around him and made pleading, shushing sounds, I suddenly realized with horror what he was doing: He was calling his mother.

CHAPTER 17

We were being chased.

Mammal.

Warm-blooded.

About the same size, shape, and density as I was. Perhaps somewhat smaller, because my physical configuration now encompassed Eli.

Moving quickly, much faster than I could even when I wasn't carrying the baby, and with him my repertoire of movements was limited to the more pedestrian.

I thought it was Meredith. I couldn't fault Eli for his instinct to summon his mother when he felt himself to be in trouble—I had the same instinct, and in the vast majority of circumstances it served our species well; one could not expect an evolutionary adaptation this fast. I also couldn't stop him from sending out the signals that would allow her own maternal echolocation instincts to home right in on him. Every time he clicked and squealed in that particular fashion, I did my best to distract him, and I had to consciously restrain myself from forcibly quieting him. His signals were becoming shorter, fainter, less frequent—whether because he was weakening or because they had already served their purpose.

Even before I'd fully processed all these data, I'd changed course. Certainly my timing wasn't what it used to be, and I never had been an expert aerialist, but I yelled, "Hold on!" to Eli, who grabbed me as though he could understand. We plunged straight down.

Our pursuer dropped, too, and then shot upward, veered one way and then the other, pulled out of sense range and reappeared where I would never have anticipated.

We shot sideways, Eli squeaking—not, I thought, entirely in displeasure—and I myself incompletely resisting the temptation to whoop. And there, in the side of a cliff rather unimpressive as cliffs go, was the unprepossessing entrance of the cave.

The reddish rock and ragged green-brown groundcover were pocked with numerous other indentations and holes, but this one, I could see once I'd made my way into it a short distance and peered farther, actually led down and back into a vast hollowed core. But some of the others probably did, too, and this one might turn out to be a dead end, and we'd be trapped. There was no way of knowing whether I was making the right decision, and, in any case, no time to dither. The pursuer was still pursuing; I could feel heat not far behind, intense enough that I wondered if there could be more than one of them.

I walked into the cave. On foot and slowly seemed the proper way to enter.

There was a short, rather broad entranceway, almost a foyer, and then an abrupt dropoff and narrowing of the passage. Instantly sounds altered. Echoes bounced back from so close on either side and above and below us, and from so far ahead of us, that they were of almost no use and I stopped emitting even faint clicks. Eli had stopped squealing almost the moment we had entered the tunnel, as if the sudden magnification and hollowing of his noise scared him.

Now we were in silence and darkness. The impression of darkness held, and my eyes closed of their own accord, there being no use for them here. The sensation of silence, though, dissolved as sounds began to assert themselves. I heard water dripping in one, a dozen different places far off this enclosed path. I knew that was the sound of rock formations being fashioned at this very instant, drop by drop, pooling calcite water leaving sediments that rose to meet the next drop of water. I heard the squeaks and skitters of cave fauna, crickets and round little voles and spiders.

I heard my own footsteps, feathery as I tried to make them.

I heard my own breathing, heartbeat, ear muscles opening and closing, and Eli's small noises, and I both heard and smelled the presence of our pursuer in the passageway behind us, which was also to our right and upward because it had spiraled down.

The attempt to sort out all the sensory data as they emerged, and to identify them if not specifically at least in relation to Eli and me, had an almost trancelike effect. I focused on minute sounds and tiny incandescent flashes of heat. With my mind I followed creatures through the mountain. I felt rock grow. So I was caught by surprise after all when Rory attacked.

The sensation was of disparate bits of sensory information suddenly organizing themselves into a clawed, toothed, dive-bombing dervish. I'd missed the pattern, missed the meaning, by over-observing the details and prematurely drawing conclusions.

By this time I'd already forfeited position and momentum. The baby Eli, still holding on to me, was hissing.

But Rory did not make contact. It took me a while, no more than a beat or two but sufficient to underscore my disadvantage in whatever contest we were having here, to realize that Rory's savage passes and complex feints were not resulting in physical contact. He was breathing heavily, laughing and hooting, cursing and whistling and clicking, generally creating as much bedlam as he possibly could. The heat of his body as it approached and then swung away set up stroboscopic shadows.

I flashed, distractingly, on wrestling matches I'd participated in as a boy, before I reached the age at which such physical aggressiveness was deemed unmasculine and moved into the feminine province, with the overall result that girls learned to handle themselves more competently as physical objects among other physical objects in the world and boys, having to think about it as I was having to do now, were less sure of themselves. I'd never figured out how to devise a fighting strategy or even take defensive action when I couldn't tell what the goal of my opponent was. In these free-for-all battles I never could anticipate whether the adversary's intention was to pin my shoulders to the ground, say, in which case my defense would have been to twist and thrust upward, or, say, to get a lock on my head, in which case an appropriate response would have involved biting and butting with my head as a weapon. It was never clear to me what constituted winning a match. I, like any audience, invariably had the impression that I'd lost.

In this contest with my frenzied nephew, I was similarly bewildered. Not knowing what he wanted, I didn't know how to keep him from getting it. With practically anyone else, I'd have assumed the intent was to steal Eli back, but Rory had shown not an iota of personal interest in the baby. Maybe he was a mercenary. Or maybe this was all in some bizarre kind of fun.

Rory raged and cavorted. Auditory shadows of his lunges flickered nightmarishly, and I couldn't reliably tell where he was from one instant to the next. The tubular sound made by the tunnel through the rock of this mountain bent and stretched in all directions, and I remembered that the girls had explored widely and deeply on that long-ago vacation, returning flushed with fear and the overcoming of fear to recount to us exciting tales of caverns and pools, lacy formations and boulders bigger than you'd expect a whole mountain to be, all of which wonders we boys would have to take their word for.

Finally I managed to gather the infant for whose sake all this dramatic activity was taking place and whose presence reminded me that it was all worthwhile. I curled my body around him, bent my head, circled my arms as far around both of us as they would go, which was nearly to overlap all the way. Then I stepped off the path.

The tunnel wall gave. I moved with some trepidation through porous rock into an underground —what? maze? labyrinth? But those words implied a puzzle built purposely to confound, and this had, of course, simply come into existence without purpose or reference at all.

Underground kingdom, as guidebooks would have it? There were no rulers, no subjects; the monarchical names the girls and women had given to some of the more spectacular formations—Princess in the Tower, King's Battlement, Queen's Throne—had logic only to the observer who came from the outside and went back out. This place could be thought of as a kingdom only in the sense that we were taught in school about the three kingdoms into which everything on earth was organized: animal, vegetable, mineral.

I stepped out into this alien place. All I could think of was that somehow I had to make Eli and myself indiscernible to Rory's hearing and heat detection, which, although quite undisciplined, I guessed to be formidable.

I needed my hands free. I swung Eli gently onto the back of my neck, hoping he would know what to do in this unfamiliar position. He lay there like a warm triangular neck scarf with fringe, and while I was grateful for his stillness it also worried me because I didn't know what it signified.

I hadn't realized until I was in Eli's constant and virtually indecipherable company how much effort adults put into trying to read a baby's moods, comply with the interpreted demands of each cry and each variation of each cry, discover or assign meaning for every sigh or frown or grin. The effort was probably a cornerstone of civilization, the foundation of the social contract. It was also, in miniature, interpersonal communication at its most difficult and self-referential.

Understanding Eli, however, was really no more difficult than understanding anybody else. Rory, for instance. I struggled to evade him, without having a clear idea why I should do so. Though he had certainly shown himself to be a violent and hateful kid, I had never known him to hurt a member of the family, and the vulnerability I'd lately glimpsed made me wonder how serious any of the talk had ever been.

There was no sound from him. Maybe I had lost him. I found a miniature cave under a braided valance of rock and crawled as far back as I could with Eli in my arms.

I held him against my chest. Just the small pressure and warmth of him were comforting. But I was afraid he would be agitated by the racing of my heart, and so I laid him down in my lap and bent over him.

Love for him actually made me weak. It also made me foolish; I so much wanted a connection with him that I ignored the necessity for silence. Something about the presence of an infant—new to the world, still new every moment to me—made subterfuge impossible to maintain. I cupped the point of his chin in my palm, kissed his flat little nose. He smiled. He smiled! Likely he was too young yet to be smiling at anyone in particular, but I indulged myself. I kissed his nose again. He smiled again. I laughed aloud. "Can you say 'Uncle'? That'll be your first word, won't it, Eli? Un-ka Jo-el." I didn't even feel silly.

When he squirmed or screamed, I tried everything I knew to please him—feeding, changing, holding. The panic response of an adult toward a crying child must be instinctive. Sometimes something worked. Sometimes, defeated, I just waited for him to either calm himself or give me some other clue, certain that with every passing second of unmet need I was damaging him for life. When he quieted, I fretted that there was something even more seriously wrong, which I was in the very midst of missing.

Rory appeared just on the other rim of the little crater that lifted its lip to form our hiding place. He didn't give any sign yet that he knew we were there.

Afraid of misreading both Rory and Eli, I took action anyway because I judged that I had to. Of course, that might not be true. Refusing to make a decision was making a decision, and so the thought of it could be equally paralyzing.

Thus confronted with the possibility of paralysis in any direction, I took both a metaphorical and an oxygenated deep breath. Keeping a firm grip on the baby, I reflected sourly that this was the reason so many men had so much trouble making decisions: the ubiquity of being wrong.

The overhang was, in fact, the fluted ceiling of a thin corridor wider than it was tall and inclining steeply downward. With alarming rapidity, I took us deeper into the deep caves. We entered an underground wilderness, which had no aura of wildness to it at all, but an impersonal serenity. This place might turn out to be a haven for the baby and me and might turn out to be our doom.

The quality of the sound in which we moved changed so abruptly that I was disoriented. I stopped. There were numerous small and distinct noises nearby and in the middle distance, and far away through rock and water and water etching rock. But there was no background noise as there always is on the surface, whether in the city or in the country, night or day. This absence was palpable, itself like a presence, itself with form and substance.

The full stillness threw each discrete sound into relief. I was reminded of a long-ago remark by some relative—I couldn't place whom, where, or when, but it must have been someone who relied on vision more than hearing—to the effect that a tree growing alone could seem somehow different from the same species in a forest, giving the entire landscape an alien cast. It was that way with sounds in that cave. I knew what most of them were—water dripping, water flowing, spiders skittering—but I heard each one so thoroughly that they seemed alien.

We moved through a curtain of rock that sounded fragile. Fragility was not a concept I would ever have associated with rock. To test it, I tried to snap off a protrusion in passing and was able to do so with hardly any effort. I shuddered.

The cave floor was pocked and scored. Tissue-thin rock curled and spiraled, seeming to sway. My heat sensors were, of course, of no use here among all this bloodless, warmthless growth that I knew but did not believe to be lifeless. The stone, sheer as taut vertical panels of fine lace, interrupted sound waves and turned them into anagrams.

I noticed, too, that I was hearing—which was not precisely the correct term—an ethereal sort of melody—which was not exactly the right word, either. I was resonating to the suggestion of music. The music of the spheres, but from the interior rather than from the cosmic space through which they move. The harmony of the universe, almost beyond hearing. I held my breath, sent urgent silent messages to the baby to be quiet, and allowed the edges of my consciousness to be limned.

Then Eli, without warning and as far as I could tell without provocation, began to squall. There was no buildup from whimper to wail to yell; he erupted from complete silence into a full-throated shriek. Still draped around my neck, though now he was squirming and in sudden danger of falling, he simply let loose with a tremendous bellow not inches away from my left ear. The cry set off all sorts of echoes, as did my anxious and quite ineffectual murmuring of his name as I lifted him down and hastily examined his little body, peered into his face, listened for some clue.

There was no external sign of new injury. He wasn't wet or soiled. Maybe he was hungry. I decided he was hungry because that was a problem about which I knew what to do, and I got a bottle out of the diaper bag. The milk was undoubtedly too cool, having adjusted to the cool ambient temperature, but he allowed the nipple to be inserted into his wailing little mouth, and he closed his lips around it and started his formidable sucking. I sighed, not entirely relieved since I knew full well that the next time he was distressed no item from my limited inventory of responses might suffice.

And then Rory came flying into the quiet, orderly, beautiful chamber, shattering it as surely as if he'd smashed the crystalline formations with a sledgehammer. In fact, he did break through one exquisite column that had only tentatively joined in midair, and his feet made deep trenches across the floor. But it was his noise and fervor, hot in that cool space, that were most disruptive.

"Pervert! Fucking pervert!" he yelled, and went straight for Eli.

When the bottle was knocked out of the baby's mouth, he made a snuffling noise of what I took to be protest, but when his crazed uncle picked him up he quieted, as though these were safe arms, as though this bigger, stronger person had his best interests at heart. Either his instincts were off or mine were. I despaired, not for the first time, at the myriad of different things we ought to know in order to live in this world and do not.

"Rory," I said in a reasonable, if trembling, voice. "Put the baby down."

"Now why would I do that?" Rory grinned, succeeded in exuding menace even as he suggested a caricature of someone trying to be menacing. He held the baby in one hand, long fingers spread up like the tines of a spaghetti fork around the little body, well away from him. If he dropped him, which seemed virtually inevitable, the limestone floor, though soft in geologic terms, would certainly be hard enough to hurt him.

I took a step toward them. Rory, predictably, took several long strides backward, lifting the child aloft and tipping him on his hand so that his safety was even more compromised.

"Why shouldn't I just off him right now? Nobody'd ever know except you and me, and neither one of us is ever going to get out of here, so it would be like it never happened, right? Ain't that what they call situational ethics?"

"Why would you want to hurt Eli?" I asked as if I really wanted to know. The mere feel of the words in my mouth brought bile.

"World don't need another nigger," Rory declared. "Or chink or spic or whatever the fuck he is."

I eased toward him, visualizing an amoebalike stretching of my boundaries to occupy a slightly different space rather than a discrete and more noticeable stepping. "What are you talking about?" I asked him, not caring what his answer might be as long as it used time and had the potential to distract him a little.

Rory held the baby up by one foot. Eli squirmed, hiccuped, and then began to howl in earnest. Rory was touching him with just his long curved fingernails, as though to keep contact between them at a minimum. Instinct urged me to keep my attention on the hand grasping the little foot, when what I really had to do was concentrate on Rory's energy, his face and breath.

He muttered, "Fucking little jungle bunny," and the epithet was so absurd that I nearly laughed.

I rearranged the mass of my body again to bring me slightly closer, and I asked again, "What do you mean?"

"Shit, am I the only one around here who knows a fucking nigger when I see one?" Rory demanded, and paused as if this were not a rhetorical question. "Or chink or whatever."

Eli had managed to twist and pull himself up and grab onto Rory's forearm with his hands and feet. I was impressed, relieved, and oddly disappointed by this evidence of his self-sufficiency. Rory recoiled visibly from the baby's touch, glancing at me to make sure I'd noted the reaction. Eli's grasp was much stronger than I would have anticipated. I saw Rory try to loosen the little fingers but he couldn't dislodge them without letting go of the child altogether, and apparently he wasn't willing to do that.

"What are you talking about?" I asked mildly again, not interested in what he was getting at but wanting to keep him going. I moved forward again. He didn't retreat, but the distance between us, between me and the baby, didn't seem any shorter and I knew dimensions were distorted by the cave walls, which were not solid, vertical, or of a single substance.

In the cavern floor between us was a pool, into which arrhythmically dripped calcite-whitened water from a high hidden source somewhere. It didn't sound as if very much water had collected in the pool. Fleetingly, I imagined years, centuries of water dripping and rock rather than water accumulating, and, because I didn't have any real understanding of the process, it seemed bizarre, unnatural. There would be, though, more than enough water for a baby to drown in if he were dropped headfirst into the pool, which seemed to be what Rory had in mind as he stepped out onto a delicate ledge and extended his arm with the baby clinging to it.

Cautiously I stepped into the water. The sound of the drops hitting the surface changed as I broke in, and both Rory and Eli reacted, Rory with a sidelong glare that I was sure meant the game was up and Eli with a tremendous shiver that I was sure heralded the breaking of his grip and his subsequent fall into the water onto the ungiving stone. Neither effect happened.

Rory said, presumably to get himself back on firm conversational ground, "I mean, he's different, right? Gotta be some colored's kid. Human."

The truth was, I'd not yet detected either definite similarities or inarguable differences between Eli and anybody else. Alexis had insisted he had David's eyes; I didn't see it. I'd heard Meredith say his voice was like his great-grandmother's; I thought his voice sounded like that of every other infant. Desperate to string Rory along, and more than a little curious, I asked, "So who do you think is the father? Ernie?"

Rory sneered as though I were the most ignorant creature he'd ever had the misfortune to encounter. "Get real. Nobody knew Ernie that long ago. Shit, there's plenty of scuzz in the world. We're a minority, you know?"

"But, Rory," I said, advancing, "he looks like you."

It was a gamble, and self-indulgent. It could have enraged Rory and made him do something to harm the baby. But he only said, "Shit," almost as if he were pleased.

"He's your nephew, you can't deny that."

"He—is—not—mine." His tone was all the more chilling for its lack of affect. With each word he swung his arm with the baby on it in a great arc, like a man signaling. Shadows and echoes leaped about the cave.

"Well, he's mine," I cried, and leaped into the motion-filled air just as Eli's grip on Rory's forearm and Rory's on his ankle both broke.

There was, of course, some slippage. Eli and I didn't make perfect contact in midair like the two halves of a trapeze act. But I landed in the water, which smelled like chalk and was gritty, and the baby's impact was partially cushioned by my body. I tried to determine if he'd been hurt, to soothe his fear, to catch my breath, and to be alert for whatever Rory would do next.

My nephew relaxed. He grinned. He cocked his head, listening and working his nose. "So," he inquired, conversationally, "what is this shithole anyway?"

Taken aback, I actually hesitated before scrambling with the baby as far away from Rory as the cavern would allow. Eli was now making a burbling noise that caused me to rest my fingers on his throat, a gesture intended to clear obstruction or heal a new wound, though I would not have been able to say how.

"Why the fuck did you bring me to a hole in the ground?" my nephew demanded, but there was little anger in his tone, an anomaly that caused me considerable alarm.

Rapidly I considered and rejected several possible replies. Finally I settled on, "These are the ancestral caves," and immediately regretted my choice, for it sounded pompous even to me, an easy target for somebody like Rory.

True to form, but more mildly than was his wont, he snorted. "Ancestral caves, my ass."

"Your grandmother used to tell your mother and me stories about this place," I told him, wondering testily what, if anything, Alexis had bothered to pass on to her children.

"Grandma?" His voice did not exactly soften or break, but there was a change in it.

As in the earlier physical struggle, I was unsure what would differentiate winner from loser in this verbal one, but I pressed what appeared to be my advantage. "Sometimes she told us legends about the origins of the species. Sometimes about the origins of the family."

There was a pause while, I presumed, he came up with something sufficiently snide. "Right. Well, maybe you came out of a fucking hole, like a snake or a worm or something, but I sure as hell didn't."

Eli was too quiet. I wanted to listen to him, but I needed to listen to Rory.

"So even if this is some motherfucking ancestral cave or something, why'd we come here? For some kind of ancient wisdom or something?"

"When I needed a safe place to take the baby, I thought about what your grandmother would have done," I said, shamelessly.

"Safe." He laughed and interlaced his long fingers in front of him, turning the cup of them inside out, stretching and flexing. "Thought you were safe, huh?"

"But you found us," I said, unwisely.

"Hey, man, I keep telling you, what are you,

stupid or deaf? It ain't me you got to be afraid of."

I knew that was not true, though I also knew now that there were other enemies. I asked carefully, holding the baby, "So what happens now?"

He answered at once, cheerily. "Now I stay. You, me, and the fucking nigger brat—don't you think we make a fine little family unit?"

Dread filled me as though I had swallowed frigid air, and a hoarfrost of defeat. I said, with more truculence than resolve, "You can't stay here."

He bristled. "Who's gonna throw me out? Huh? You? You and what army?"

And where would he go? I did not want to be thinking this; of all the people in the world for me to worry about or mourn, I would have put Rory low on the list. But against my will I understood that he was in grave danger. I thought of Sebastian. I thought of David, sickly in all manner of ways, more and more the longer he lived in that world. I rested my fingertips on the row of punctures under Eli's skull, slightly hardened nubs of scar tissue in the soft flesh; who knew what vital fluid had already been drained from this infant? I thought of Miles. I thought of the generations of men and boys before us, and had the flash of an idea that this might be the wisdom I would find in these caves. I understood that Rory, terribly damaged as he was, would be quite lost—would be destroyed, would destroy himself and others with him—if he did not find a way to save himself now.

Still I could not bring myself to welcome him. I simply sank back against the wall, rough as if it had been embroidered, and buried my face against the baby, and said no more.

CHAPTER 18

We began our lives in the caverns, and I marveled at the ability of our species to adjust.

We could live almost anywhere; if we could not adapt the environment to suit our needs, we adapted ourselves to the environment. The tongues of some of my cousins were exactly the length of the flowers whose pollen they plundered. The skin and hair of those who lived in colder climates were thicker and darker than of those who lived in the tropics.

We could subsist, even thrive, on a wide range of diets, from finicky—one particular fruit at one particular stage of ripeness; a certain cocoon, but neither its larva nor its moth; the blood of mammals only—to the array of choices on the various levels of the food pyramid. We could survive almost any loss. We could love almost anybody.

Whether this adaptability should be regarded with pride, survival of the fittest meaning not so much of the strongest as of those who make the best fit, or with shame, as proof that we were perpetual easy marks for cosmic bullying, was arguable.

I lost track of time. Not of time itself, precisely, but of its familiar divisions and differentiations. I would have expected, had I ever thought about living my life underground, that I would be able to tell night from day, springtime from autumn, by my own circadian rhythms: When I needed to sleep it must be morning; hunger should be the signifier that evening was coming on; an urge to migrate ought to indicate the change of seasons.

But babies wake and sleep, eat and are hungry, with no deference to any rhythms but their own, those of their weary and discombobulated caretakers or those of the planet. It took only a few cycles of interrupted sleep, punctuated by much longer spells of unwelcome wakefulness during which I could have slept if I had been able to adapt fast enough, for the world outside the caves—indeed, outside the increasingly symbiotic pair of us—to recede into a sensory blur, where it seemed likely to remain permanently out of focus.

But Rory was there, too, and could not be forgotten for long. Sometimes he would disappear for substantial periods of time—nights, I supposed; weeks—and at first I thought I would be able to put him out of my mind. Instead, I found myself wondering where he was and what he was doing; then I was worrying about what kind of trouble he'd managed to find; then I was virtually obsessing. When he came back—he always came back although I did not always know it right away, much to his delight when I was seriously startled—relief at his return was so mixed with intense anxiety at having him among us again that the two reactions seemed, when it came to Rory, all of a piece.

He had, or would show to me, absolutely no respect for our environment, which had inspired in me, at first, such reverence and which still awed me, though I had become more concerned about protecting it in order to protect myself and Eli than for its own sake. Rory would have none of it. I came upon him one time spread-eagled on a huge slab of rock encrusted with smaller formations; I had never seen lichen or coral, but I had the impression of roughness growing on a rough surface. My nephew had attached himself to the rock face like yet another growth. "Rory! Get off there!" I called, and wished I hadn't, for, predictably, my exhortations only made him worse.

He wiggled his butt, gave me the finger with one hand and then the other, pivoted his hips and shoulders in their sockets until he looked like a spider against the rock, and scuttled higher. I thought he would go all the way to the top, but apparently physical challenge wasn't the point.

The point was, specifically, to deface. He plucked at the encrustations with nails and teeth and managed to dislodge many of them as if they had been wads of gum stuck there by other unruly children as intent as he was on messing things up.

Then he turned himself around so that his head was downward, maneuvered himself onto a thin loose slab, and slid down as if on a sled. He left a shiny swath of smoothed rock that showed clearly and would show for a time long in any but geologic terms where he had passed. "Bitchin!" he shouted, and the caverns echoed.

Appalled, I stood holding Eli at the base of the outcropping and reflected bitterly that Rory was not the person I would have chosen to share my exile. In retrospect, almost anybody else seemed preferable, but I knew I would not have chosen any of them except my mother. I would have welcomed a lifetime alone with her and the baby in this isolated, potentially serene place. But my mother was dead, and Rory was here.

Rory was not finished. Without turning his back to me or making any other effort at privacy or concealment, he urinated and defecated on the rock face, the floor, and even the delicate formations like long braided hair that hung across one end of the chamber. Fetid steam rose. The ammonia odor of his urine and the rich, acrid smell of his guano made me cough and lightly cover the baby's face, a gesture I found faintly laughable even as I made it. "Well," I said, "why don't you show me how you really feel?"

He stood back, readjusted his clothes, and surveyed the area he had marked. "Cool," he said proudly. In fact, he had altered the contours of the rock in ways that, as time passed, would be no more or less interesting than patterns and formations fashioned by dripping water, layered sediment, earthquakes, the burrowing and building of those who lived here. So, was this defacement, to be loathed and avoided, or creation? Was it my responsibility to protect the world from Rory, or to stay out of the way as Rory and the world changed each other?

Rory was a force to be reckoned with, although the nature of that reckoning escaped me. He made sure his presence was as unpleasantly intrusive as possible. His practical jokes were unfailingly mean-spirited—or perhaps someone with a sense of humor more intact than mine would have been more appreciative. I was infuriated by the strange noises that I was almost sure were produced by him but that I had to investigate on the slim chance that some even more dangerous creature was down here with us. I was wearied to numbness when he broke and stacked rock formations to alter the sound dimensions of a chamber or contours of a path. I was seldom amused.

In particular, I disliked Rory's interference with the stability I was struggling to establish for the baby. He did everything he could to keep us off balance. When Eli was asleep and I was just starting to hope I could doze off, too, Rory would do whatever it took to wake us both up. Before the baby was responding to loud noise, he would poke him. If I was quick and smooth enough to keep the baby out of his reach without waking him myself, Rory would lob pebbles at him or start a miniature avalanche that showered rock dust, or collect water in his cupped palms—which must have required a longer attention span than he ever demonstrated when he wasn't doing mischief—and throw it in Eli's face.

If we were awake and Eli was feeding, Rory would sing. Through the haze of my exhaustion and annoyance, I noted that he had a lousy voice. He sang lullabies. I marveled dully that he knew anything so sweet and calm; I would have expected heavy metal or grunge rock. He must have learned these songs from Ernie. His lullabies were often far more effective than mine. Eli would stop his play with me, which was never very enthusiastic, or would close his mouth against food from mine. His eyes and ears would drift shut. He would squirm around until his position approximated that of an infant in a nursery. Before I could decide whether to intervene, he would be fast asleep, which more than likely meant he would be awake when I wanted him to sleep.

Nothing I said or did, no objection or reasoning or attempt to explain my needs and Eli's, no consequences I could come up with made Rory stop; the point was to be obnoxious. I tried pretending it didn't matter. Whether he saw through that or was simply on a roll by then, his actions were not modified by lack of response, either. I was quickly reduced to waiting for the occasional and unpredictable lapse in both boys' behavior that gave me a chance to do, however incompletely, what I needed to do.

Something about being in the rarefied underground atmosphere, and about the rarefied circumstances that had brought and were keeping us here, encouraged rarefied thinking. I came to fancy that we were enacting in microcosm the development of the social contract. A rather vague but compelling theory took shape that civilization arose out of the tension and then the balance and then the tension again between chaos and order.

When I could regard myself and Rory in this removed way, as standard-bearers in a dynamic process that was older and larger and far more important than either of us, our adversarial relationship took on a wider meaning and I thought I could stand it. There were times when I was even almost glad he had followed us here.

I was also fond of him. Much of the time, this affection was as abstract as my appreciation of the roles the two of us might be playing in history; but there were times, enough to keep me going, when I clearly perceived that Rory was lovable. Not so much under all the ugliness, both affected and real, as mixed in with it, there were strands of sweetness and vulnerability.

"How's the kid?" he'd ask. I never allowed him anywhere near Eli, of course, though the more time passed without another threatening incident the more consciously I had to remind myself what had happened on Rory's first appearance in the caverns.

I would wait to see what the trick was, how I was being set up. When no trap showed itself, I would answer cautiously, "He seems to be getting better."

He would nod, pass his hands over his eyes and ears. "Good. That's good." More than once, I was sure I detected tears.

I had to resist the temptation to regard Rory as all one thing or another. When the goodness in him showed, I wanted to believe that all the unpleasantness—the vicious racism and homophobia, the free-wheeling hostility, the usury and maliciousness—were nothing but defenses, and that prolonged exposure to unconditional love would banish them; in an even greater leap, that I had that sort of love to give, and indefinitely.

When he reverted to his more accustomed demeanor and I was wary or downright afraid of him again, then it was easy for me to decide that I had been a fool ever to have entertained charitable notions about him.

Neither of these extremes, however strong and recurrent their simplistic allure, was accurate: Rory was all of these things, a mosaic without a theme, a self incompletely organized. Most of the time he just drove me crazy. The constant necessity of figuring out how to deal with him caused me no end of anxiety. My chest ached virtually all the time. My hands trembled, and my heat detector seemed not to be functioning at full capacity. In addition, Eli was behaving worrisomely. I did not know whether this was a turn for the worse, but I could not rid myself of the apprehension that something was not right. His movements were alternately jerky, putting me unhappily in mind of Sebastian, and too fluid, almost jointless. His head lolled on his neck, and the soft spot under my compulsively measuring fingers felt, if anything, larger and squishier than before. His hearing seemed to me to be impaired, though I had no clear information about developmental stages and certainly had no idea what I was searching for when I inspected his ears. I was in over my head.

I began to experience homesickness, which, considering what I had come to understand about my home, was downright peculiar. I realized that I was homesick for the home I'd thought I had, which made only slightly more sense.

I found I would fixate on one thing or a cluster to mourn, and then, when the worst of that was past, move on to another. I missed the sound of rain, which was nothing like the sound of underground water constantly dripping. I missed the smell of open air. I missed card games, hot coffee, clean clothes. I spent a long time grieving football. And I missed people, individually and en masse, whom I'd thought I'd be glad never to see again: Alexis. David.

There was always more to mourn, because I was mourning the loss of an entire way of life. I was scrabbling not to adjust to this change, which was, my whole being protested furiously, too much, too much. Another evolutionary mistake, surely—since so much of life is change, why do we resist it so hard?

In particular, I missed my mother. Try as I might, I could not entirely believe she had ever hurt me intentionally, although I also could not quite believe she had not. I thought about her a great deal, the same thoughts over and over, until I was no longer thinking of her but of the thoughts themselves.

There were times when I would probably have been incapacitated by grief, maybe undone by it, if I had not had Eli to take care of and Rory to watch out for. I resented their myriad demands and did not meet them well, but they kept me going.

I did not want to bestir myself from the slightly concave spot on a wide flat ledge, not unlike an Anasazi cliff dwelling site, where we had been roosting for a while. Eli showed no signs of hunger or other distress, and he hadn't produced his calling-mother sounds for some time, but it must surely be time to eat. I was vaguely considering the possibility that we would both starve to death down here, and that that might not be so bad, when Rory offered, "I'll get dinner this morning if you want."

I waited. I tried to anticipate deception, and found my mind too dulled to keep hold on any specific trepidation. Really, I did not much care what he did. "Fine," I said.

"Cool." He sped off, and very shortly he sped back. At my feet he deposited, with a campy flourish, some spongy substance that might be plant material, edible but without usable nutrients, or might even be some kind of mammalian or amphibious or insectoid creature with blood.

My mouth watered. "What is that?" I demanded.

"Dinner," he said, as if explaining the obvious. He edged backward and watched, all but leering.

I nudged at the pulpy mass. I scanned it. There

was no sign of life. But my senses had not been reliable about interpreting data lately. I broke off a piece of the material, which smelled only damp, and put it on my tongue. Bitter. Burning. Impossible to swallow. Hard to dislodge, and a residue remained in my mouth. I choked and spat it out. "Rory, what is this? It's some weird kind of mineral, isn't it?"

"Shit. Busted." I heard him make a face.

Outrage broke through and I started toward him. "You little son of a bitch. What if I'd fed that to Eli? You could have killed him."

He leaped off the ledge before I could get to him and hovered, with a great deal of noise and motion, just out of my reach if I wanted to keep my feet on the ground. "Oh, for Christ fucking sake, lighten up. I knew you'd test it first. If you hadn't, I'd have told you. What do you think I am?"

I was beside myself. I screamed at him, setting off wild echoes. "Get out of here! Get the fuck out of here and leave us alone! Nobody wants you here!"

Rory executed a few turns and somersaults and then went off down the narrowest of the corridors that led out of this chamber. He made it clear that he was in no hurry. He called back, "Now I'll get dinner. Trust me!"

I kicked at the porous rock, which I fancied to be much like a hardened amoeba, until it slid off the ledge. There was a long pause, and then I faintly heard the splash as it struck water below. The sound was most unsatisfying. I hit the wall with my fist, which hurt. I went back to the baby, who was stretched quietly in his blanket on the ledge.

This time Rory did not come back. I waited much longer than I should have, because the thought of hunting in these convoluted passages with Eli in my arms or attached to me somehow was intimidating. There had been no indications of prey near us for some time; either I would have to range far afield or it was time to move again. I kept telling myself that if only I could count on Rory to find us food, life would be so much easier, and it really was not a lot to ask.

But we slept and woke and slept again, and Rory had not returned, making it necessary for me to worry about him as well as about food. At last I bundled up the baby as best I could and trussed him against my chest. Probably it would have made more ergonomic sense to put him on my back, but I was too nervous to have him out of my direct sensory range. We set off. I kept collecting data about location and route, hoping but doubting that I would be able to find the way back here again. The passage was tubular enough to be called a tunnel, and it bored through the mountain at right angles, then in curlicues, then straight. We had not gone a hundred yards before

I was certain I had chosen the wrong path, and I turned around to head back. But now there was a multiple intersection where I did not think there had been one before, and no way of knowing which branch to take.

I chose one, knew at once it was a mistake, turned back and took the other, which was manifestly also not right. From somewhere even deeper in the mountain, I could hear Rory, taking full advantage of the complex echo chamber made by the caverns and the tunnels and corridors that connected them. He whooped like a rodeo cowboy, sang and shrieked like a rock star, and, I thought, called my name. I could not have reached him even if I had been so inclined. Finding myself oddly reluctant to cause a commotion and call attention to myself down here, I said, "Rory," hardly above a whisper. Far away and high up, Rory hit a sustained falsetto warble, but it could not have been in response to me.

I emitted a series of clicks, and opened and closed my ears. Echoes came back too close from both sides and above and below, and did not come back at all from up ahead. There were sparks of body heat from creatures that could have been prey, but I was not nearly quick enough to catch them; otherwise there was only bloodless stone, whose beauty now seemed cruel.

Then I realized that Eli was gone. The blankets and rags hanging from my chest swaddled nothing. Disbelieving, I clutched at the fabric, still warm from him and from me, so roughly that I would surely have harmed him if he had been there. I dropped to the damp, chalky floor and tore the bundle loose. He was not there. He must have fallen out, though I could not understand how that was possible. He must have worked himself free of the restraints. I had lost him somehow and been unaware of it.

The alarm I sent up then shattered the silence, and I thought I heard fragile stone shatter, too. I screamed and shouted. I beat myself against the walls, ceiling, floor, until they were all the same continuous surface, and I threw pieces of that broken surface in every direction. For all that, the attention I was able to call to myself was paltry, and I knew I would never find my baby that way.

But I did not stop until Rory came. From a distance away, he answered me scream for scream, and he threw himself around the long thin space as I did. He might have been mocking me, but I believe he was not. Rapidly he closed the distance between us, and perhaps I moved toward him, as well. We met as though colliding, held each other as though locked in combat, and waited for the terrible echoes to subside.

CHAPTER 19

"We'll never find him."

"We'll fucking find him."

His specious reassurance heightened my apprehension of doom. I sighed and held my head.

For what seemed time without beginning or end but doubtless was not, Rory and I had been hunting for Eli—each for his own purposes, and I could not fathom Rory's. But I was convinced that I needed him; I could not possibly find Eli myself, or know what to do if I did or did not, inside this mountain. There were too many rooms, nestled inside each other like Chinese boxes, strung together like beads irregularly spaced and sized, or not accessible at all one from the other. There were too many forms, made of rock but constantly changing, rock dripping down from ceiling or growing up from floors or shooting out in loops and spirals and angles that moved in place, I swore. Dripping;

growing; shooting—action verbs not usually associated with rock. It was too bewildering.

And the mountain was only a small part of a range, which itself was only the visible portion of a huge geologic feature, with innumerable strata and ecosystems of infinite variation because of innumerable histories. Or, maybe, we had been hunting for Eli, time without beginning or end, inside the whole of the earth; under the crust, through the mantle, toward the molten and unstable core.

Flying and crawling, sending out frantic signals that went unanswered and usually unreturned, it was easy to get caught up in the self-perpetuating spirit of the hunt and lose track of its purpose. I was never at risk of forgetting about Eli, but he himself grew steadily less engaging than the machinations of the expedition both mad and methodical, frantic and careful to a fault.

I had pledged not to miss any crevice or any milky pool, anything that could be a roost or a grave, any dark corner or mysteriously illuminated space. I found it impossible to know which passages and rooms, sleek formations and rubble fields we had already searched. One direction was much like another.

That day we had eaten better than usual, Rory having come upon a nest of newborn mammals whose identity I did not know but whose blood sufficed. We killed them, I think; they were too small and new to have blood to spare, and we had both lost the delicate self-control to be sure we were taking only what we needed. Having caused harm to those tiny alien beings—never knowing the extent of the harm I caused—has come to stand for the range of moral compromises throughout my life, giving rise to considerable guilt. But at the time, I was ashamed mostly because I was not hungry and Eli was somewhere in this maze, hungry or worse.

The extremity of the circumstances made me reckless and unkind. "What do you care? A fucking little nigger brat. Or spic or chink or whatever."

He stiffened, threw something in my direction but without much conviction. "What do you know about it?" he muttered.

"Not much."

"I fucking loved Ernie," he declared, and I understood this was not a non sequitur.

Profoundly, I did not want to know this. I was shaken to realize I had not thought about Ernie one time since we had left Ambergen. Rory, apparently, had; I would not have guessed he had it in him. Even more uncharacteristic was the content of his statement and his willingness to say it to me. Love, I thought ruefully and in awe. What many disparate things we call love, for lack of a better vocabulary. Through the shiver of horror and sorrow that shook me, I managed, "Great. What do you think that counts for now?"

I felt his regard, expected it to be angry or sad or fearful, but could be sure only of its intensity. He turned away. "I'll find the kid, okay?" he flung over his shoulder as his strong avial muscles flexed and stretched to carry him off. It might have been either a promise or a threat; most likely, he himself would not know which it was until he made good on it. I made a helpless, desperate move to stop him, but he was out of my range before I could even say his name, which was all I could have thought to say.

I was alone. I had not been alone since I had been in the caverns. I had not really been alone in all my life. For a while I heard my own breathing, and then I did not. For a while my heart pounded in my ears, and then, as if some deeply internal muscles had closed off the sound, I was not hearing my heart any more.

There was slight outward pressure on my cheek, like a plunger laid lightly against it. I moved my head, meaning to turn away but somehow instead turning toward it. The sensation was mild, even gentle, but unnerving in its unfamiliarity. I put up my hand, palm out and the backs of my fingers aligned with the long curve of my jaw. If some other living thing was in this space with me, I could not locate it like this.

Cautiously I moved my hand outward, a millimeter at a time as though reluctant to disturb the air itself. For long moments I encountered nothing. The soft pulling against my flesh continued and my cheek tingled in the spot now belatedly protected by my hand.

My fingers arched and splayed. I allowed them to extend to the full length of the phalanges. The tip of my middle finger grazed rock. I moved it slightly downward and found the rim of a depression, into which air was being siphoned as though someone on the other end were inhaling strongly and without interruption.

Something about coming upon a cave within a cave, about the discovery that I was nowhere near bottom, sent a shudder through me. I stayed in that position for some time, balanced between curiosity and fear, and finally made my decision because Eli might be in there.

I braced myself and, for courage, bared my teeth. I plunged my hand into the hole. Its diameter was big enough that I had to rotate my forearm to follow its roughly curved inner surface, and as far as I could tell there was no end to it. I had expected to be met with claws, or with some sort of disgusting detritus, or with slithery eyeless things. I was shocked to encounter nothing.

Ma used to tell variations of a story about the wind in the caves. Sometimes it blew in and sometimes it blew out, through tunnels that could be as small as your pinky or bigger around than the fattest person you had ever seen. In some of the stories, our ancestors had blown out of the caverns through just such corridors, transit from one world to another. There had been one tale about a boy trapped inside the mountain in a tube of rock—in Ma's illustration it had looked a lot like a straw—where the wind blew in and out at the same time and with the same force, suspending him forever. I did not remember this story being sad or awful. The boy had been transformed, eventually, into some other sort of boy who could live happily in a tunnel supported only by wind.

But in real life, if Eli had fallen or been deposited in a hole like this, it was unlikely that I would find him. Probably I would never even know. My skin crawled and I rubbed my shoulders against rough stone like a lufta, as though to dislodge some parasite. Hair rose uncomfortably all over my body, making me itch to smooth it down.

I withdrew my arm. From fingertips to elbow, air seemed still to be breezing along it, and I wrapped it close to my torso. My hand ached.

Now I heard the unmistakable whirring of wings. I heard the clicking and squealing of someone echolocating, not very expertly but with great determination and intimidating energy. Mammal, I had time to think; warm-blooded.

Danger, I realized belatedly, and then it was upon me.

Claws tearing open my clothes and my flesh. Soft hair, soft flesh against my belly and under my skin, secretions flowing with my blood. Seductive predation, life-threatening sensuality.

Tongue in my mouth, into my throat, the brushlike tip of it across my uvula activating both my gag reflex and sexual arousal. Teeth under my jaw, nipping, puncturing, and the headrush of being sucked. It had been years since I had felt that sensation. I could almost remember when I had felt it before.

I tried to push the attacker away, but I was off balance and slipping in the chalky water that glazed the smoothed floor in this part of the caverns. Slashing down and sideways with my own fangs, I pulled out hair, sweet-tasting and fragrant. The attacker hollered wordlessly, a childish yelp of fury and surprised pain, and I knew who it was. "Meredith."

My niece attacked me as if we were not family. Not, though, as if we were strangers: Her movements against me were wild and blatantly erotic, her nipples erect, my penis erect in involuntary response. Her long slim segmented fingers probed into my ears, stimulating, then hurting. I jerked my head away, and she had her thumbs in my mouth, claws raking the organs on the roof and palate, fingers jointed upward and outward to my nose where their heat seared the cold hairless flesh.

I grabbed her thin shoulders and twisted her backward, intending to fling her off me. Instead, we both lurched halfway around, still joined, and now I was on top of her. Her breath smelled wonderfully of blood, perhaps mine. The heat of her passions—rage, lust, some female thrust I would never comprehend—was luscious in the clammy air. I had not known how much I missed body heat, and I was appalled to discover it now.

I tried to pull away. She held on. "Meredith, Meredith, what are you doing?" I panted.

She was not talking. She was hissing and squealing, primal expression below or above language. She wound her fingers in my hair and jerked my head down to hers in a fierce kiss that left my lips and tongue bloody when I had freed myself.

"Meredith, listen to me. He's not here. Eli's not here. He's lost. Rory's out looking for him now."

She did not react. She was lost in her own emotion, transported by it. I felt her gather herself, and then, from nearly flat on her back, she sprang up at me.

I got my forearm under her chin and pinned her against the stone floor. The back of her head hit hard, and I heard her sharp intake of breath. This was Meredith, my niece, my sister's child, and a young female; I let up just slightly, fearing I had hurt her.

The impact of the top of her skull under my jaw knocked my head back and loosened my grip on her. It also bared my throat to her. Her fangs sank through the hair and skin, punctured the striated flesh underneath, and instantly drew blood. The anticoagulant in her saliva started working immediately, and twin spouts flowed into her eager mouth.

At the same time, I felt myself on the verge of ejaculating. Horrified—mortified, which was more than a little ludicrous under the circumstances—I did my best not to let it happen. But of course by that time it was utterly out of my control.

Groaning, I came. Meredith caught the semen, too, rapidly and greedily moving her sucking mouth from my throat to my spouting penis and then back again, to make two new puncture wounds under my right ear.

I collapsed. I lost consciousness, though I think not for long. When she was finished, Meredith detached herself from me. I felt her go and had some dim apprehension that I should stop her, but I was in the grip of a physical and psychic numbness that prevented me either from moving or from knowing whether I had moved.

Silence assaulted me. Stillness invaded my ears and deafened me, filmed my eyes with gray plush and my nose with a sticky patina. Quiet pressed in on me, threatening to displace me as water is displaced by a heavier, denser object. The upper world had never been silent. I was afraid to make any sound, and afraid not to. I felt nothing on the inner or outer surfaces of my skin. I seemed to be as blind as creatures who had never lived anywhere but underground; I might have lost my eyes altogether, in an evolutionary vestigializing of those parts rendered superfluous, one after another.

But there was an odor focused and sharp as a puncture wound, and a beacon of heat. "Eli." I may have spoken it aloud.

When I was a boy, the younger brother of a classmate was crushed by a tree his father had sawed down. I had been not much affected by the death; I had not known the child, and my classmate never talked about it, didn't act any differently that I could tell. But I had been terribly impressed by the part of the story in which the father had, like Paul Bunyan, single-handedly lifted the enormous trunk off the body of his son. It had been too late, but the effort, the superhuman strength born of great parental love, had moved and troubled me.

My mother explained about adrenaline. I wondered whether she would have done the same for me, but did not dare ask; if she'd said no, I would have been hurt and embarrassed, but I would not have believed a yes because I'd had to ask for it. I wondered whether my father—long since gone by then—would rush to save me if he knew I was in trouble. I had never been in trouble. I wondered whether, when I had children, I would have the chance to prove my love for them in such a doomed, heroic way.

Now, with that sort of effort and an adrenaline rush not unlike that of flying, I roused myself because Eli needed me. I heard noises in the walls and ceilings around me, and I thought distantly of predators and of prey, then realized I was hearing Rory and, amazed and moved, recklessly paused to listen. I heard scrabbling, flapping. Clearly, I heard his voice, though not any words. His noises had no directionality or any other context, except that they seemed close by and coming from everywhere at once. Then they stopped. Then they resumed, somewhere else.

The sense of smell is useful for identification but not much good for navigation. I was, however, able to isolate the pale and erratic pulse of Eli's body heat, and I set off along a corridor I had not known was there. The passage quickly became too small for me to travel through upright, then too small for me to crawl. I wrapped myself into a serpentine tube and wriggled, smelling the damp, smelling Eli and the danger he was in.

Having appendages, though, I was not efficient

at slithering, and I brushed against something unstable. Like nothing so much as a toppling supermarket display, small objects, jagged but lightweight and carrying the impression of hollowness, tumbled over me. The clatter they made was brief, and muted by my body pressing against them and limiting their space to ricochet, although my instinct was to draw back.

They smelled not like rock, not like wood. They were bones.

Obeying an impulse I made no effort to understand, I freed one hand and scooped up as many bones and bone fragments as I could hold, then let them run through my fingers. I bit into one. It was empty.

I heard music. I could not be hearing music. I pushed ahead, imagining the epidermal layers I was sloughing off among the bones, the trail if anyone or anything cared to follow. I heard music.

Not quite a melody, I thought, and then heard the melody: narrow intervals between notes, a sound like the blues. Eli could not be making that sound, not yet. I kept going.

There. Something was there. Ahead and below, a whirlpool in complete darkness and total silence. I eased myself up onto all fours, held my breath, and tried to take in everything at once.

At first I received such a roil of impressions that there was no hope of sorting them out. I thought I would explode with them. I thought the mountain would burst open from such a buildup of internal pressure, or a new complex system of caverns and corridors would be hollowed out on the spot. This fancy was both pathetic and fallacious; nothing so grandly inaccessible happened, of course.

Individual data began to come clear. I was not to be spared the obligation to act.

Rising heat wrapped around diminishing heat, cold not spreading but deepening, at the heart of a mass of ferocious radiant heat.

I eased forward. Knowing I was taking a terrible risk, the nature of which was beyond me, I sent out a straight line of echolocating clicks, cut it off, and waited for the echoes. They flew back at me as though clawed and taloned, too quickly and too dense to inform me of anything except what I already knew: Something was there, and part of it was Eli.

Emanating from the mass was the needlelike odor that had helped to lead me here. I had smelled that odor before. It had dread about it. I could not place it.

Rory was whistling. This was nothing like the ethereal minor-key music I had heard and then lost before. This high-pitched, strident tunelessness looped all around like a frayed and tangled ribbon. Perhaps, trapped, he was summoning help, which would be hopeless, pointless.

Or perhaps he was signaling that he thought he had found Eli, which he had not because I had. Or perhaps he had abandoned his self-appointed task altogether and was simply indulging himself in the high of being lost.

Then I knew what the odor was, and I heard sucking and swallowing and a seeping sound like water draining out of a hose, and I knew who was there, and I lunged.

Meredith did not draw back from her son when I hurled myself at them. She held his limp little body in a fierce maternal embrace, and her fangs remained sunk in his fontanel. I screamed as I hurtled into mother and child, willing the sound to travel through the pocketed and tunneled mountain, boring its own pathways if necessary to reach Rory; willing him to help. He did not.

My trajectory was slightly misdirected. The skewed impact of it jammed Eli hard into his mother's belly. She gasped. He made no sound or movement.

I brought the heel of my hand down hard onto her forehead, fingers clawed over her skull as though they could penetrate. Her teeth popped loose from Eli's head, and the cloying fragrance of his brain fluid spurted.

"He's my son!" she hissed. The outrush of air burbled through the viscous liquid in her mouth. "He belongs to me! You had no right! Who do you think you are?"

I wrestled the baby free. He made no noise or movement. I whirled and raced across an open space that turned out to be much smaller than I had judged, and when I ran up against a barrier, incomplete but towering far above my reach, I had no choice but to face Meredith. Eli was limp and cold in my arms.

Like a comic book superhero, Meredith had struck a pose on the rim of a little crater, legs spread, arms wide, webs draped like a cape. The heat from her body pulsated like a strobe light out of control. Her voice bellowed and screeched just at the edge of intelligibility. In one of those moments when everyday perceptions suddenly jump just slightly off track, revealing truths that are there all the time but are not always true, I was struck by how grotesque were the auditory, visual, tactile, olfactory images of our species. Really, we were very odd creatures.

Rory had found a way to throw his voice. Screeches and bellows bounced wildly, their echoes layering to create the illusion that he was everywhere and nowhere. The caves rang with him. The mountain kept him inside.

Afraid myself, I imagined that Eli was terrified. I whispered that we were in this together, that I would not leave him, which may be the truest pledge we can make to one another.

Then Meredith, who was alone, took a great

running leap. She hurtled high all the way across the cave and smashed into the far wall.

After the great clamor of the approach and the impact, there was great silence. Eli was making no sound. I had virtually stopped breathing. I heard water dripping again, here and at numerous other spots near and distant. I heard Rory, whistling and singing, maybe sobbing, and his feet apparently running in place.

But nothing else moved. Certainly Meredith did not.

Finally I went to her, this ruined child. At first I crawled across the damp and gritty crater floor on my belly, but both Eli's weight, which I would have considered inconsequential, and the angles of my own body too severely impeded progress. I was cold, and the baby was frigid against me, stiff.

I got to all fours and moved that way to the place where my niece had destroyed herself. It must have been deliberate, I thought; she had been too sure of herself for this to have been an accident. The suicide of someone so young was tragic; the thought of Meredith, my niece specifically and personally, killing herself on purpose made me gasp with sorrow. But there was something noble about it, too, and I found myself hoping it had been deliberate, making a choice to believe it had been since I would never know one way or the other, a gift to her son from a child-mother who could not give him anything else.

Quite a distance up, where I could not touch her without scaling the wall myself, dimly illuminated by some stray diffuse light like gauze, her body was spread-eagled against the rock face like a thrown glove, darker against dark, heat escaping as if from the stone itself. There was blood, but not much. Something I didn't know about, some mysterious fluid or physical force, was adhering her body to the wall.

Her face was pressed into the rock, hidden from me. At the time I thought that was probably just as well; I did not want to see the expression on her face at the moment of her death. Since then, though, the image of a blank visage, features obliterated beyond all recognition, has haunted me, and sometimes I have taken great pains to sketch in details, remembered or imagined, in the face of my niece, so young, that keeps floating up in my mind.

I wondered how long she would hang there, and how anyone else coming upon her would imagine that she had died. I wondered if she ever would be discovered, and if, not having witnessed her life or her death, any explorer would even know what she was.

In my arms, Eli chirped softly and twitched against me. The top of his head was open and oozing. He was watching me with his tiny eyes, and his outsized ears cupped and trembled, listening. "I love you, Eli," I told him, but I could not keep him from slipping away.

Rory had sent up a wail. Through the porous rock he sounded close by, but I would never see or touch him again. His beautiful, chilling lament followed me, or led me, through the mountain, until I found myself standing, baby in my arms, in front of the claw-marked wall. If I had consciously thought to bring Eli here, and deliberately tried to find it, I never could have done so, and it would have receded and magnified into personal legend.

Cradling Eli in one arm, I spread the other hand, then pressed my wet face against the etched expanse. Like those so desperately adaptable before me, I found a niche. I smoothed and poked at it to make it ready, though it was by nature ready and my efforts altered it only superficially. My fingertips and the flat of my hand came away powdery.

Gently I laid the tiny body in its place. There was no sense trying to cover it, and no shroud more suitable anyway than air, water, powdery dust. There was nothing to say. I lay at the wall for a while. From all around rose and fell Rory's disembodied keening.

CHAPTER 20

"Joel."

Eli was calling me. I had to wake up. I wasn't asleep, and I couldn't wake up. The music of the caves was a bluesy, mournful, dripping sea of rock, at the same time terribly liquid and terribly solid.

"Joel."

It wasn't Eli. Eli was dead. It was my mother. My mother was dead, too.

I wrapped my wings more snugly around my head and torso, scraped claws against flesh as I brought my arms and legs even tighter in, rounded my scoop so it would fit up under me smoothly. I held my breath and clung to my spot on the wall, where I had landed without choice or purpose.

The back of my neck was pierced. The pain was like hard water falling on soft stone. I was pried away from the wall. I was lifted and swept through the air, disconnected except to the fangs puncturing the folds of skin at my nape.

I was carried like a newborn. I received no information about how or by whom I was being transported, much less why; no sound or odor, no visual cues, not even any heat except the points of fire where I was held. Increased air pressure, heavy on the bones of my face and in the pockets of my lungs, hinted that I was being taken deeper into the earth, and, correspondingly, everything narrowed.

Eli, I kept thinking. My short, intense relationship with him had been predicated on an extreme power differential, and, though the imbalance now was reversed, I was put in mind, painfully and confusedly, of him. Of Eli. Now it was I at the mercy of virtually everything and everyone else, I who would be hurt or nurtured wholly at another's whim, I who could not communicate beyond the most basic of pleasures or aversions, I who would die if left alone. Eli.

"Joel." I had been deposited onto ground that was too hard and too damp, and my mother was lying beside me. "Joel," she said again, "tell me more of The Dream." When I didn't answer, because I couldn't, she brought her face very close to mine and hissed, hot breath, "Surely you haven't stopped dreaming The Dream."

"BECAUSE OF HIS PASSING," I managed to say. It was gibberish to me.

But Ma cocked her head. "His passing? Whose?"

This was beyond me. I meant to shrug, but instead my entire body shuddered, kept violently shuddering, and she swaddled me. The sensation was familiar: the leathery wings around me, her breath and her voice. But she radiated no heat. She radiated instead, in strong waves that tugged at me like a living magnetic field, cold that was more than the absence of heat, more than its inverse, a positive property in its own right. Cold. Dark. Dense.

" 'Her' passing, maybe? Could it have been 'her'?" She shook me a little in her impatience.

It could have been. I told her so, but she was not appeased. I said, "Ma," the infant's prelingual verbalization not intended as communication with another person until another person acknowledges it, and which, like all communication, would not mean anything if someone else were not there to determine that it did.

Ma said eagerly, as if she'd been wanting to tell me this for a long time, "I didn't die. I passed over."

"Alexis killed Sebastian," I told her in a rush. "Meredith killed Eli." Then I realized that—incredibly, tragically—she wouldn't know who Eli was, and I explained, "Eli was her son."

Ma lay still for a while. I didn't know whether she'd heard. I could not get warm against her.

The profound cold of her was beginning to make my bones ache, my head feel empty, my heart and breath slow. I tried to pull away and she wouldn't allow it.

I said, "I thought you were dead. I've mourned for you."

She jerked, as if I had startled her or as if she were silently and mirthlessly laughing, neither of which seemed plausible. "Your mourning hasn't been wasted. I'm an Old Woman now."

At first I didn't know what she meant; she'd been an old woman for years. But then I understood, the common noun became chillingly proper, and I struggled in earnest to free myself from her. She would not allow it.

The cave reverberated. The floor and ceiling, close against me, vibrated as if drilled. The jagged wall skimming the ventral irregularities of my body was trembling, making my teeth itch and the skin burn around my heat detectors. Along my dorsal surfaces, where my mother cuddled me against her, the buzzing was even harsher and more insinuating.

Cold. Not the cold of death but the cold of intense, deep-set life, inverse life, cumulative life turned in on itself. I was past shivering. My bones ached. The fluid in the cavities and sacs of my head had thickened and was expanding, mounting pressure outward against the plates of my skull, beginning to push them apart.

I curled up. I lowered my head. I flexed my avial muscles, clenched my fists and feet, rolled my scoop into a hard and flexible baton. Then, as suddenly as I could manage, I arched my back and twisted, breaking my mother's grip. She gave a hoarse cry, "Joel, don't!" and I felt like a rebellious child, but I scrabbled and flung myself away from her in the only direction not blocked, which was forward, into the narrowing passage, deeper into the mountain. Ma called after me, grazed my ankle with something sharp, teeth or claws. But she could not hold on.

The walls of the tunnel were soft, and purchase was easy to find. I was, in fact, changing the form of the solid rock and hollowed space through which I was making my way, digging, scratching a trail. The tunnel buzzed like the aura of an earthquake. I was all but deaf, and there was no heat to detect.

There was cold. Behind me, my mother, and ahead of me, a solid, porous and dense.

The cold was more solid than anything else, and I fell into it. I heard a prolonged, desperate and oddly musical sound, like plainsong pleading, and the echoes of it everywhere, through the segmented tunnels like finger bones through the mountain and through the bones of my own phalanges clawing now at cold turgid air. My mother was screaming.

I fell into an impacted mass of cold living flesh.

Rancid odor billowed at my impact, the miasma of life so pure and concentrated it was something other than life, something deeper. Tissue-thin skin burst and from every fissure, every orifice welled thick liquid that sprayed and coated me.

I slid, deeper through the layers of ferocious cold toward the intense bead of radiant heat at the core, toward her barely beating heart. Something sharp punctured the top of my skull, and the buzzing rose to thunder.

I felt the sloughing of the cave wind across my exposed brain. Cold penetrated and expanded, and siphoning began like the draw of an immense engine. Pain and terror peaked, then swelled farther into ecstasy, toward oblivion. The Old Woman held me and sucked, and surrender to her was to be an epiphany.

I was jerked backward. The Old Woman's fangs pulled free of my brain, fluid spurted, and with it, agony. The segmented fingers at my temples burned. My mother clutched me against her for a moment long enough for me to feel her racing heart, skyrocketing temperature, panting, and to know that she had put herself in mortal danger for me.

From the Old Woman, there was dense silence. Then the buzzing began again, shot upward and outward until it honeycombed the whole mountain, the world, and the bloated mass of her swelled with eerie rapidity into the tunnel toward us. The exposed soft surfaces of my brain, dried out as they had been, still sent bizarre sensory messages. I saw the approach of the Old Woman in a way not really visual, but vividly, in more than three dimensions. I heard her through my follicles and pores. Overwhelmingly, I detected—not heat, exactly, and not exactly cold, but some other quality of vivified energy. And there was pain.

The fangs reached me again, although from no identifiable mouth. There was penetration at countless points—the base of my throat, the hollows behind my ears, the throbbing hairless flesh over my heat detectors, my navel, my scrotum, the insides of my thighs. Sucking began, a cold molten wind. I was being drawn out.

"No! He's mine! He belongs to me!" my mother cried.

The vibration stopped. The sucking stopped. The Old Woman kept herself wrapped around me and her fangs inside, but all motion ceased.

Very quietly, perhaps beneath the level of language altogether, my mother said, "Let me have him."

The Old Woman withdrew. The layered blanket of cold was folded back, exposing me to ordinary underground chill, which was far more acute. My puncture wounds burned with cold, with escaping heat, and those in my skull geysered. As my viscous exudate pooled and sedimented, a field of stalagmites grew up from the floor where my head lay.

Ma pried one flat hand under my head to catch some of my escaping brain fluid. I heard it gather in her palm and cupped webs. Then she withdrew her hand, brought it to her mouth, and drank.

She had not inserted her fangs, which meant she hadn't injected anticoagulant. Blood from the body wounds was already starting to clot, and bloody fluid from the head wound flowed more slowly. Images still flooded my sensorium in bewildering juxtaposition, but I got myself up on all fours.

Ma came to me. In a tender maternal gesture resonant with the threat of violence, she took my head in her long hands and bent her own head over me. "I love you, Joel," she gave me to understand; I don't think she spoke. Then she bared her teeth.

Perhaps I would have fought back. Perhaps I would have surrendered. But at the instant before her hollow teeth penetrated my brain, my mother turned her head away from me, flung me behind her into the labyrinthine passage leading outward, and leaped into the Old Woman's heart.

I hesitated, but not for long. A great sibilance

rose, hissing and buzzing, and then the sound, like the beating of a punctured heart, of immense sucking. The force of it created a pressure against which I struggled, and I scuttled away.

CHAPTER 21

Alone somewhere in the caverns, as I had been now for a long, amorphous time, I clung to a wall. The rock was porous and giving; it molded itself around me.

I had been practicing, acclimating myself to going incrementally higher and higher. Having started at the bottom, I knew where the edge of the wall was at that point, but otherwise it seemed boundless. There were sensations of curvature, of rotation. It was like climbing the inner surface of an infinite sphere. Now I must be very high indeed, but I still did not detect any roof above me, and I knew that I could go much higher still.

Like someone suspended between vast sky and vast ocean, I was acutely aware of how small I was. To any observer, from any vantage point, I would be barely discernible. But I felt expansive. I felt limitless. There was a transformative quality about this perspective, both frightening and calming.

My wounds had healed, over vast internal change. The range of motion of my hips and shoulders had gradually and with considerable discomfort extended so that now I could turn my limbs outward from my torso until they were nearly flat. The rock surface felt furred, although I didn't think it was. My flesh felt porous.

I pushed off. I had trained, and was able to hover just above the surface at variable speed, not a natural move. I rocketed some distance, then whirled, pulled up short, shot upward and then downward, and proceeded back the way I thought I'd come at a much slower rate, like an echo partially absorbed.

The millions of claw-marks, ancient and recent, ageless, ticked past, frames in a film just beyond the rim of comprehension when I flew fast, hash marks as if from some not quite accessible ledger when I slowed.

I must have passed many times over the niche where I had laid Eli's corpse. It would probably be mummified by now, internal organs and fluids—precious enough to have led to his maiming and death—dried out in the aridity of this place, body husk preserved by the chill. I had no need to view it, and little horror of doing so. Eli was anywhere I thought him to be.

Eventually I lowered my scoop and my bare

feet. My claws strafed the soft rock, which gave in satisfying grooves. I made a few long horizontal passes, then vertical ones. I carved arcs and angles, circles and cross-hatches and straight lines.

I was thinking about it too much. Performance anxiety and a reluctance to appear the fool—though to whom I had no idea—were getting in the way.

I took a deep breath, thought deliberately of my mother, and propelled myself against the wall with hands and feet clawed, putting enough downward spin on the maneuver to send me into a long slide that, like the skilled roll of a bowling ball, hooked to the left just a bit at the end. I could not quite control my momentum and did not stop soon enough, so the upturned tail of the letter was too long, but it was still a recognizable J.

With the sort of giddy triumph brought on only by success at a personally symbolic task that would mean nothing to anybody else, I gave a silly little jump and fairly darted around in a circle that grew wider in diameter and deeper in circumference with every revolution I made. Like a car on a very fast track, I kept picking up speed, until I was dizzy both from the circling itself and from the increasingly canted position I had to assume in order to take the endless turn. It required a conscious effort of will to stop the incising of the O, and I was out of breath and tired as I stretched and stepped over to start the E.

In this way, I clawed my full name into the cavern wall. The limestone accepted my graffiti—whether defacement or art or nothing more or less than signature—rather more easily than I had anticipated. This caused me to speculate that it would give them up easily, too, although the survival of the other claw-marks would seem to belie that assumption. I did not particularly care, though perhaps I would when the work was finished.

Jumping over from the downstroke of the U, I had started the final S with the bottom downward curve and had gathered momentum going up, slaloming back and forth. I was flying flat-out and out of control as I rounded the top bend and came off the final downward stroke. My feet were bleeding. My hands were cramped. My spine and its attaching bones buzzed from the prolonged jarring. There was more to do, but I was exhausted and needed badly to eat, sleep, and heal.

Meaning to find a roost somewhere—like all those before me who had also left their signatures here—or, failing that, to drop to the floor far below, instead I landed on another part of the wall and music chimed. Startled, I bounced back into midair and nearly fell before my fingertips found another rough spot to clutch.

Music again, clear pure notes like bells in a minor key. The same music I had heard the night Rory disappeared into the hidden caves and Meredith and Eli died.

I was reluctant to shut off any possibility of hearing that sweet sound again, but I clicked my tongue rapidly and, acting from tragic necessity, closed my ear muscles against all auditory stimuli other than the echoes I hoped I had produced. They came back in a jittery stream. Not having cared much for quite some time about navigating or about identifying anything else in the world with me, I had to repeat the process several times before I got any usable information.

Even when data began to array themselves in interpretable ways, I could not make sense of what I was learning. Trembling, I managed to find a slightly rougher spot on the rough wall, barely wide enough for me to rest on, either a roost someone else had once used or a clawed place where someone had been desperate to find one. I crouched there, flattened and wrapped into as small an object as possible, and sent out signals one more time, a veritable expedition of precisely modulated clicks and squeals that would return with their own tales of the world beyond.

Nothing I had located anywhere around should have been capable of producing music. I thought that Ma had had a story about music in the caves, made by the caves themselves, but my memory of it was so vague and deep that I might well have told the tale myself.

The only new oddity my reconnaissance had encountered was a peculiar formation farther along the wall and higher up. The range of designs among the various formations in the caverns had already presented itself to me as infinite, so the existence of this one was not a surprise. A thick fluted fringe where sediment-laden water had, apparently, dripped heavily down the rock face, it was, compared to the lacy draperies and complex helictites I had almost become used to, aesthetically not especially impressive.

But it seemed to be the source of the music. In response to the querying sound waves I produced, even the echoes were faintly musical.

Physical pain and fatigue, together with an apprehension of being insistently invited to discover a miracle, took me out of myself. I crawled and rappelled and clumsily flew in the direction of the dripstone formation. It took a long time. I lost my way and found it again. I was nothing but my body, heavy and transformed with pain; I was nothing physical at all but only yearning spirit.

My forearm bumped into one of the calcified drips, thick as I was and much longer. A clarion note sounded. I caught my breath. I kicked, and my shin struck another mass, which rang.

Feeling myself part of an ancient ritual, playing the earth itself, I maneuvered until I was hovering just above the resonant hillocks, then dropped among them. Even my fall made music. I lay in an open space and gathered all four limbs and my scoop tight to my trunk, then shot them out like the points of a star. Five glorious notes sounded, a series of flatted fifths in a mournful, heavenly, bluesy descant.

For the first time in my life, I made music. I composed wonderful melodies that were lost even as they were created, riffs that disappeared into the topography and atmosphere of the caverns, ephemeral variations on constant themes. My fists pounded. My feet kicked. My fingers and toes raced up and down the minor scales. My wings, fluttering, made a light trill with an Oriental cast, then thundered in Wagnerian crescendos. Eventually I was rolling and writhing among the dripstones, finding myriad ways to move against and with them to create harmony and dissonance, syncopation and stately rhythm.

"This is so cool," said Ernie.

I had finished the phrase in which I was engrossed before the shock of his presence registered with me. Still, I was unwilling to stop. Luxuriantly splayed, I slid over a dripstone swelling like a harp, and asked, rather dreamily, "Ernie?" although I knew it was.

He said, "Yeahhh," in a husky underbreath.

Despite my efforts to stay in my altered state,

orientation to time and place was returning. I realized that Ernie was standing on the floor of the cavern looking up at me, and that there was no way he could get up here. I said, "What are you doing here?"

"Following Rory," he answered readily, and burst into a perfectly pitched and broadly emoted rendition of "I Will Follow Him."

There was an answering call, musical only in intent, closer to an off-key yodel than a song. Under me, the stone vibrated. I felt obliged to ask "How did you find us? What's going on at Ambergen?"

"They were all going up north someplace. Someplace cold. I loathe cold. It's cold in here. Your sister is a really pretty lady, Joel, but she's a crazy lady, you know?"

"She's entitled," I observed. "She's lost all three of her children and her only grandchild." It was actually the first time I had thought of it in those terms, and I thought to pause for a moment in tribute to Alexis, or to send her, though she would never know, a bit of my music, which, with all the zeal of the new convert, I was certain would bring her comfort. Experimentally, I shifted position, and a few notes undulated.

But Ernie sang out, "Rory!" and my meditative mood was shattered. From directly beneath me, apparently separated by only a thin leaf of lightweight rock but unable or unwilling to get out to us, Rory bellowed in response. Whatever word or phrase he used was incomprehensible, though I assumed it was Ernie's name and some kind of order or plea.

Ernie had moved into a graceful ballet position, en pointe and lithe figure extended nearly horizontal, arms out like wings, hands arched, lacy dreadlocks falling over his face like the most delicate cave formation. When he heard Rory's voice, he froze. I marveled that he could hold the pose so steadily and for so long.

Rory summoned him again. My face and chest vibrated with the resonant call, my back and skull with the higher registers of Ernie's reply. My habitual impulse would have been to shield myself. I could have slid down out of the ray of passion that was streaming back and forth between them. I could have climbed higher, or sideways; I could have hidden inside one of the depressions I had made for the letters of my name. Instead, I stayed still and waited to see what would happen.

Little happened for quite a while except the calling back and forth. Ernie did lower his leg and arms and sink onto the floor. Rory seemed to move a little, or I did, because we were not so perfectly aligned on either side of the thin wall anymore.

Then Ernie slid himself—still graceful, still shrieking melodiously in rhythmic counterpoint to Rory—toward the base of the wall a little to the right of where I hung. I twisted so that I could cock my head and hear what he was doing. He was scrabbling. His long gaudy fingernails were digging into the limestone, and clouds of powdered rock drifted up. I thought about how the dust was altering the cavern. I thought about how we all were, just by passing through.

Rory must have been clawing from his side, too. It did not take long for them to meet in the middle, and when they did the wall trembled with their meeting. Heat traveled upward and I felt it spreading and being absorbed. I absorbed some of it myself. Then I listened to them go away through the mountain, not singing now but talking excitedly, Rory's deeper, harsher tones laced with Ernie's higher, sweeter ones.

I did sleep then, and I ate, and I slept again. Then I went back to work. My feet and hands were extremely tender now that their torture had been interrupted and resumed, and it was all I could do to use them again. I could have found or fashioned tools, I supposed, but it seemed important to be as close to the work as possible, to exchange raw materials between my body and the rock.

I inscribed the numerals of my birth date and the hyphen that followed, but I left the death date blank. It would have been presumptuous and cowardly to pretend I could know what it was. I just made sure to leave plenty of space. Perhaps somebody else would fill it in, or I myself might have enough warning. Most likely, the space would remain blank. I rather liked that.

I slept and ate again before I started on the epitaph. Excitement interfered for a while, and I had to take some time to settle down, to calm and mute my rising expectations and welcome whatever emerged. I thought about Eli. I thought about Rory. I thought about everything I had lost and given up, and was sad, and then was not.

I flew across the cavern and turned. The section of the wall I was working on had been only subtly disturbed by Rory and Ernie's tunneling and reunion; the letters of my name were slightly slanted now, as though italicized. Haunting voices came and went, and I heard music, but not, I thought, from this wall; there must be more dripstone elsewhere, or other geologic features still alien to me. I listened for a while, and then I closed the muscles inside my ears and did not listen any more.

It took me a long time to finish the part of the epitaph I knew. More than a few times while the arduous work was in progress, I fell asleep, on the cross piece of an A or an H, on the tine of an E, nestled in the curve of an S or the cup of the U. I did not sleep deeply or for long, and I did not eat at all. I did my best to dredge my consciousness, so that the rest of my epitaph would show itself to me.

But in the end, I came no closer to finishing the sentence than I ever had in any iteration of The Dream. BECAUSE OF HIS PASSING, my claw-marks on the wall read, and though they are tinted with my blood, they will say no more.

BECAUSE OF HIS PASSING

I rather like that.